TRUCK DREAMS

Gary H. Baker

ISBN: 1456306405

ISBN-9781456306403

This book is dedicated to all truck drivers everywhere.

It is also dedicated to the memory of two spirits from thirty-seven years ago. They were dancing together in a departure corridor at the Honolulu International Airport. They were Yvonne and George. Spy, Dog, and I were watching as they enchanted us.

A huge thank you goes to Jim Harstad and Gary Everist for their help with the manuscript and their encouragement. Thanks to Jane Brown for her excellent proofreading. Debbie Baker is the prettiest lady in Edgewood, Tennessee, and she has been essential in every step of the writing of this book. Thanks, darling. I love you, and I owe you.

About Big Bubba Buck's Belly Bustin' BBQ Bliss:

If you find yourself driving interstate 65 in Kentucky and you open your window and detect an irresistible barbeque aroma, you'll know you are close to Big Bubba's. And if you feel a sense of friendly southern hospitality magically tugging at you and leading you down the exit ramp at mile marker 65, Munfordville, and then pull you into Big Bubba's, don't panic. It happens to the JETS all the time. The JETS, you will learn, are a key component of the Truck Dreams story.

Come on in to Big Bubba's on your next trip through Kentucky, and like the JETS, say hello to Robert, April, Jordan, Marjorie, Amanda, and Cort. They will invite you to sign the JETS membership board. It might be the best feeling you've ever had while signing your name to something.

About North 40 Truck Stop

Eight miles west of the Tennessee River you'll see the big sign for it. Its exact location is Interstate 40 at mile marker 126 on the Music Highway between Nashville and Memphis. What will you find in this big southern truck stop? A warm welcome from the friendliest people I've ever met out on the road. You'll also find great food and a sense of peace and quiet that is sometimes hard to find around a truck stop. I write this in order to say thanks to the good folks that allow me to hang out at the North 40 and do an occasional book signing. So, the next time you're in the neighborhood, stop by and say hello to Kendra, Betty, Kayla, and myself, and if you think about it, check to see if Paul Remers or Rambo is there. If they are, tell them, "Welcome home and thanks for your service."

I'll see you somewhere out on that big road.

Gary H. Baker

PROLOGUE

Holliday, Tennessee
The North Forty Truck Stop
12-11-09

I met Paul Remers in a truck stop. I overheard a conversation he was having with someone else. "I'll be going back to work next week," he said. My quick appraisal of him didn't reveal anything that might have suggested a recent injury or anything of the such. But there was something in his voice... I was eight feet away from him. I looked closer at his face. Clean, sharp bone features, high cheekbones, blue eyes, my age, or better. And the eyes, the blue eyes, had hurt in them.

"How you doing?" I said to him.

"Aw, alright. How 'bout you? I talked with you here a couple of months ago. You remember?"

He was right. I had seen him here a couple of months ago. We had talked for just a few short minutes. "Yes, I remember you. It might have been the last time I was here. Did I hear you say you were going back to work?"

"Yes, my wife died two months ago. I've got to get back to work."

I sensed the physical loss he was going through, the actual absence of coffee and talk with her in the morning, the words they often traded of caring and shared commitment and reflection on the many years they'd been together. All of that gone now that she had passed. It was two months ago, and there was still hurt in his eyes and in the way he moved, and in the way he sat down with me at a small table.

"You've been off the road for two months now? I bet you've missed it and want to get back."

"Want to? No sir. I been out there thirty-eight years. That's enough. There ain't been a day I wanted to go back. I just *got* to."

"Thirty eight years... Things have changed on the road in thirty eight years."

"Yessir, I remember back then a truck driver come in to a place like this..., I never paid for a cup of coffee. They's glad to see ya'. They respected you. 'Course drivers back then earned respect."

"Knights of the highway."

"Yessir, that's right. If a four wheeler or another truck broke down, why before you knowed it, there'd be two, three more trucks to stop and help out. You don't see that anymore. And drivers was good to give the right-a-way. Yessir, did it all the time."

Our conversation turned to CB chatter. Paul remembered an incident from the past: "I asked the guys I was talking to on the CB to get off channel nineteen. You know, all the nonsense and dirty talk up there. So, I said, 'Let's go down to twelve', or maybe another channel, I don't remember. We were talkin' about God, or praying, or something, so we went down to twelve, I think it was. So this stranger keyed up and said something stupid like, 'You a bunch of sissies, got to go down to twelve.' Then he said, 'I think I'll just pull over and get out and wait for you sissies and do some serious ass kickin' when you come by. But I doubt you'll stop.' Well that just kinda' got me fired up a little bit. I said, 'Where you at mister? I'll stop.

You're talkin' like you're pretty tough and mean. I think we'll just find out how bad you really are.' I turned my truck around and went back where he said he'd pulled over." Paul stopped and waited for my response.

"Another CB Rambo I bet. He wasn't there was he?" We both laughed.

"No sir. He was gone. But I'm kinda' glad he was. You know, I got in trouble enough. I should a learned not to fight a wannabe man. It used to happen all the time. I'd call out some CB Rambo's bluff and hurt 'em pretty bad. I was Navy SEAL and if I got into it ... well, I'd always be the one thrown in jail, not the other guy."

I got to thinking about Paul's age. "You must have been in the SEALS in the sixties."

"Yessir, early sixties. They didn't call us SEALS then. Frogmen, UDT."

"Yeah, I remember that." He wasn't going to volunteer any more of his military memories. They never do – the ones that were there in the Nam. The ones that were really in it never brought it up. Oh, they would sometimes talk a little, share a quick story if someone else brought it up - someone like me – a rear echelon mother_____ - REMF.

My kind would talk and talk and talk about all of our harrowing war adventures: the time our unit almost did so and so, the time you almost had to go up on the line, the time in Saigon you just knew that bar girl was a V.C. spy. Or, in my case, the time our ship was in Danang Harbor and we saw U. S. war planes come screaming out of the hills, the ordinance they left behind still booming back in the hills.

But the guys that were really in it never brought it up. So, if I wanted more, I'd have to ask for it. " How old are you?" I asked.

"I'll be sixty-six."

"Yeah, so… you were in Vietnam."

"Oh yes sir. I sure was there." The hurt in the blue eyes intensified.

We talked a little about Vietnam in generalities, nothing heavy, but I noticed he was going back there as we talked, and I noticed the hurt in his eyes was growing. Somewhere along the conversation something came up about blacks, and he went all the way back. "You know, some people just don't understand about blacks. Why they's the best there is. They's the best we had. We weren't *like* brothers. We *were* brothers."

The growing hurt in his eyes turned to open weeping and tears. I felt ashamed that I had brought this on. But like most other times I'd got this close, I kept going because I honestly believe that if they can talk about it that it will help and maybe, eventually, if not get them past it, at least get them a little more comfortable handling it – not it handling them. So that's what I told him. "I've been around a few vets in my time and I might be wrong, but I think it helps to talk it out."

The look in Paul's eyes told me he didn't disagree.

"I talked to a guy not long ago. He told me he was one of a very few who was listed as both KIA and MIA. He really got my attention. His eyes held things that nobody should ever have seen. He held them and you could be certain he'd hold them until the day he dies. Paul, this guy told me he's not good around people. He said the reason is because he's a master bullshit detector, and when people start running off at the mouth about things that are bullshit or just don't matter, he can't handle it. If he stuck around, he'd end up hurting them. So he just doesn't stay around people for long. Do you ever feel like that?"

"Well maybe a little, but I go to the Lord. He always gets me through."

"Paul, tell me to get lost if you want to. If you want me to shut up, I will."

He didn't say anything.

"Tell me what happened."

"There were five of us. We were UDT Unit 3. We were in a dugout and a grenade came in. He rolled over on it. None of the rest of us were hurt bad. I took his automatic weapon and was spraying everywhere with it. I caught a bullet right here." He pointed to his upper left leg. "It didn't hit no bone. I didn't even feel it."

He wept and the tears slowly trickled, "He took it for the rest of us. He was a black man. We were brothers in Nam. The rest of us was white. We were brothers. We'd do anything for the guys around us."

"What was his name?"

"Washington."

"You remember the rest of them? What their names were?"

"Yes sir." It was amazing to see this strong-looking man weeping and telling me this story. You'd have to see Paul to understand. A handsome man by any standards. A strong man, even though he was coming up on sixty-six and he had a slender build, you could see the strength in this man. And not just the physical strength – the spiritual strength. The stories he told me about God calling him to the altar to preach, sometimes with no warning at all. One day God called him to get up there where the preacher was and tell the folks about salvation. When he got up there he told the preacher, "God told me to come up here and preach." The preacher looked at him in glorious wonder and sat down in the first pew. Paul preached for half an hour.

"There was Jimmy Fleming, a feller named Roberts, Charles Terrell, and me, and Washington."

"Do you remember Roberts' first name or Washington's?"

"No, I'm gettin' old I guess."

The next day Paul called me and said that Roberts was Bennie Roberts and that Washington was Clovis Washington.

"But he didn't get a medal for what he done. You know, he was just looking out for his men. He was our leader. He saved us all. But he never got a medal."

"Paul, are you telling me he was never put up for anything?"

"No, he never was."

I didn't ask why. I could make a good educated guess why, but I didn't go into it. I got to thinking. We were both quiet for a moment or two. I was still thinking. "Paul, I don't know. I'm just thinking. Listen, how would you feel if somehow we try to get some long overdue recognition, some respect for Mr. Washington?" I didn't realize at the time that those two words, recognition and respect, were totally inadequate, and that the correct word should be honor.

He looked at me, but I could see he was still half way around the world. "Yessir, I'd like that."

For the first time in thirty minutes Paul Remer's beautiful blue eyes lit up. A spark of joy and anticipation sped through them and led me to write the following:

Dear Reader,

Somewhere in Vietnam in the early sixties the leader of UDT Unit 3, Petty Officer First Class, Clovis Washington laid down his life for four men he loved. If the honor he deserved from a war weary nation was ever bestowed upon him, we don't know about it. Let us now pay that honor and let us rejoice in the hope he gave us by his sacrifice. For as Paul Remers reminded me from scripture, the words of Jesus - "Greater love has no one than this, than to lay down one's life for his friends." John 15:13

Gary H. Baker

CHAPTER ONE

Ronnie Matlock stayed down low, hugging the ground. They were coming for him; he was sure of it. And if they found him, they would kill him. He was just as sure of that. After they killed him he'd be gutted and cleaned and then roasted and eaten. He was doing all he could possibly do to stay alive. He didn't particularly enjoy the image of his juices dripping over a fire while they licked their chops and slowly turned the eight foot long pole he'd been skewered on.

There was a rustling in the brush forty feet away to Ronnie's left and he heard voices somewhere off to his right. If it was the North Coast Gang, there were probably a dozen of them. If it was Toros and his gang, there were probably six or eight. Ten seconds went by, the longest ten seconds he'd experienced in a while. He'd heard nothing but sensed they were getting closer. Then he made up his mind. He eyed the decaying, mostly rotted log eight feet off to his right and he slithered along becoming one with the ground and making no noise. It took ten seconds to reach the log and thirty seconds to conceal himself under it as best he could.

As he was trying to cover his hiding place with leaves, limbs, brush, the rotting log itself, the thing he most feared about the consequences of his decision to go for the log wriggled just a bit, a foot in front of his face. It was nearly impossible to be sure of its color, black, tan, mottled brown, or something else, but there was no mistaking the slightly lustrous oily sheen of live snake. The fearsome serpent was about four inches wide at its mid-section and seemed to be undulating away from Ronnie.

Despite the snake's presence, Ronnie's senses lent themselves to the voices, the voices that were very close now. "We're going to cook you Christian. We're going to eat you. Come on out. We know you are here. Come on out now." Toros had killed several Christians in the last six months. He and his gang devoured the carcasses after gutting and cleaning them. A four hour slow roasting was always the method of cooking. They had no kettles or other utensils for boiling the human meat.

Toros had four men with him today. He'd left the other three back in camp. The five men stomped around in the thick undergrowth looking everywhere for a sign Ronnie might have left. Nor did they neglect to look into the trees above. The prey Toros and his gang sought certainly was capable of climbing. The other four echoed the same plans and predictions Toros was making, "Yeah Christian, we are very hungry. We are going to eat you. Come on out."

Ronnie's guts might have been cooked already. They were rolling and burning and threatening to erupt, but he noticed the snake had moved on out; at least, the one snake. Were there more?

He wiggled a couple of fingers to the right of his face, making a slight peep hole through the leaves he'd used to cover his hiding place. A set of legs to go with one of the voices was maybe nine feet away; no shoes, only rags wrapped around his feet. Ronnie caught just the hint of movement a foot and a half away from the man's feet, then the snake struck at an ankle and hit solid on it. The fangs were in good and the sacks released the venom.

The scream caught the others off guard but they converged to the spot. "It's a rattler! It's a rattler!" wailed the victim. The others beat the snake to death with their clubs. "Let's get outa' here. Where there's one of these, there's usually a whole pack of 'em." They picked up the dead snake, and its live victim and trudged off through the thick undergrowth. At least they'd have snake for dinner tonight and maybe some human meat if their comrade died.

Ronnie waited a full thirty minutes before coming out of his hole. He knew perfectly well they could have stayed close, setting a trap, feigning their withdrawal, waiting to ambush, to kill him, roast him , and eat him. He slowly crawled around on all fours for a few minutes, careful to remain silent, and extra careful not to crawl over another snake.

He crawled a little farther, thinking it would probably be safe now to get up on his feet and high-tail it back to his camp. He must have been crazy this morning thinking he could simply stroll through the woods on a leisurely hunting trip, hoping to add to his growing inventory of dried meat, or possibly bringing back to camp that big snapping turtle he'd spotted a week earlier. In that case he'd have turtle stew tonight. But he'd been somewhat careless, a rare thing for Ronnie, and he'd been spotted by one of the scouts from Toros's band of cutthroats. What a ghastly crew they were, the goblins of civilization, the human form of a predator Raptor, the bile and excrement of mankind. Monsters, all of them.

Yep, Ronnie Matlock, Coon Dog to those who knew him, had been careless this morning. Straying further from his normal operating area than he should have, and worst of all, not painting his skin with the mud and bark juice camo he usually employed. He reminded himself again, *it ain't like it was at first*. Two years ago when he was sentenced to the island there weren't many of them – the banished. There was plenty of room to hunt, mind your own business, tend to your own affairs. But now, who knew how many were on the island? He could estimate with a fair degree of certainty that there were at least four or five hundred; four or five hundred of society's worst; serial rapist, child molesters, those who practiced incest, drug traffickers, serial killers, Hannibal Lecter types, terrorist, and others.

Who would have thought that the proponents of the Banishment Law were right all along? They had preached for years and years that heinous crime in the United States would decrease dramatically as soon as some teeth, real teeth, were put into the punishment of those found guilty of the most abhorrent, the most ghastly crimes imaginable. The criminologists, courts, police, the entire criminal justice system, used the technical term of deterrent – real punishment that would make you think twice before raping, mutilating, or murdering someone.

Almost immediately the numbers of the worst types of crimes started to reverse. As soon as the banishment law was passed and people saw that the convicted criminals really were shipped off to a remote island, never to be seen again, never to get a sniff at an appeal, or a nine by six cell, or TV, or radio, or weight lifting in the yard, or letters, or family visits, or food, or clothing. As soon as the people saw that the banishment was real, the type of crimes one could commit that would land that individual on a banishment island nearly came to a halt. It seems that a real deterrent had been the answer all along. Who would have thought so? Especially the astounding turn around in drug abuse. When drug traffickers began to see their brethren shipped off to a banishment island with no possible hope of ever returning, most of them either sought legal occupations or at least shifted the contraband they smuggled to that which would not get them banished if they were convicted. And of course, with no supply, the demand dried up.

As far fetched a notion as it seemed to be, it was true. The United States had finally won the war on illegal drugs. Of course there had really never been a war on drugs. There had only been the occasional headline of a cocaine bust or a meth lab taken down by local police. There had been the calculated and measured perception that there really was a war on drugs. Just feed the populace a few headline grabbing victories over the sleazy dope peddlers every now and then. Keep the real story hidden – the chain of corruption, pay-offs, kick backs, and bribes running all the way from street cops, D. A.'s, and judges, up to the highest elected offices in the land. Keep the real story hidden.

But these things weren't on Ronnie, Coon Dog, Matlock's mind. At the moment, he was preoccupied with staying alive. He was trying to read the wind for any scent of Toros and his gang. Very cautiously he angled off westerly through the thickest of the brush and undergrowth. He was good in the jungle. He kept off the trails. He always went the route least expected, always the most difficult route. He'd done it as a U.S. Navy SEAL in Vietnam and, he'd done it in the woods of Appalachia for years and years, and he'd done it as a boy playing the role of beagle hound in Alabama when his daddy went rabbit hunting.

He paused, sniffed at the sticky, hot air, perked his ears, and slowly did a three-sixty scan, his senses reporting everything copasetic. Still, he knew his foe could be relentless, could still be hiding in ambush. He'd seen them fake retreat before. For city boys they weren't too bad in the woods. Of course when surviving in the wild one hour at a time was your only concern, you learned quickly, not only to fake retreat, but also to set ambushes, plant punji stakes, make crude weapons, and learn to hunt and trap game. Killing humans? That was an art they had all become experts at long before they ever set foot on the island.

Coon Dog had watched them the day they killed his friend Red Man. Coon Dog was hidden in the bush sixty yards away from their camp doing a little SEAL type recon. It's always good to have some intel on your enemy. He saw them behead and butcher Red Man, the body eventually looking like a grossly oversized rabbit on the skewer. Blackened and shriveled up on the skewer, the once six foot Red Man had become a five foot Red Man.

The Red Man, he'd made a big mistake. He was crazy, and he didn't really know what he was doing the day he walked right into Toros' camp reading scripture out of the open Bible in his hand. The Bible was given to all the men sentenced to the banishment island. In fact, it was the *only* thing given to them.

The Red Man prided himself on his split culture - Yaqui shaman and evangelical Christian. You never knew if he would induce the Crow to whisk him off to the spirit world or if he would recite scripture from the Gospel of John. Either way, he was sure to get your attention. He'd gotten Coon Dog's attention. Red man, Coon Dog, and Big Joe Gallick comprised the fourth group of criminals to be placed on the island. The first three groups had preceded them by two months and of their total number of sixteen, there were eleven survivors by the time Red Man, Coon Dog, and Big Joe Gallick showed up.

Red Man, like Coon Dog, possessed survival skills that would see to it he'd have enough to eat. Likewise, building a shelter from the elements and crafting animal skin clothing proved not to be a problem for Red Man. One day, not long after his arrival on the island, Red Man happened upon Coon Dog in the deep woods off toward the east side.

"That's a good one," he said.

Coon Dog was busy skinning a big doe. He was shocked anyone could have come up on him undetected. He went for his flintstone knife he'd made the first week he was on the island. He held it chest high, tip straight out, ready in an instant to attack Red Man if he moved an inch closer. Red Man didn't move. Only his eyes vibrated with life, something flowing through them. What was it?

"There are not many left like that one. The others are learning fast. Soon, I think, the deer will all be gone. One year, maybe ten months. They will be gone." Red Man's eyes still swam in a strong unidentifiable current.

Coon Dog eased the flintstone knife down a little now. "How long have you been here?"

"Three full moons. Eighty-five days to the white man."

Coon Dog's mind was racing. *They did put off two others the day I got here! Here's one of them right here. I wonder what happened to the other one?*

He'd been correct when he'd thought he'd heard one of the marines on the dinghy say, "We got to get moving, there are two more." Then the marines asked him if he could swim, and when he said he could, they pushed him out, two hundred yards from the shore. The Bible, sealed in plastic to stay dry, was all they gave him.

Still, he wasn't about to warm up to this strange Indian just yet. He didn't say anything. He waited for Red Man to speak up again.

"How long have you been here?" Red Man shot the same question right back at Coon Dog.

"Eighty-five days, three full moons," flintstone knife still about half mast, still tip pointed out, hand still tight on the handle.

"Well then… there were at least three of us on that day. I talked with another. We counted the days back. It was the same, the same number of days. And now you. Yes there were at least three of us that day."

Coon Dog lowered the knife to his side but didn't put it away. "I think it was only three. The marines that put me out said something about two others."

"Two Marines in a dinghy? And did they make you swim in?"

"Yes," said Coon Dog.

Red Man's eyes flowed with something strange. A man of two worlds was likely to do that. "The other calls himself Big Joe Gallick. Irish all the way. The Bronx, I think he said. He is dying. His camp is maybe a half day from here."

The two men both wanted all the information they could glean from each other, but it wasn't easy for Coon Dog to take a few tentative steps in the direction of a solid conversation with this man. Coon Dog hadn't spoken to another human being in the last eighty-five days. Not only that, what kind of a man was this strange Indian? What had he done back in the world? What kind of despicable bloodletting had he carried out which landed him here on the banishment island?

CHAPTER TWO

These fleeting memories of his introduction to Red Man didn't last long. Coon Dog was still wary of and half expecting a surprise attack from Toros and his blood goblins. He was still moving slowly toward the west, toward his camp. He called the camp Jabez Junction, named after an old truck driver he'd known back in the world. He had other camps scattered around the island. He never stayed in any one of them more than three days at a time. If he could have stayed in one all the time it would have been Jabez Junction. From there, the west, he took some pleasure in the sunsets at the edge of the sea. The vast Pacific opening up in front of him, he'd search the timeless patterns burned in the clouds. He absorbed what they had to say to him – endure, your chance will come to join us. He'd become intimate with them and spoke to them when a favorite hue would be missing from the ten thousand or so selections in the eternal palette - maybe a light indigo with yellow ocher, maybe a burnt orange with slight gray streaks. "Ah my dear cadmium and slate gray, where are you tonight? Has The Father sent you off to another galaxy for the evening? Maybe another dimension, another time warp?"

Coon Dog had become something of a philosopher lately. He'd never had any interest in any such nonsense in his life prior to the banishment island. But the time he had spent with Red Man had kindled some degree of metaphysical curiosity, though exceedingly difficult to nurture, what with four hundred or so cannibals constantly on his trail. Yes indeed, it's difficult to consider where you come from, why you are here, and where you are going when your throat is about to be ripped open, even for a Christian like Ronnie, Coon Dog, Matlock.

Movement up ahead on his right. He crouched low. Voices? None he could make out. He stayed down. The jungle was still wet from an earlier shower. He ran his fingers through the underbrush at ground level and mixed the moisture with the soil and applied it to his forehead, cheeks, neck and forearms. He was very dark from living in the wild and catching the sun daily, but after the mistake he'd made this morning, he was determined it wouldn't happen again. More movement. He couldn't see it, he could hear it. Still no voices, but somebody or something was moving up ahead. He pulled his knife and stayed low. *Stay here, wait, let it pass.* He felt the bump, bump, bump, bump in his finger tips, his wrist, his neck, his forehead, and in his groin. Always in his groin he'd feel it. He often wondered if others felt it there. *Wait, breathe easy, become one with you surroundings.* One of his SEAL instructors used to say, "You need to get lower than the piss on the ground, you need to make negatory sound, if you don't want to be found."

Movement again, closer now, maybe twenty feet. This wasn't a human. Coon Dog was sure of it. Its maneuvering was too smooth, too feral for a human. *A cat. Has to be a cat,* Coon Dog told himself. *He's got my scent. He'll be here in a moment. How big? What kind? Bobcat, Cougar, Jaguar, Panther? Curl up into a ball. Play the old possum game.* He'd done it before. Chances are better than running. Knees to chest, arms tight around knees, head to chest. Tight, tight, tight, get tight, knife in hand. *There it is, still coming slowly, eight feet away. Black, it's a Panther, male, one hundred- fifty pounds, almost as big as my one- seventy. Two feet away, emitting an angry, hungry growl. Getting louder, aggressive, trying to make me flinch. Paw testing my back side. Trying to roll me over. Teeth on my shoulder. Getting ready for a bite? Now sniffing me up and down, teeth again back up on my shoulder. Maybe I better make a lunge at his throat. If I miss, it's all over. NOW! No! No! Wait, wait until he sniffs down lower, if he sniffs down lower again. Maybe I've already missed my best opportunity. No, there he goes back down again. NOW!*

Coon Dog unleashed the lethal tension in his torso and whipped the flintstone surely and swiftly at the Panther's throat. When it tore through, he kept it going hard and up high into the cat's brain. In an instant it was there and trying to penetrate the cat's skull from the inside out. Coon Dog's arm was all the way in the cat, almost up to his elbow, and already the cat's death spasms were slowing down, and while Coon Dog's eyes burned with sweat and cat blood, the death spasms came to a halt.

Coon Dog skinned the cat and buried the carcass. He didn't need the meat, and he didn't want the carcass to draw attention to his location. The vultures would be seen for miles. But he cleaned up the panther hide as best he could and took it with him. Many would have identified the cat as a leopard and it might have been. There were reports of dark skinned leopards in this part of the world. But to Coon Dog it was a panther, and now he brought the skin with him as he made his way westward. There would only be three hours of sunlight left so Coon Dog decided to clean the skin up a little more. He knew he'd not be able to return to Jabez Junction tonight, so he stopped at the next stream he came to and washed the panther skin and scrubbed it as clean as he could on the inside with sand and rocks from the creek. Most of the membrane and layers of inside fat came away quickly, but he had to work hard on several spots. Then he hung the skin to catch what was left of the sun to dry it as much as possible. Tomorrow, when he brought it into camp he would clean it again, then stretch it tight and allow it to dry in the sun for at least two days, more if necessary.

The evening was closing the shutters on the pale sun. Coon Dog took the panther skin with him and climbed a slight ridge behind him, stopping often to perk his ears and nostrils. It took maybe fifteen minutes, and when he was on top, he climbed a eucalyptus tree to get a look at his surroundings one last time before the sun was blocked totally. Yeah, that's what he thought. Skinny smoke from a campfire was visible back to the northeast highlands. It was roughly four miles away. He'd seen smoke there before. One of the gang's hunting camps no doubt. Toros? Maybe. It could have been another gang. They didn't worry about fires giving away their locations. They usually traveled with enough men to set up decent perimeter watches. And if another gang wanted a rumble in the jungle after the sun went down, so be it.

Coon Dog worked his way back down the ridge about halfway. He gathered a small heap of dried grass and leaves and stuffed it back behind an exposed boulder on the down slope. He had just enough overhang to protect him from rain. He crawled into his home for the night just as the dying gray turned to black. He folded the panther skin to form a cushion for his head. Before reclining back into the grass and leaf mat, he opened a little leather pouch he had tucked away in an inside pocket on his buck skins. The oily mixture was very effective as a mosquito repellant. It had taken him four months to get it right. After experimenting with every root, leaf, bark, and berry he could find, he finally found a combination that worked. He ground down several types of tree roots and added wild onions, eucalyptus leaves, and wild flower clippings. Just a few dabs of the concoction on his wrist, ankles, and neck were all he needed. Mosquitoes had no interest in whatever nutrition his blood might provide them. He slumped back into his mat and laid his head down. Weary, so weary … for a moment or two there was nothing else. Just lying there, eyes closed, deep slow breathing, letting the day's activities, the deadly maneuvering he'd been involved in, letting it all slip away. Nothing but weariness.

Many nights he'd pray before catching the sleep he chased. Other nights he'd meditate on old memories until, alas, the meditation became a dream. It was a trick his cousin Toby Etheridge had told him about a few years ago. Coon Dog had never really tried it until he'd become a truck driver, and then he found it did work. He'd usually start his meditations from a well used inventory of the major chapters from his life. The list included his youth, the days he'd spent learning the lessons of hunting and fishing in central Alabama from his daddy, Horace Matlock. The list also included chapters from his time in Vietnam. These he never chose to meditate on, but they would become dreams never-the-less. There were the chapters of his three ex-wives and many ex- girlfriends. But the dreams that sustained him the most were his truck dreams. These were dreams he marched back to over and over again. They sustained him in a way the others couldn't. They not only held him captive for awhile, the other dreams could do that. His truck dreams or shadows of unconscious thought contained a promise. The others never did that. The truck dreams promised something still good about America, something that could still be found that belied the conventional take on 21st century American culture. His truck dreams provided a promise that if you keep moving, keep driving, you will eventually come across what America used to be, and what it still could be. It wasn't easy and you'd have to keep driving relentlessly to find it, but it was there. It sure was. An America that always existed, and for people like Coon Dog, always would if *he* had a say in it. You just had to keep moving , keep driving to find it. Tonight Ronnie Matlock's truck dream featured CB dialogue that was neither memory nor fantasy. It was a tangled mix of both of those things, and in the dream's conversations, he couldn't ascertain whether or not he was actually one of the six or seven speakers. He might have been, but he couldn't tell for sure.

* * *

The dream started and St. Louis was thirty miles behind. The truck driver locked his seat belt, turned on his head lights and his running lights, turned his C.B. on, and pulled out of the north bound rest area. It would be a long night. He was bound for Canada. He lit up a smoke and keyed his mike, "Big truck coming out of the north bound pickle park."

"Yeah, come on outa' there cowpoke. Plenty of room for ya'."

"I appreciate it driver. Anybody need a hole in the north-bound pickle park, there's about four holes left."

"The only hole I need is one that's got two legs on it."

"I heard that, I did." A different driver shouted on his microphone.

"Now fellers, I gotta' make Canada by mornin', so I expect ever'body to hammer down and keep the pathway open."

"Copied that driver."

"Drop in with us Canada. We headed for Dee Troit."

"I ain't goin' to Dee Troit." a new voice added.

"Shut up Curly. You ain't goin' nowheres."

"I ain't? Then how come I'm pulling 42,000 pounds of dog food?"

"I guess to feed that wife you said you got."

"Naw, 42,000 wouldn't begin to feed her."

Everybody laughed at that.

A new voice entered the jumbled conversation. "Attention truck drivers! Attention Truck drivers. This is Sergeant Julios P. Cornpecker, Illinois State Trooper. Now boys I've been monitoring channel 19 for a few minutes and it sounds to me like you might be trying to form you up a convoy. Now, us troopers here in the Land of Lincoln don't allow no trailer park trash truck drivers to run no convoys through our great state. No Sir! Never have, never will. I'm warning you now. I strongly recommend that you back 'em off and shut 'em down. That is unless you want to spend the night in the pokey with Smokey, all paid for by the good tax payers of the great state of Illinois. That'll about do it gearjammers. I'm sure you'll seee the wisdom of my words. If you don't, well... then you'll be the recipient of some good old Illinois hospitality. But not 'til after I clean the highway up a bit with your no-good fat truck driver asses. Sergeant Julios P. Corpecker signing off. Aloha, Asta La Vista, Chow, Au Viter Sein, A Riva Delchi, and like they say down yonder in Tennessee, I'll holler atcha' later."

"Cornpecker, you ain't going to stop no convoy. Get your stupid chicken shit ass off the radio."

"You tell him Tex. I ain't heard Cornpecker in quite a while. I guess he's been busy trying to keep that horny Great Dane of his outa' his wife's bedroom."

"No, the way I heard it was Cornpecker liked to get it on with the dog while his wife watched."

"Yeah, I think I heard about that too."

"Dagnabbit fellers, do I have to go all the way to Canada listening to this trash?"

"What's your handle cowpoke? You ain't one of them twinkle toes good buddies are you? You sound to me like maybe you been reading one of them industry magazines that's always yakin' about CB etiquette or some such nonsense. Are ya'? Are ya'?"

"No, I ain't no good buddy, and my handle is Old Soft Shoe. It's just that all the juvenile chatter gets old. You know? Doesn't anybody besides me get tired of it?"

"Tired of it? What's the matter with you Old Soft Shoe? Haint nobody made you turn your CB on. No sir. I don't think nobody climbed in that cab with you and made you turn it on."

There was a pause in the conversation. The night wasn't as lonely now. A decent argument had been started and so far no tempers had flared. Ten or twelve big trucks were rolling north, each driver having paid the price of membership in this club many years ago. There were no rookies in this caravan of 72 footers, only seasoned truckers, most having driven over two million miles in their careers. From a distance of a mile or more you could see them coming, the string of headlights resembling some elongated sea creature flashing double phosphorous beams at almost perfect intervals. A four-wheeler would scoot past them in the hammer lane every now and then. The trucks would slow down a tad for a construction zone periodically, and occasionally a driver would drift a half foot or so out of the center of his lane. But this convoy had a steady and soothing rhythm to it. If it had been a song instead of a string of big trucks, it might have been <u>Amazing Grace</u> – slow, easy going, not in a hurry, but with certainty and sureness, on its way to a destination.

Blackbeard broke the silence, and when he did, the feel of the <u>Amazing Grace</u> convoy was certain to change its nature, if only ever so slightly. "RRRRRRGH Mateys", a deep and gravelly Caribbean pirate's voice shattered the short reverie and took control of CB channel 19. "RRRRRRGH, shiver me timbers and blow me main-sail down. RRRRRGH! I was bound for the fine, deep port of Montego Bay, where the island lassies await and the promise of rum and peaches and avocado has got me licking me chops. Alas, I strayed upon your strange voices as if my charts had failed me; as if I'd been on a southeast heading, making for cover in Trinidad, running hard to avoid the devil himself. Yes landlubbers, it was then I heard your strange voices. So listen well, and heed the words of Black Beard. RRRRRGH, put your machines in full sail Mateys, and set your course for the Caribbean. Aye, come with us. We will plunder and ravage every craft we come upon. Whatever flag she flies, it makes no difference. Our swords will open many a throat, and many will fly over the side, a feast for the sharks."

A North Carolina flat bed driver cut in on Black Beard, "Black Beard, I think you caught a case of something that went from your crotch straight up to that no account brain of yours." An oversized trailer with a sailboat strapped down good and tight flickered its running lights on and off two or three times and Black Beard's voice disappeared for the time being.

"Awk! Awk! Captain clammed up. Captain clammed up!"

"Crap, that stupid bird of his picked up the mike."

Things got quiet again. A few minutes later the driver bound for Canada, Old Soft Shoe, turned his CB off and reviewed his route and trip itinerary for the next few days. Five hours to Chicago, turn east on 80/94. Four hours to Detroit, the sun would be up by then. Two more hours into Canada and finally deliver his load of electronics and appliances to Port Burwell on the shores of Lake Erie, take his ten hour break and dead head back to Battle Creek, Michigan. There he should have a load of auto parts waiting for him, and then a quick delivery of maybe five hours to Belvedere, Illinois.

Old Soft Shoe had been around the block quite a few times. He'd driven about every kind of rig a man could drive: doubles, triples, auto haulers (parking lots), oversize, tankers, reefers, day cabs, cab-overs, containers, straight trucks, crane rigs, and up to twenty axles. He'd been in forty-eight states by the time he was twenty-four, and that was forty something years ago. He'd been a driver trainer, and he was very good at it. He had a good way with the wannabe drivers, and he was a patient man, something that most trainers were not. He'd hauled about every kind of freight there was, all the way from women's lingerie to lead which weighed seven thousand pounds for a piece the size of a bathroom commode. He'd hauled frozen seafood, frozen pizzas, and a whole list of other frozen foods including ice cream, vegetables, cookie and cake mixes, beef, turkey, pork, chicken, gator meat, and rattlesnake meat. He'd hauled dry foods of every description, and dry goods of every description, explosives, steel, finished and unfinished lumber, furniture, auto parts, aircraft parts, large and small appliances, legal drugs, and every kind of alcohol, domestic and imported.

A young driver once asked him, "What's the largest single piece of freight you ever hauled?"

"Well, that's easy. The largest was an elephant for the zoo, and the smallest was bees. You know, honey bees. We'd take them from Texas in late spring up to Wisconsin and South Dakota. About early fall we'd take them back to Texas for the winter. It was the funniest thing. When we'd stop for coffee and fuel, you know, well, the stragglers, the bees that got blown out of the hives would be hightailing it back to the cages, the bee houses, the hives, and they were mad as fire. You didn't want to be outside the truck when they started arriving. The truck stop people just hated to see us show up with those bee hives."

* * *

Ronnie, Coon Dog, Matlock woke up. The dream was over. A pack of coyotes had awoken him with their wild and furious yapping. He looked out from his semi concealed ledge with the rock above his head and caught the shadowed trail of clouds snuffing out a gray half moon. He crawled out slowly and gathered a handful of rocks. He waited a couple of minutes to see if the coyotes would resume the chorus. When they did, probably fifty yards away, he let the rocks fly in their direction. That's usually all it took to shut them up. He rubbed his eyes and stretched a little and was thinking about the truck dream that seemed so real. Sergeant Julios P. Cornpecker and Blackbeard had showed up in his nocturnal visions on many occasions, but "Old Soft Shoe" was a newcomer to the parade of truckers who sailed through his dreams regularly, just as if they'd been old friends.

He'd thought about lying back in his den for a little more sleep but decided not to. He took another look at the position of the moon and realized the dawn was less than an hour away. Now would be a good time for prayer, he thought.

He went to his knees. "Well Father, here I am again, just an old bag of bones trying to hang on. Thank You Father for the many blessings that I don't deserve. Thank you for all the many opportunities I've mostly squandered away. But I ain't through trying Lord. One of these days maybe I can be what you want me to be. I'm going to try, Lord. Please give me the strength and the wisdom to do your will, not mine. Yes Father, I'm sure there are things you'd like me to do, even on this wretched island where men and beast want to eat me. I accept the Blood of Jesus to cleanse my soul. I know without His Blood, I can never be the child you want me to be. And Father when I truly become that child, maybe then I can do your will. You know, Father, You've been talking to me about Toros and how I should witness to him. Well Father, I'm a bit confused about how all of this stuff works. You know, witnessing. I know what it means – to tell others about my relationship with Jesus and how I know that only through His Blood can we be saved. I understand that part. But Toros, I can't figure how I'm supposed to approach him. I mean, he really does want to eat me. He said it in no uncertain terms just yesterday, and of course we saw...., well, I saw, no...., I'm sure You saw it too. He ate Red Man and many others. I know that when You speak to my heart about witnessing to Toros, that You really mean it. Well...., I guess I'll just have to keep praying on it. I know you'll show me the way it is to be done. And yes Father, I do want men like Toros to hear the Truth and be saved. I know it's possible. I know that's why Jesus died, to save the very worst of us. I know that if I can be saved, well..., I know anybody can. Show me how to do it father. I'll do my best to witness to the truly lost on this Earth. Lead me, guide me, show me how Father. Show me how."

Coon Dog looked up at the moon again, now just a wee bit lower in the sky and emerging from the drifting, dark clouds. Still a few stars twinkling and a hint of pre dawn pink was trying to rise from the east. He bowed his head again.

"Father I ask this morning you be with those I've left behind – Myrna, Katherine, and Janey. Be with them. Protect them and send Your Spirit to be there for them. I was a terrible husband to all three of them Father, but now I know I need to pray for them. Take care of them and I pray their hearts will be open and they ask Jesus to take them."

He paused, put his hands to his chin for a second, and continued, "Father please help me with my plans for escape from this island. I think I might be able to pull it off. I need your strength Father. Be with me every day. And Father when I get back to the world, I pray that I won't go after those evil men that are responsible for my being here. Yes, I pray for their souls too. May I be led to do Your will, and not to seek selfish revenge."

He set his face in a tight, determined look, and continued praying, "Father be with Toby, and Jabez, and Windjammer, and Big Montana and all of the Jets. Protect them from evil Father. Cover them with the Holy Spirit. Be with them. I thank you for it Father. And be with our troops Father, where ever they might be, and our leaders, and our country. Help us all be what you'd have us be. Show us the way Father. Thank You. And Father please be with my brothers I lost back in the Nam. I pray they are all with You, and let them know I think about them every day. Thank You Father, thank You for all the blessings. I pray You will use me today. Use me for something good, something to fulfill Your will. I love You Father. I love You Jesus. I love You Holy Spirit. In Jesus Name, I pray. Amen."

He dwelt there on his knees a while longer, no longer praying with voice or thoughts, but by just kneeling and absorbing the feeling, the power, the reality of spending time with God.

The Jets was the Christian truckers group he'd been a big part of back in the world. The acronym JET stood for Jesus Express Truckers. His cousin Toby Etheridge and an Appalachian trucker named Pete Thompson, everyone called him by his CB handle, Jabez, were the original members of the JETS. Later, a sixty year old surfer named Windjammer got involved, and after that an out of control sexual predator named Big Montana got involved with the group. Big Montana was lucky though. Jabez stopped him one night from committing another rape and about ten of the Jets helped pull him out of a trap Satan had set for him just as he'd started to reach out to Jesus. The trap involved Big Montana's participation in an international sex slave business. The two masterminds of the operation were Ted Sciaffano, a New York City crime boss, and Vladimir Fedoseev an ex KGB field agent. They were the two that Coon Dog had prayed he wouldn't take revenge on when and if he got back to the world. They were the reason Coon Dog was convicted of two rape/murders. They had set the entire conspiracy up. They framed him in such a way there was no out. They'd gassed him and had a doctor remove DNA laden sperm, and of course planted the evidence on the two hapless female victims. Simply killing Coon Dog would have let him off too easily. They wanted to see a key member of the JETS get sent off to the banishment island. After all, it was the JETS who were responsible for their downfall and prison sentence a couple of years before the banishment law was passed. After serving only a year and a half and after greasing the hands of two states attorneys and two federal judges with ten million dollars, they were free once again to return to crime and of course to go after a key member of the JETS.

Most of that stuff only came up in Coon Dog's prayers. The rest of the time he was busy trying to stay alive. He was lucky yesterday and he knew it. He almost got caught by Toros and his gang, and then the panther. Yes, he was lucky.

Now he looked back to the east. A solid pink and crimson glow was rising. The sun would break the jungle's horizon in twenty minutes or so. He removed his bedding and scattered it carefully back in the leaves and grass from where it had come from. No sense leaving a hint to others as to where he'd spent the night. He'd be able to remember the location though. He might need it again in the future. He unfolded the panther skin and after notching a couple of holes in its edges with his flintstone and cutting a thin two foot long strip of it, he tied it around his shoulders and draped it over his back. The inside, still damp, was on the outside, so as to catch the sun for additional drying. Coon Dog appeared to be wearing a cape, only of panther skin, not fabric. What a sight he was, standing there in the early light. Six feet tall, about a hundred and seventy pounds, he wore a wood cross hanging from a buckskin strap. His hair was black and gray, whacked off to two inches, the same as his beard. His buckskin britches and vest were dirty and bloodstained. He wore ankle high moccasins with four layers on the bottom for his walking comfort. And now, before he moved out, he cut a six-foot long, three inch sapling for a walking staff to replace the one that got lost in all the fracas of yesterday. Yes, he was a sight to see. He actually was a quarter Cherokee, but this early morning on the banishment island three hundred miles west of the Mexican state of Nayarit, Coon Dog looked like a full blooded North American Indian that might have lived here a thousand years ago. The island was no doubt a rugged and desolate asylum. In Spanish it was called Isla de la Lejania – Island of remoteness.

CHAPTER THREE

Coon Dog purposely left prints in the mud of several creek beds and then aimed off into jungle vegetation that led away from the true direction that camp Jabez Junction might have been found. These and many other precautions he'd always taken had so far protected the camp from visitors. He'd traveled about two miles. The mid-morning sun's intensity reminded him once again of a place in Southeast Asia, forty years ago, where like this island, he had been hunted by the bad guys. But now he would take back to the route and leave no signs all the way into camp. Would his ploy continue to protect Jabez Junction from the cannibals? He sure hoped so.

An hour later he could see the blue Pacific through a clearing. He worked his way down a gradual slope spotted here and there with small trees and plants. Finally he came upon low cliffs and farther away enormous boulders that worked their way from the surf's edge back into uncountable finger inlets. Some extended fifty yards back toward the cliffs, and some as much as a quarter mile. Few coastlines anywhere in the world were as rugged as this one. He knew the best route over and through the boulders. The route he chose dropped down to the many water inlets, hundreds of pools and eddies, and occasionally tiny strips of sand bars and beach. As he trekked through these lower areas that were catching the ebb and flow, the rise and fall of the surf patterns, Coon Dog pried mollusk mussels from the sun soaked rocks. He ate them live and raw until he was close to the cave. Coming off a sand bar he entered a fresh water pool that leaked over a rock ledge on the left, into an ocean inlet. On the right was the entrance to Jabez Junction. Sheer fifty foot vertical cliffs protected the hiding place from above, and down at ocean level the entrance was hidden by eight or ten huge boulders. Coon Dog worked his way through them and into Jabez Junction. He came in slowly and cautiously. In a few minutes his eyes adjusted to the dim splintered light sneaking in from the opening. He took off the panther cape and left it near the entrance. He scanned the rock room quickly and went directly to the back wall and filled a large wooden ladle with clear spring water that trickled down into the cave from a fresh water stream that flowed out of the highlands above.

The room was sparse. He'd built the wooden recliner he slept on most of the time. On it were stretched doe skins which were tied off tightly underneath and a couple of doe skin pillows he'd fashioned and stuffed with dried grass. One he used as a pillow for his head and the other as a support under his knees. On a rock shelf on one side of the cave he kept a few tools he'd fashioned and a few weapons. He had two tomahawks, another flintstone hunting knife, two spears, and a bow and about fifteen arrows. He didn't keep any firewood stored in the cave because he didn't build any fires in it. But he did have a fishing net he'd made from vines. It was maybe ten by ten feet and when he used it he weighted down one side of it with small rocks. He'd throw the net and drag the catch back to him with straps attached to the unweighted side. He'd tried spearing fish, but by trial and error determined his net casting provided more food.

Assured that everything was in order, Coon Dog turned to exit the cave and picked up the panther skin on his way out. He climbed over a few boulders and waded through a two foot pool before he began his work on the panther skin again. He soaked it in the pool, then stretched it over a sun drenched smooth boulder about waist high and the size of a buffalo. It was the perfect work bench. The membrane side was exposed to the sun, the outside skin stretched over the heated boulder. He went to the sandy bottom of the pool with his hands and scooped eight, maybe ten piles of wet sand up on the skin. Next he scrubbed the sand across the skin's surface with a small piece of doe skin he'd brought with him. He cleaned it like this several times, rinsing it thoroughly each time. He took the panther skin with him as he made his way to the freshwater pool, fifty yards away. There he immersed the skin in the salt free water and rinsed it thoroughly. He stretched it over a boulder to begin the sun drying.

He was quite proud of his new black panther skin, and he knew that after three good days of drying he would possess a valued addition to his meager wardrobe. He wasn't even sure he wanted to wear it. There was a sneaking suspicion entering his mind that maybe this valuable panther skin had a much greater destiny than being a mere article of clothing for a wild man on a deadly island of the doomed. With that thought fixed in his head, he wound his way through the maze of boulders and climbed back up to the edge of the jungle. Was anyone waiting for him up above? Was he about to make another mistake and walk right into a trap? Without thinking about it he went into HWWLS mode – hide, wait, watch, listen, smell. Ten minutes later he came out and went to the highest vantage point he could find. He scooted up under some thick jungle ferns, thick enough to protect him from the now boiling heat of the mid-day sun.

He sat down and looked out to sea. He knew he'd see it in about a half hour. Well, at least he thought he'd see it. It made its southbound pass everyday about the same time. One of the two Spruance class destroyers that cruised off Isla de la Lejania 24-7-365, it represented the jailer to the men on the island. That is, all the men except one.

Prior to passage of the banishment law, the proponents of the law emphasized the simplicity and the economic benefits of dispatching society's worst monsters to the banishment island. There would be no cost outlay to build, maintain, or staff the island. On the contrary, federal, state, and local governments were currently spending somewhere in the fifty billion dollar range annually to pay for new prisons and jails , and all the cost of maintaining and staffing the old ones. The proponents of the banishment law further pointed out the savings to tax pay-ers by eliminating lengthy appeals, commuting capital punish-ment executions, and the like. All told, the estimates were that in the system before banishment was enacted, the average cost per day to incarcerate a heinous criminal was roughly fifty dol-lars, and after banishment was enacted the cost would be under three dollars per day. All that would be required to keep the blood sucking cannibals from escaping would be to continu-ously assign a couple of U.S. Navy destroyers to patrol off the island. If an escape plot was mounted and the sharks or the high seas didn't stop the escapees, then the destroyers would. How much more simple and cost effective could a prison be run? It couldn't.

Coon Dog waited. He was thinking about the crew of the destroyer. They were young, most of them – the techies, the deck hands, the weapons systems specialist, and the clerical and ship services types. The senior petty officers and the officers were older, late twenties up to the mid forties. Coon Dog had sailed with many crews back in the day. He'd been on carri-ers, LPH's, troop ships, cruisers, destroyers, and swift boats. He'd even had a deployment on an oiler when the sixth fleet commander, Admiral Harrison, had thought it wise to conceal the whereabouts of certain elite SEAL teams. Coon Dog figured the captain of the destroyer that should be passing by anytime now was probably a commander. But most of his thoughts were on the youngest members in the crew. Was there a young Christian on board who would help him? For the escape plan Coon Dog was building, there would have to be.

CHAPTER FOUR

Fifteen miles off the coast of Isla de la Lejania the *USS Nolin River*, a ten year old destroyer was barely visible from the island.

"Bring her another ten degrees southeast, Quartermaster, and maintain 16 knots."

"Aye, aye, Sir."

The O.O.D. (Officer of the Deck), Lieutenant Troy Wilkerson, was standing at the chart table in the pilot house. The coffee in his mug was luke-warm and stale. *Why can't the officers' mess make decent coffee? Even the black mud they drink down in the crews mess is better than this stuff.*

"We'll make that same course adjustment every twenty minutes, Quartermaster, and maintain 16 knots. That should keep us close to the 10 mile arc."

"Aye, aye, Sir." The quartermaster, Chris Remington, was a twenty-three year old third class petty officer. He'd run cross country in high school, played golf, and liked to shoot pool. Off duty he listened to Alice In Chains and Sound Garden. He might have been described as post Generation X. Like other recent generations of young American sailors, he flirted with a variety of socio-politico theories and movements, not settling in any one camp until much later in his life. For now it was go to sea, learn a few things and think about the G.I. bill and college when he got out of the Navy.

CHAPTER FIVE

Coon Dog had waited for half an hour under the ferns, and then he spotted the destroyer. If he hadn't been in the Navy, he never would have seen it. Just barely, every 30 seconds or so, he could make out the hint of the super structure, and the bridge, bobbing up between ocean swells. Before he made his way down the slope and into the boulders that led to Jabez Junction, he debated what to do with the rest of the day. He could fish or sharpen up his tools and weapons, or he could work on the escape raft he had hidden down the coast a couple of miles. Instead, he decided to go swimming. All the running yesterday and the battle with the panther had left his muscles knotted up. Nothing like a good hour long swim to smooth things out – not just the muscles, the mind and soul as well.

He'd had his spear and flintstone knife with him when he'd climbed to the observation spot under the ferns. Now, on the way to the swimming hole, he used the inverted spear as a walking staff. He stayed up high above the cliffs and boulders just in the edge of the jungle for nearly a half mile before dropping down and starting to worm his way through the inlets, coves, and ocean cul-de-sacs, all of them strewn with and in some cases hidden by the boulders.

The "swimming hole" was narrow and close to a hundred yards long. It wound its way through rock walls thirty feet high in some spots and the more common ten and fifteen foot boulders for most of the way. It could not be seen from above, and of course, that's why Coon Dog used it. He'd seen a shark in it on only one occasion. With it being only forty-five feet wide, he felt he'd have time to scutter up a rock to safety if a shark were to appear. He laid down the spear and removed the knife scabbard and laid it down. Then he dropped his buckskin pants and dove in from a ledge about fifteen feet above the shimmering, undulating turquoise pool below.

The swim was just what he needed, long, lazy laps from one end of the pool to the other. The tension, knots, and trouble of yesterday slipped off him as a cool mountain stream might have trickled over a rocky creek bed, cool mint growing in the eddies and wild flowers stretching toward the sun on the banks. He didn't think about anything. He just let his body take over, that ancient rhythmic dance of a babe in the womb – the swim.

Eventually he gave in to the lateness of the afternoon and climbed up the rocks using a few handholds and wedging himself between crevices as a rock climber might do. He found his things, slipped back into his buckskin britches, and scanned his surroundings quickly. Could a cannibal have followed him down here? His mind was already back to survival for another night of concealment. Don't let them know where you stay. His stomach was starting to think about a few things as well.

He hustled back to Jabez Junction and grabbed his fishing net. He worked his way down the rocks toward the sea itself. There were several areas he'd had luck in. The best place was where the rocks flattened out at the water's edge. At low tide and when the ocean swells weren't bad, he had a good place to cast the net and draw it back in quickly to see what he might have caught. After his third cast, he pulled the net toward himself and could see from a distance of maybe twelve feet that he'd gotten lucky. A six pound aku was tangled up in the net. If he could get it to him without letting the net open, he was about to enjoy raw aku, what the Japanese call sashimi. He drew it closer, the rock- weighted trailing edge of the net doing its job, not allowing the fish a back door escape route. He gutted and cleaned the aku and ended up with four eight inch long, heavy strips of raw, beet-red sashimi. He placed his meal in a pouch, gathered his net up, cleaned the knife and started back to the cave. Had anybody seen him fishing? He hoped not. He was hungry and wasn't interested in sharing his catch with a cannibal, and he certainly wasn't interested in another harrowing misadventure through the jungle with half a dozen man eating savages on his trail. He made it back and realized for the tenth time already today that his plans for escape needed to be ramped up. How much more of this could the take?

He added dried seaweed and wild onions to the menu, finished off the sashimi in ten minutes, and washed it all down with five ladles of good spring water trickling down the back wall of the hideaway cave.

Still an hour or two of sunlight left. What to do until dark? He liked to stay busy and to work all day right up to sundown. It helped with his sleep. If he could avoid napping during the day and stay busy, he usually got a decent night's sleep. The blood thirsty gangs tended to be more active at night. They built fires and stayed up late, hence you'd often catch them catnapping in the daytime. Coon Dog would occasionally build a cooking fire, but it was always in the daytime, and it would always be done quickly and only in an area where he had excellent escape routes.

He walked to the rock shelf where his tools were kept. He sharpened his flintstone to a fine edge as he did every two or three days and picked up a heavy mallet, an awl he'd made from bones, and some small rocks he'd been collecting. Finally he was ready to spend more time on the panther skin. He headed out of the cave, and on his way he was thinking about what he wanted to do with the skin. It was strange. He didn't have a vision. He did not have a plan at all, but when he got to it he started working on it as if he had blueprints and schematics directing him. He'd always been a fine craftsman of leather, pelts, animal skins and the like, but he usually had a pretty good idea of how the piece would shape up, what its function would be, what exactly it would end up looking like. But not this time. He removed the skin from the drying rock and ran his hands over it and seemed to be feeling it for what it might become. He pulled it slowly down the side of his face and wrapped it around himself. He held it high, getting a better take on its overall dimensions then laid it down and looked it all over again, and then picked it back up again.

Then he started cutting and shaping. The skin was plenty dry enough to work with, and Coon Dog was surprised how supple and luxuriant the short black fur felt to the touch of his fingers. Still he worked without a real plan. Oh, he was beginning to sense what shape it was taking, and what kind of garment it was going to become. But it wasn't because of a conscious plan he was working from. His hands worked independently, not as part of his thinking. It was a strange experience. Coon Dog couldn't ever remember anything like it in all his years.

When he'd done all he thought he could do on the skin, he took it up to the jungle and climbed up through the canopy. He flung the skin up as high as he could go. He made sure the thick tree foliage would conceal it from prying eyes down below. A couple of days of sun up there would dry it thoroughly and make it ready for its final cutting and shaping.

CHAPTER SIX

Coon Dog sat on a boulder facing the quickly disappearing sun. Layers of heavy cloud banks protected his eyes from the radiant energy. Sections of the horizon fairly exploded with color while other areas whimpered a sullen gray-blue song. He stretched and smiled out to his best friends – the colors of sunset at day's end. What other friends were there on this God forsaken island? Certainly not Toros and the other blood thirsty cannibals, society's banished monsters. Not the snakes, the sharks, or the panthers. His one friend, Red Man, had been eaten by Toros and his gang.

Coon Dog didn't often let Red Man's memory linger. But tonight, sitting here by the sea, Red Man's memory squatted down next to Coon Dog, and it wasn't going away. Coon Dog allowed Red Man's spirit to be present as he started thinking to himself. *Wouldn't it be nice to be on the southeast side of the island tonight and have that wide three mile stretch of sandy beach all to myself? Walk it leisurely just as if I were a Florida tourist on the white sands of Panama City or Fort Walton Beach? Maybe jog a mile or two at the edge of the water where the sand is packed perfectly for each footfall? I could look over my shoulder and see each footprint dissolve behind me as a new beach wash from a new wave gently erased it. But no, that would be impossible. I'd be totally exposed to the cannibals. I could get away with it in the early days. Me and Red Man had done it together a couple of times.*

Then he remembered most of the conversation he and Red Man had on one of those beach walks. "Coon Dog. Ha, that's a funny name. Your mother thought you'd turn out to be a good hunter," Red Man said.

"No, no. My daddy called me that. It's a nickname. My real name is Ronnie Matlock."

"Ronnie Matlock, or Coon Dog, which do I call you?"

"Take your pick."

"I think I will call you ...let's see...I will call you Island Dog. Will it be all right to call you Island Dog?"

"Hell, I guess so. Call me whatever you want to. What should I call you?"

"I am Lonely Bear-Brave Bear. You can call me Lonely Bear-Brave Bear."

"I don't know if I can remember all of that. How about I call you LB?"

"No. That not good. You call me Lonely Bear-Brave Bear."

"Okay, it'll be Lonely Bear-Brave Bear." But in Coon Dog's mind it would be Red Man, plain and simple, because this fellow prisoner had the reddest skin he'd ever seen.

"Is it safe to walk the beach in the open?" He started to say LB, but thought better of it.

"I think it is safe today. The crows have not warned me of anything today."

"Have they warned you before?"

"Yes."

"And did the cannibals show up."

"Yes."

"Are the crows always dependable?"

"It depends on one's experience."

"Could I learn to hear and understand the crows?"

"Maybe a young white man could. But you, Island Dog, you might be too old."

"That figures. But I also figured I was too old to get framed for raping and murderin', but here I am."

"It's a good thing."

"What's a good thing?"

"That your people set up this island, this banishment island. Yes, I know you did not rape and murder women. The crows would have let me know. But for the others ... yes, for them this island is a good thing. Here they will die. And why should the government spend the people's money to keep them alive in a prison? I don't often agree with the government, but I do this time. And yes, I'm sure you wonder why I would say that. Do you not wonder?"

"Well Lonely Bear-Brave Bear, I uh ... yes I guess I might wonder. I mean ... you know ... you yourself must have done something to get a ticket here."

"Yes. I knew you wondered about that. What I did to get here had to be done. I could tell you about it, but you would not understand. It is like the crows. You are too old. There are other worlds you are not aware of. Even my own people don't understand. That is why they seek out those like me. I have spent my life in the study of and the practice of powerful medicine. Your people call me a witch doctor and say I practice the occult, but they have no idea what my medicine means, where it goes, how it works."

They walked a good way down the beach, quietly, not talking. "So, tell me. Why is it a good thing this banishment island has been set up? I have told you only that I believe it is a good thing because why should the people spend their money to keep evil men alive. There is a better reason. Do you know what it is?"

Coon Dog was thinking it over. He remembered several years ago that the advocates of the banishment law said it would put to rest the seemingly never ending debate and divisiveness on capital punishment. He'd go down that track. "Some folks said that putting a man on a banishment island is the only way to make sure that the man will be judged by God. I got a cousin named Toby. He told me one time when we was talkin' about it, that he'd been sitting on the fence for a long time on capital punishment. You know, there were times he was one hundred percent in favor of it, but there were other times he'd get to thinkin' about it, and you know what he said? He said, he could not be the executioner, you know, the prison guard that pulled the switch. Toby's a strong Christian, and he just felt that only God should decide if a man should die – even a man that's done some mighty bad things. Yeah, Ol' Toby, he got into the debate on the banishment island pretty strong there for awhile. He was all for it. Is that what you were asking about? The better reason to have a place like this is that only God would make any final decision on a man's life?"

"Yes, yes, that is a good part of the reason. Your cousin is a wise man. And did you and Toby talk about another good reason – the deterrent to would be criminals?"

"Oh, yeah. Toby talked a lot about that. And look what happened after folks saw that banishment was real. The last I heard before they sent me here was that first degree murder was almost unheard of. Rape was down by eighty percent, so were all sex crimes, and would anybody ever have believed it? Drug abuse was almost dried up."

"But you, Island Dog, you are here with men who deserve to be here. You should not be here."

"Well no, no I don't deserve to be here, but I'm not going to stay here forever. I plan on gettin' off."

"Yes, I sense there are men praying for you and for your escape. Tell me about these men. I sense they have a strong connection to the Great Father, The Lamb, and The Great Spirit."

"That is exactly what they have my friend. They are all truckers. We call ourselves JETS. That means Jesus Express Truckers. I drove with them for a few years. They are amazing. I've seen them do a few things that are...well...let's just say they've done some things that would be described as miraculous."

Red Man stopped walking and turned to look out to sea. "Miraculous. Yes, what a strong word! And do you dream of these men, these JETS?"

"Oh yes. Almost every night. But the dreams sometimes are very confusing. You know ... most of the time I'm not sure who the people are in the dreams. Sometimes I'm sure it's the JETS. Other times I'm sure it's not them. And almost always, I can't tell if I, myself, am in them or not. It gets crazy sometimes."

"I'm sure it does seem crazy to you. But listen Island Dog. You are not too old to learn from these dreams. There is wise counsel in dreams. A man your age surely knows this. And your Bible, our Bible, what does it have to say about dreams? Were there not many visions that the prophets Jeremiah, Micah, and Daniel received in dreams? And before them Abram was the first to have a vision from God. He would have more. Then Jacob dreamed of a ladder reaching all the way to heaven. Paul was in Corinth and dreamed the Lord would protect him while he preached there. If these men could learn from dreams, then should you not be able to do the same?"

Coon Dog pondered the question, "Sure, I reckon I can. You said *our* Bible. You are a Christian?"

"Yes."

"You think maybe my dreams are trying to teach me something?"

"They are trying to do *something* to you. All dreams are. They may teach, warn, encourage, manipulate, entertain, threaten, protect, or distract you. They are always doing something like that. They don't just happen. They are not the subconscious overflow of daily activity as many of your psychoanalysts believe."

"You sure about that?"

"Yes."

"So let me see if I got this right. You are a medicine man, I think they call it a shaman. You talk to the crows. You are a Christian. You did something that got you banished, but it had to be done, and I wouldn't understand it. And now you tell me you know more about dreams than psychologists do?"

"I am what I am."

"Well, okay, you are what you are, but isn't there something inconsistent about what you are saying?"

"What is inconsistent?"

"You say you are a medicine man and you say you are a Christian. How can you be both at the same time? I read my Bible ... well, I mean I used to read it. One of the cannibal gangs ransacked my camp and besides taking everything in it, they burned my Bible. Did the Marines give you a Bible when they put you ashore?"

"Yes, I still have it."

"Well, what I mean is ... when I read it I don't recall anywhere it saying God's children are allowed to be sorcerers, medicine men, seers, or anything of the like. How do you get off thinking God will permit you to be involved in that stuff, and then receive you into the kingdom of heaven when you die?"

"Ha! Yaaaha! Ha! Ha!" Red Man fell to the sand laughing uncontrollably. Deep rolling belly laughs had him tied up. He tried to get back to his feet, but the laughing had him earthbound. Now crying laughing, sobbing laughing, the kind where it's hard to breathe. He reached his hand up to Island Dog and barely got it out, "Help Me." As Coon Dog pulled on the Indian, Red Man yanked him down to the sand and rolled over on top him, laughing harder than ever. Coon Dog was not amused and had his flintstone up under Red Man's throat.

"Ha, ha. This is funny as hell. Get off me you phony cigar store Indian."

Red Man rolled off him and got to his feet, the laughter subsiding. "I'm sorry ... it's just ..." He almost started back in on the belly whomper laughing, but was able to regain a bit of sanity. "I'm sorry. It's just as I was saying earlier, ... um, um, um." He almost started again, but finally regained control. "Earlier I said there are worlds, let us say realms of existence that most men are not aware of." He paused and waited til Coon Dog put the flintstone away. "I have found ways to enter some of those worlds. I don't think I was born with this ability. I might have been, but I don't think so. Medicine men in my tribe have passed this knowledge on for many thousands of years. So, your question was, I think, before I lost control ...oh, your question was how can God allow me into heaven knowing I have skills as an Indian spiritual man, a medicine man? It is an easy question to answer, but first let us talk about some things that the Bible says."

Red Man started walking slowly down the beach again. Coon Dog was walking with him but stayed a few feet further away than he was before. "There is a story about Saul and David. Saul has lost favor in the Lord's eyes. He had tried to do things on his own and avoided the counsel of the Lord.

Eventually Saul seeks the help of a medium, one who can com-
municate with the dead. The medium is able to pull Samuel up
from the bowels of the earth. Are you familiar with this story?"

"I think I read it, but I don't remember anything about it."

"Yes, well Samuel speaks to Saul and tells him he will die
soon, and David will become the king. These things do take
place. The use of a medium is central to the story, and I have
always felt that I am in a similar position to that medium.
King Saul seeks out her skills to bring up Samuel from Sheol,
a deep dark place in the earth. Will this medium be restricted
from entry into heaven? For after all, Moses was instructed
to stay away from mediums and familiar spirits. Will she not
be treated any differently? The story does not deal with that
question. As for myself, I think it is the same. I will not
know my ultimate destination after my death until I get there.
But I can tell you this Island Dog. It does not worry me. I
have already been on the other side. I much prefer my earthly
existence."

Coon Dog got up from the boulder he'd been perched on
and took one last appraisal of the fading sunset. Misty gray
blue shadows would hold just a few moments longer. Most of
the crimsons and violets had already faded. He worked his way
back to Jabez Junction and wondered at the Red Man memory
he'd just had. Could it really have been only two years ago? It
seemed more like another lifetime.

He entered the black cave and felt his way over to his frame
sleeper with the skins drawn tight over it. He applied some
of the mosquito repellant to his neck, arms, and feet. He laid
down and positioned one of his dried grass pillows under his
knees and another under his head. He immediately started
thinking about driving a big truck. That would be the easiest

way to drop off to sleep tonight, not rethinking the strange other world psychology of a whacked out medicine man who's been dead for two years. He drifted off to sleep and another truck dream was under way.

....

The truck driver always thought I-81 in the Shenandoah Valley was the prettiest interstate in the country. Now he knew he'd put I-80 in Northern Pennsylvania right there with it. He tore out of New Jersey one night in early February, glad to be out of the nonsense and calamity of twenty million people or so, linked together, glued together. God help them, stuck together, from the tip of Long Island to Northern New Jersey. Crossing the Pennsylvania line at the Del Water Gap and rejoicing in the clear moonlight sky above and the good mountain driving ahead, he said to himself. *Thank you Father for getting me out of there, out of the clutches of foreigners, congested traffic, gone mad traffic, impossible traffic, confusing road signs, incorrect road signs, no road signs at all. Thank you for getting me out with no delays, problems, screw ups, missing paper work, wrong turns, loading or dock problems, angry drivers of trucks and cars cutting me off, honking at me, throwing obscene gestures at me, cursing me. Thank you Father for not allowing the ordinary things that happen in and around New York City to happen.*

He didn't thank God the Father for the almost flub up with the African gate guard at the shipper's truck yard in Newark. He pulled into the yard and noticed the signs, six of them, directing him to one of six lanes to drive through. But which one? He also noticed the other sign that said "Check in on CB channel 4". He flipped his channel selector to 4, keyed his mike, and spoke loudly, "Security, do you copy? Mid State

Trucking checking in for pick up." No response. He kept trying. No response.

Finally another trucker cut in on his CB and said, "Mid State that there gate guard don't speak no English. Take lane two and pull on up yonder on that there scale. The guard is right there in the shack next to the scales."

He slowly went through lane 2 and up a ramp to the scales. He stopped at the stop sign, didn't set his brakes until the weight print out on the machine inside would be printed. Then he got out of the cab and walked the twenty five feet to the guard shack. The tar paper black man inside saw him coming but didn't look his way or go to the closed sliding glass window where any and all business would be handled. The driver waited outside in the cold for a minute and finally tapped on the window even though he knew the man inside knew he was there. The black man begrudgingly came to the window, opened it and said, "Uah paapa urrhh nid. Nid uurk purmt."

The driver said, "Say again please, I don't understand."

"Uah paapa urrhh nid. Nid uurk purmt."

"The driver said, "I'm sorry, it's me. I don't hear well. Please say again. I'll get it this time."

"Uah paapa urrhh nid. Nid uurk purmt."

Two minutes later the truck driver deciphered the half African, half New Yorkeese lingo. "Your paper work need. Need your New York permit." The man's nature wasn't mean. It was indifferent. At least to the driver that's what it sounded like. The man's eyes told the real story. "Mister, you are going to have to understand me. Not the other way around. I know what you want – to pick up your load and get out of here. But you will have to do what I say if that is to happen."

So now that the truck driver was out of there rolling westbound in Pennsylvania on a beautiful clear night, the twenty million or so confused victims all behind him, he looked up into the midnight sky and thanked God. There was snow in the mountains, and the skinny leafless trees were looking like beard stubble in the moonlight. Oh it was all so beautiful. He was out of there! Good highway ahead, open road, no traffic, 65 mph, but he'll sneak it up to 68. Rolling now. Out of there. Road sign says Scotrum, PA, or was it Scrotum? Another says Lake Harmony. *You got that right. I'm feeling harmonious.* Nescopeck Mountain, Lime Ridge, Roaring Creek, White Deer. *I'm rolling now. Yessiree!*

The driver moved easily through the mountains. Up a long grade leveled out on top for a distance then back down the western slope. The rig might have been sailing. Effortlessly it took the mountains on, one at a time. The driver was confident and smooth with the wheel in his hand. Rolling westward, sailing westward, it was all the same. He was the captain of this ship, and he was in total control. What little traffic there had been was gone now. The truck, the driver, the mountains, the road, the stars and the moonlit night – that's all. No distractions. Nothing to do but roll. Nothing to do but sail. Feel the highway, feel the wheel, feel the truck react to your control. Feel the driving. Oh, what a night!

A little later a few scattered cars and trucks began to share the highway with the truck driver, and not long afterwards the truck driver was pulling into the company truck terminal. The terminal manager said they were taking his truck out of service and the driver would have to catch a ride home with another driver. The truck driver went into the driver's lounge and asked around about getting a ride. Nobody was going his direction it seemed, so he went outside to the yard and asked a few men if they were going his way. "No. I don't even have a load." "No, my truck is being worked on." "No, I'm waiting on a ride myself."

It was still dark and he was about to give up, but he spotted a couple of men working on the trailer lights of a rig that was in the terminal's outbound lane. The driver of the truck being worked on was standing there watching. He had a turban on his head and a long gray beard.

"Hey, you got a load going south? I'm trying to get a ride home."

"Ah, yes. Yes. I going south. We get lights fixed, we go."

"Okay, thanks a lot. I'll get my things."

"Ah, yes, get your luggage."

The truck driver went back to get a couple of bags of personal stuff in his truck that the terminal manager said was being taken out of service. A few minutes later he and the turbaned driver were pulling out of the truck yard and headed for Georgia.

"My name is Singh Khutar." His voice was high and squeaky.

The truck driver said, "I'm Bill." He was thinking, *Great, I'm riding with a Muslim or a Hindu, or some other kind of a raghead. He stinks. I can smell him from way over here. His voice sounds like a bird chirping. This truck is the pits. The passenger door doesn't work. This seat feels like a dozen springs are coming through it. Look at the trash on the floor and all the clothes and junk strewn around back in the sleeper. What a mess!* "This isn't a company truck is it? How long you had your Freightliner?"

"Oh, I have it over two million miles."

"Really. When did you overhaul the motor?"

"One point four million I do overhaul."

Bill was quiet for a minute. He felt the vibration of the big motor running through the cab. The steady, reassuring, pulsating throb of four hundred fifty or so horses, running smoothly. He looked over at Singh, his seat up close to the steering wheel, not back away from it like most drivers he knew, himself included. Singh seemed to be in a natural and comfortable position even though he was up close to the wheel. Bill watched as Singh shifted gears occasionally on a hill, and for the life of him, he couldn't detect any bump or power shift when the shift was made. And he noticed that when Singh flashed his lights on and off to give the "come on back over" signal to trucks in the hammer lane, the spacing he allowed before giving the signal was the same each time. Then he noticed that the speed Singh was running was just a little slower than most of the trucks on the highway and as a result, Singh was never tailgating, was never on his brakes, and was never accelerating out into the hammer lane to pass somebody. He realized that these things provided Singh with much better fuel mileage than most of the drivers he knew.

"Have a tangerine." Singh had grabbed an open bag of fruit from somewhere in the chaos of food, clothing, and junk behind his seat and was holding it out to Bill.

"Thanks." Bill took a tangerine but waited before peeling it. He held it in his hands for a moment and was looking around for a trash bag. He noticed that Singh was already eating a tangerine. He began peeling his and when he had all the peels in his hand, he used his other hand to open the vent window.

"Are you too warm?" Singh asked the question without taking his eyes off the road ahead.

"No, I'm going to toss these peels out."

"Oh no, no. Just lay them up on the dash by the windshield. The heat from the defroster will make a good aroma out of them." His sing sing voice seemed pleased to make this announcement.

Bill laid the tangerine peels up on the dash near the windshield and took a large section of tangerine into his mouth. It was very sweet and very delicious.

They rode on through the night, stopping for fuel just before sun-up. Bill was returning to Singh's truck from the rest room and noticed that most of the other ten or twelve drivers around the fuel islands had returned from their business inside carrying large bags of pre-dawn breakfast – burgers, fries, sausage biscuits, chips, candy, shakes, hot dogs buried in ketchup, mustard, onions and relish, and any quick snacks they could cram into the bag – cheese crackers, lots of cheese crackers.

As they continued driving toward Georgia, Bill was thinking about all the drivers he knew who kept their seat slid way back from the steering wheel, and he glanced back over at Singh who was now slowly eating maybe the third tangerine of the long night. Bill had to smile a little smile then returned his gaze to the road ahead.

Some time passed, maybe several weeks and Bill the truck driver was back in the mountains. A nor'easter was shutting down everything. Parts of Virginia, Maryland, Pennsylvania, and New York were buried under two feet of snow. Bill was pulling a load to Boston and had decided to avoid the I-95 corridor, so he was two hundred miles west of the coast. Little did he know that was the epicenter of the storm, where most interstates and secondary roads would be closed. It being too late to adjust his route, he settled into the dangerous task of negotiating mountain roads packed with snow and ice. The first couple of hours weren't too bad. At least he had decent visibility. He maintained 45 mph on level roads and on uphill grades and only dropped to 30 on the downhills. But the snow started getting heavier, and Bill noticed there were only a few vehicles still on the roads and their lights were getting harder and harder to see. He thought he saw a sign indicating a 3 mile downhill grade, but he wasn't sure. Just to be safe, he cut his speed down to 20, and he switched his four way emergency blinkers on, but it didn't make him feel much better because now the wind whipped snow doubled its intensity. He was in a blizzard, a whiteout. Visibility was nonexistent. Not even a faint flicker of lights from other trucks and cars. Outside his windshield his headlights hit the wall of blowing snow and careened right back at him. His years of experience screamed two instant warnings - GET OFF THE ACCELERATOR and DO NOT GET ON THE BRAKES. *But I can't see, and I'm going downhill with 43,000 on, and my speed is picking up.* Oh did he ever want to hear a secret voice in him come out just once, just once now, and say *It's okay, just a little brake will be okay, just a light touch to hinder your advancing speed. It's okay, go ahead just a light touch.* But that hidden inner voice never came out, and he knew what he must do. Get it over on the shoulder where the foot of snow isn't packed down to a skating rink. Get the rig over there. *But I can't see! Tough. Do you want to die or do you want to use your only option to slow this thing down?* He ever so gently aimed it right. If he went too far it was hello guardrail and a thousand foot tear through the hardwoods. At the funeral they would say he was brave for having tried to bring it down the mountain in the whiteout. They never would have known he was doing everything in his power to stop it dead on the shoulder and sit it out. In either case he would still be dead.

He felt the steer tires bite into the deeper snow on the shoulder and he started slowing a little – 27, then 25, a little more to 22, then 18. He still couldn't see a thing outside, only white where the headlights bounced off the wall of snow. His speed dropped to 12 and then 7, and he had a glimmer of hope – maybe he'd live to see another day. It didn't last long. He didn't feel like the truck was moving, but it had to be. He now was reading 5 mph on the speedometer. Twenty years of driving, but he'd never had this happen before. He could not tell if he was moving or sitting still. Was he out of control? Was he rolling, sliding, spinning? He didn't know. There was only the whirling whiteness all around. There was no such thing as a sense of distance, or depth perception, or speed. He opened his window and stuck his head out and tried to look down to see if he was moving. Nice thought but to no avail. The whiteout was in control. Finally the speedometer reached 0, and he set his parking brakes. He climbed halfway down and cautiously put one foot down through the snow to try to hit something solid. The ground, it *was* down there. He got back in the seat and tried to slow down his heavy breathing. Then he changed his shirt. The sweat on the one he'd removed had a little different smell than usual. Raw fear was reeking from it. *Hm,* he thought. *Twenty years. Never happened like this before.*

Bill the truck driver was joined by others now in Coon Dog's dream, and the dream was taking a turn toward the bizarre.

"Speed, bennies, pep pills, west coast turn-a-rounds, that's the thing all right. I used to pop em' down like candy. I'd run three thousand miles easy. Then I'd pop some more and turn around and head home. Couldn't sleep when I got there , so I'd go right back out. Did that for about five years."

Then a foxy looking lady walked into the diner where they were drinking coffee. She looked at the drivers sitting around the horseshoe counter and said, "Hello boys. Who wants to give me a ride to Grand Junction?"

They pretty much ignored her except Bill. He got up and was going to touch her, but she became a black panther and gave him pause to continue toward her. Then she became a sleek, shiny, apple red Pete 309 dressed out in brilliant chrome from nose to rear end, top to bottom, and she was running hard on 94 westbound in Wisconsin, thirty miles from Eau Claire. The CB jumped loud with, "Push it fellers, push it! We gonna' roll tonight."

"God A'Mighty, there's Jabez. He's in the cab of a heavenly chariot. Look at him fly! Why the angels can't keep up with him."

And three more were behind him, but they weren't chariots. They were big trucks. They roared through the stars and the mountains, and they never stopped. They went through heavenly canyons in far off galaxies. They exploded through sparkling purple vapor curtains a million miles across. They were truckin'. "Hey Jabez, we comin'. Slow down, we comin'".

"Can't slow down boys. We rollin'! We rollin' clean and good! Can't stop. Come on boys, can't stop!"

The astro convoy picked up new drivers and whipped through untold dimensions of time and space. Then, just as suddenly as it started, it came back to earth and was working hard, pulling the nearly 20 mile grade, westbound on 70, inside the Utah line heading for the 70-15 split. Some of the trucks would be turning northwest toward Salt Lake City, and some would be taking 15 southwest toward Las Vegas, then over Mountain Pass and down into the L.A. basin.

The trucks all had heavy loads. There were no speed demons in the hammer lane. Tachs were pushing 1600, all of them running about 5th or 6th gear. One less experienced driver was beginning to lose power. He went to the CB. "I'm losing rpm's, but the speed seems to stay up. It almost feels like an injector might be messed up."

He got several comebacks, all making a legitimate suggestion or asking an appropriate question: "Try dropping a gear."

"Is your turbo running?" "You got good fuel?" "Are you over-heating?" And so it went.

But nothing he did would correct the problem. So by necessity, he began slowing down. His tach and speedometer were both going down. As trucks began swinging out on the hammer lane to pass him, another CB voice offered its opinion. "You know, I was running up this grade a few years back, and the same thing happened to me. I was losing rpm's but not speed; then they both gave up. I was slowing down and eventually I had to stop."

"Well, what was the problem?"

"Never did figure it out, but I can tell you what I think it was."

"Tell me."

"When I stopped, the first thing I did was check the fuel pump. It looked clean, no clogs or dirt in it, and the fuel level was where it was supposed to be. I checked everything else I could think of, but nothing seemed out of whack. I tried pulling the grade again, but no luck. I pulled over on the shoulder and tried to think it through. I knew the elevation was six or seven thousand, a heavy load, and every other factor I could think of, but my thinking wasn't going to get that load up that grade. I tried again, but still had no power. I was going to call for a wrecker to come get me, but my cell was out and I didn't have a qual com. I laid down for a nap, and two hours later I fired it up and off I went, no problems, plenty of power. You know what was wrong with that truck? It needed a rest. That's all it was."

"Aw, I don't know about that."

"I'm telling you, that's all it was. She needed a rest. Just needed to take a little breather, just like a human. Now that was the first truck I ever gave a name to. She's been Ol' Sleepin'

Nelly ever since. Try it mister. Pull over and give that truck a two or three hour snooze. She might wake up ready to go and climb right on up this grade."

"All right. I'll give it a shot. But what should I name her?"

"How about Ol Sleepin Nelly the second?"

"No I got a better one. How about Old Lard Ass Who Needs Sleep?"

"Yeah, that sounds good."

Coon Dog awoke abruptly. The cave was pitch black. He could hear the ocean a hundred yards away. Did he hear anything else? Did he hear men whispering? No, he was secure in the knowledge that he'd never seen another human within two miles of this location. Sometimes while out on hunting trips or recon, days and nights he'd spend away from Jabez Junction, he would purposely leave signs of his presence. His thinking was that the cannibal gangs would waste time and effort on locating him in that area. It was pretty good thinking, but little did Coon Dog know that after two years, Toros was getting wise to the deception.

Coon Dog lifted himself off the sleeper and made his way in the dark to the back wall. He filled the large wooden ladle with the cool sweet spring water trickling down the wall. He drank his fill, then carefully maneuvered his way to the opening. He went to the first sea water he knew would flush his urine away quickly. No sense leaving his scent, even here at the place he felt he was the safest, even in the middle of the night. But there was nothing he could do to hide the gas he expelled.

CHAPTER SEVEN

That same night that Coon Dog had felt confident about his privacy at Jabez Junction, Toros was three miles away sitting near the campfire gnawing on a human bone he had been heating over the fire. If you got them glowing hot and dipped them in water and returned them to the heat several times, they would soften up a little. It was a femur and he'd been working on it for several nights. The big knobby end that had once fitted into a man's pelvis was gone, and another inch or two down the shaft was also gone. At his side were his weapons. One was a crude tomahawk with a blunt rock attached to one end, his beating weapon. Another was a real Indian tomahawk he'd taken off Red Man's body. Lastly he had a spear ground down to a pretty fair point on one end.

He wore crude moccasins that were rotting off. Even new they weren't comparable to the craftsmanship that went into the moccasins Coon Dog made and wore. Toros wore tattered and torn dungaree jeans that all those dropped on the island arrived with. The ones Toros wore were from a new island arrival of approximately three months before. He'd been eaten within three days of his arrival.

If you'd seen Toros back in the world, before his banishment and in between prison stints, let us say in a public mall and he was on probation, you'd probably flinch. You were ordinary Joe eight to five, wife, kids, a den in the burbs. Let's say you were strolling down the main corridor of the mall supposedly window shopping while your wife was in J.C. Penny's on down the way. Really you were eyeballing all the young women, playing fantasy games with each one. Then suddenly you saw Toros and another man that seemed to be with him, but there was something very strange about the two of them. Toros got your attention first. He was standing ten feet away, his back half turned to you. You noticed the tattoos and the cord like ripples in the back of his neck above the long sleeved tee shirt, and below the knit cap with only a short bill on the front. You noticed the cap covered either a bald head or stubble of a wiry nature. Was he a black man? You didn't think so, but you were not sure. His skin color is somewhere between mulatto and Puerto Rican. Turned halfway sideways you don't get a good look at his face, but you do notice it's a hard face, a very hard face. It even looks like the swelling and bruises of many a fight over many years has stayed on his face, has never gone away. You realize that even if you could get a good look at his face, then you wouldn't really see what's under the scarring and swelling where the eyes are supposed to be, and you realize with some shock, you wouldn't want to. Then you notice the younger guy with him, thinner and obviously younger. No hard face, but definitely not a soft face either. Maybe it's a face that has seen plenty of fights, but has found a way to stay out of most of them. You notice immediately this younger guy is black, not pure deep black, but like most, something less than that. And then you notice the peculiar way in which this younger guy reacts to everything Toros does. He's the bottom of the pecking order, the underdog, not the alpha dog. Toros turns to look at something, he turns. Toros strolls a few feet down the corridor, he follows. Outside the mall in the parking lot, Toros puts a cigarette in his mouth, the younger guy immediately produces a lighter and lights him up, and only then, he lights his own smoke. That's all you see of the two of them, but you, Joe six-pack, wife and kids, den in the burbs, even with your minimal knowledge of life on the seedier side, you've seen enough prison movies to know what the story is with these two men. A hardened con gang leader and his young bitch. Toros looks mean. He looks real mean.

But Toros isn't in a public mall tonight. No, he's three hundred miles off the west coast of Mexico on the banishment island of Isla de la Lejania. The five men around the fire with him are gnawing on human bones also, but not on any femurs, the largest bone in the human body. Several have ribs, and a couple of these zombies of death are trying to chew out sustenance from the skull bones. They see that Toros is about ready to say something. They won't mutter a sound until they are sure he's finished.

"It's a good thing I have done tonight sending out Hector and the Sergeant to locate the Christian. It is time we find him. Two years now he's tricked me. He's left that sign of the cross everywhere and we've been fools to search near it. Yes, he's played the game well, but now we are here, close to his hiding place. Here he leaves no signs. His trickery is over. And tomorrow morning when Hector and the Sergeant return to camp, we will either prepare the Christian for eating or we will eat Hector and the Sergeant."

The others knew that if Hector and the Sergeant didn't get lucky and kill the Christian and drag him back, then none of them would ever see Hector and the Sergeant again. They would disappear. They wouldn't be crazy enough to return to camp with no food. They knew it, but of course would never voice that knowledge to Toros. It had been this way all along. If Toros ordered you out of camp and to return with something to eat, and you returned empty handed, well ...everyone knew who would be gutted and placed on the spit to slow cook. It had actually happened twice, the hopeless victims too tired, to worn out to fight anymore, too overcome with their own starvation and lack of will to live. The mornings they returned empty handed, they simply waited near the fire for Toros to kill them and do the rest of it.

Down in the inlets and boulders by the ocean Hector and the Sergeant moved slowly. It was an overcast night, no moonlight or starlight.

"The spring must trickle out down here somewhere. I think Toros is right. The Christian probably stays close to it." Hector was leading the way. He knew that to fail tonight meant retreating into the jungle to try to survive on his own. He also knew that if that were the way it would shake out, that he and the Sergeant would eventually square off and that the winner would eat the loser. Staying in the gang had probably kept him alive so far. Other than the Christian, they weren't aware of any other non gang members that had survived more than a couple of months, except Red Man.

"What's that?" The Sergeant whispered.

"What? I don't hear anything." Hector strained to filter out anything from the steady ocean sounds of waves a hundred yards away and tides rolling and swirling against the rocks all around them.

"No, not sounds, the smell."

They both turned up the olfactory unit a notch and stood motionless. It was gone as quickly as it had arrived.

"I smelled it too. He pissed and farted. If he'd taken a dump we'd still be smelling it."

"And he pissed into the water. It's gone now."

"Yes, he's close by," whispered Hector.

The Sergeant pulled Hector away, and slowly they climbed up out of the boulders and crept through the grass above until they reached the edge of the jungle. "We will get the rest of them and be waiting for him in the morning when he comes out."

CHAPTER EIGHT

What a night of truck dreams! Old Bill and that raghead, Jabez and some wild bunch, WHEW! I wonder what Red Man would say I'm supposed to learn from all of it. Coon Dog stretched long and contorted his body around a couple of times before stepping down off his sleeper. He noticed the sunlight already sneaking in the opening of the cave, there was just enough light to head for the spring water on the back wall. The dreams must have really sapped him. He was usually out of the cave before first light, but not today.

He was naked as he walked out the entrance. He would go to the same inlet he'd relieved himself in last night after dreaming. Did he actually think he heard voices last night? No, impossible. It must have been part of the dreams. After peeing, he'd come back and put on his buckskins and moccasins and have a breakfast of pemmican mixed with spring water.

Out of the cave now he was making his way through the first three boulders. The fresh water pool was just to his right. His heart froze! A cannibal was thirty feet above the pool, back turned to him, scanning the area feverishly. Coon Dog looked around. Another cannibal was seventy yards away on the other side of the boulder strewn inlet. His instincts told him he could not go back to the cave. If there were two of them, there were more. In the cave he'd be hemmed in. They would discover the fresh water pool and in short order follow it back to the cave. He had a choice. Up over the rocks and a mad dash to the jungle. No weapons. Running through four, six, or eight of them. Or the sea? *If I make it through the boulders to the breakers, I can swim out quickly. None of them would dare swim out after me.* What to do then? He'd worry about that when he got there. GO! He darted through two boulders very close where he couldn't be seen and stopped to collect his wits. He peeked back and saw a third cannibal probably sixty feet above the hidden entrance to the cave. He was pointing down at the fresh water pool or was he pointing at *him*?

GO! He tore out from the boulders and hit a thirty yard stretch of open sand. Halfway through he saw the fourth cannibal off to his left up on another boulder and even though it was at an angle, the cannibal was between Coon Dog and the sea.

"There he is! There he is!" Coon Dog heard the fourth cannibal screaming.

Spears, clubs, and tomahawks, that's all they had. No bows and arrows. The fourth cannibal was climbing down, trying to get into position to intercept Coon Dog.

Coon Dog could see he was going to be cut off. He picked up the only thing he could, a rock the size of a grapefruit and headed straight off, right at the surprised cannibal. The cannibal got his spear up in enough time to put it right through Coon Dog's belly, but Coon Dog dodged it and hit the cannibal chest high knocking him back against a boulder. A half second later the rock found the side of the cannibal's head about ear high. Then it found it again, and again, and a fourth time for good measure.

As the cannibal slumped downwards, his blood and brains already mixing with sand and sea water, Coon Dog ripped off the rotting shirt the cannibal wore and wasted no more time. In sixty seconds he was in the ocean swimming hard against the current and the waves. At fifty yards out he looked back over his shoulder and saw Toros and five other cannibals on the edge of the rocks, all screaming at him. "You will die Christian, and when you wash up, we will still eat you!"

CHAPTER NINE

Coon Dog was glad he'd yanked the ragged shirt from the cannibal. It was indispensable as an eye shade while he floated on his back. He'd folded it over to get it as thick as he could, then he tied it behind his head. At first he attempted to shield his entire face with the rag, but quickly realized he was performing water board torture on himself. He didn't need that!

Now it was mid morning, probably another three hours to high noon. After his escape, he'd swum out about a mile before deciding to roll over to the survival float. Windjammer, one of his old truck driver buddies and a member of the JETS, had told him a story about using the survival float one day off Makapuu Beach in Hawaii. Windjammer was about a quarter mile out and resting comfortably, just his face and chest bobbing up high enough to allow him to breathe easily and of course hold his breath for buoyancy. After a while three companions joined him, each one sporting a dark grey dorsal fin. They showed no interest initially, and Windjammer was about ready to head back in toward the beach taking it nice and easy, not creating a ruckus with panic swimming. He actually thought the sharks had moved on, but then one of them swam up close and nudged him on the thigh. In his surprise and shock Windjammer flailed at the water and nearly drowned.

Coon Dog was thinking about Windjammer's story and about the lesson it contained – don't panic if a shark bumps you or gets real close; they are probably just probing for blood or some other weakness. *Well sure,* Coon Dog was thinking. *We swam with sharks in SEAL training just to get used to it.*

Training was one thing, this was another. This was the open Pacific. *I am alone, cannibals who know I'm out here are on the beach, just waiting. A U.S. Navy destroyer is circling out there another fourteen miles. If they pick me up, they'll put me right back on the island.*

So Coon Dog did what came naturally. He laughed at his predicament, and taunted the sharks. *Here sharky, here sharky, sharky! Come on Sharky! Come and get me! Here I am! Come on sharky, sharky. I bet you're real hungry! Come on and get a bite of ol' Coon Dog. Come on sharky, come on now!* His taunting was silent. He didn't say it out loud.

Then Coon Dog did what didn't come so naturally to him. He prayed. Praying was an activity he hadn't done much of before becoming a JET. Oh, he'd done a little praying as a youth and even in Vietnam, and occasionally for the next sixteen years of his nineteen year Navy career. Then he quit praying until he'd become a JET. His Navy career was typical for a Vietnam vet. After his second tour in Nam, he got a cushy assignment. Then the ordinary routine began to settle in - rigorous training and remote duty to some far off hot spot, or a super sensitive secret mission which never made the evening news. At the nineteen year mark Coon Dog found himself with a SEAL team based out of Rota Spain. He was a Chief Petty Officer and the team counted on him as much as when he was a young buck. He might not be able to swim as far or as fast as the young guys, or survive for countless days in the badlands, but when the going got tough and a truly expert weapons man was needed, it was usually Coon Dog they looked to. One day Coon Dog got a letter from back home reporting bad news. His father, Horace Matlock, had made a turn for the worse.

His lung cancer was no longer treatable, and the doctors gave him less than six months to live. Coon Dog immediately went to the personnel officer and requested a transfer back to the states so he could be close to home when the time came. The personnel officer said that as much as he wanted to approve the request, he just couldn't do it. Coon Dog couldn't believe what he was hearing. After nineteen years of honorable service, a clean record, three purple hearts, four Navy Unit Citations, a Silver Star, and about fifteen other assorted metals and accommodations including his POW status for two weeks in North Vietnam, the brain trust of the United States Navy would not allow Chief Petty Officer Ronnie Matlock to be transferred stateside so he could be close to his father when he died.

But Coon Dog didn't stop trying. On his third and final visit to the personnel officer, Coon Dog was prepared to take matters into his own hands. He walked into the personnel officer's private office and snapped off a crisp salute, "Chief Petty Officer Matlock requesting a moment of your time sir."

"Come on in Chief, but if this is about your request to go stateside, don't waste your time. There's nothing I can do."

"I beg your pardon sir. There is something you can do. My father is going to die soon, and I need to be close to him. You could sign the approval for my transfer sir,"

"No, Chief, I'm sorry. That's just not going to happen. Now, I'm dismissing you chief. You need to turn around and walk out that door."

"No sir. Not on your life. I'm going to be with my father one way or the other. Let me ask you something sir. How many bullets have you taken? You ever spent a night in a bamboo cage in North Vietnam sir? You ever been dragged out to a binjo ditch and thrown in head first? You ever swim six miles in the Bering Sea waiting for a chopper to pull you out?

You ever hid in the jungle in Panama for a month and a half two hundred yards from an enemy stronghold? Just asking sir. Cause I was thinking, if you had done these things and let's say, a lot more over a nineteen year period, well … I'm just thinking. And let's say you never, not once, ever asked the Navy for any special favors. Well sir, do you think it would be unreasonable for you, yourself, to ask the Navy for just one little favor – to be close to your father when he died?"

"Just asking sir. But you don't have to answer, because I already know the answer. And sir, you don't have to worry about not signing the approval for my transfer. No, I wouldn't lose any sleep over it sir, because I'm going to make that totally unnecessary. I quit your stinking Navy. And if you are starting to think you'll have the shore patrol stop me from leaving the base and boarding my civilian flight home, sir, I wouldn't do that if I were you. Sir, there are six major news outlets back in the states with the details of everything we've just talked about. If they don't hear from me in the next forty-eight hours, they are going public with the story – the story of how a decorated Vietnam POW can't be transferred stateside to be near his father when he dies. How do you think the Admiral would like that sir? How about the Pentagon?"

So after nineteen years of honorable service, Chief Petty Officer Ronnie Matlock quit the United States Navy, fully aware of his forfeiture of the government pension he would have started drawing just twelve short months away. Being close to his father was more important to him. And right about that time was the last time he prayed to God, until he became a JET nearly eighteen years after he'd quit the Navy.

Fourteen years, a long time to be away from God. It was a red pony tailed hitchhiking preacher on a cold Virginia day that triggered Coon Dog's return to prayer and to God. Coon

Dog picked him up and took him to Little Rock and saw something in the rough cut highway preacher that inspired him to tell his cousin Toby Etheridge that he wanted to join the JETS. The preacher's name was Larry and his hook was that you knew he was "sold out" to God. He avoided the entrapments many preachers accepted. He didn't need a church building or a salary, or even a shelter. He told Coon Dog, "I don't have a car because I think this is where God wants me to be. Out here with the lowest of the low. Living with people who are down and out. I feel like I can give them a glimpse of a loving God working through me. I'm not sure I could do that in another setting. All I seek is wisdom to see where God leads me, and this is where He's led me."

Yeah, that was the trigger, then he joined the JETS which was really pretty simple. You only asked Jesus to take you and did your best to serve the Father as you felt he directed you. Not really heavy stuff, but oh was Coon Dog surprised at the sense of freedom that came over him. A lot of the baggage from Vietnam and the rest of his Navy career ceased to haunt him. For the first time in his life, he seemed to have a purpose that wasn't military related or dealt with the wreckage of that same relationship.

Now, a mile off shore, he prayed. "Well Father, they done chased me outa' Jabez Junction. I pray you'll keep me afloat 'til dark and see if this old SEAL can swim in and make my way to another camp. Father I'm sorry I killed that man back there, and I hope I don't have to kill no more. In Jesus name I pray."

CHAPTER TEN

South Louisville was working class and was best known for the International Harvester Plant, the Ford Plant, and the G.E. Plant. Central Louisville was better known for Churchill Downs, the L&N train yards, and some of the world's best known distilleries. East Louisville harbored a German neighborhood, a Jewish community, and the high bred cultural elite. West Louisville contained some of America's most hazardous chemical industry producers and turned out many good prize fighters including one heavyweight, Muhammad Ali, who many think was the best of all time.

But if you were looking to win or to lose money shooting pool, you headed to south Louisville and a pool hall named Lefty's. There were some money pool halls in west Louisville and some close to Churchill Downs, but Lefty's was the place the fever pitched nine ball shooters would show up.

You could see it in their eyes when they walked in the door. They wanted fast paced nine ball action. It was the fix they craved, the fix they had to have, junkies with a nine ball habit.

They played on the first table, up front close to Lefty's little four foot high, eight foot long counter top from where he would control the room. He had a stool behind the counter but was on his feet when the room was full and busy.

In the summer of '65 nine ball was only a dime a rack. Neighborhood high school boys spent some of their beer drinking money at Lefty's, not drinking, but shooting pool. Lefty would not tolerate drinking, fighting, or any other kind of trouble. Gambling, that *was* tolerated. In fact, that's about all you did at Lefty's. If you didn't have a little money up on the rail for a nine ball game, or an eight ball game, or a bank game, then you'd gamble on the coke bottle coming out of the coke machine. Four guys buy a quarter coke and whose ever bottle is stamped on the bottom from the furthest away bottler wins a quarter or fifty cents from the other guys. Tonk and poker games flourished up on Lefty's counter top. When you looked out the large front plate glass windows and saw the cops cruise by, the cards and money were swept off the countertop quickly.

The parents around the neighborhood didn't object to the pool hall. They knew Lefty meant business when it came to keeping troublemakers out. But pool shooters, the best around Louisville, came with the nine ball fever.

One of the neighborhood kids was a seventeen year old named Taylor Spaid. Lefty liked Taylor and taught him all he knew about shooting, which was a lot. For the next year Taylor was in Lefty's all the time. If he wasn't in school or delivering papers, he was down at Lefty's shooting pool. The old salts would come in, and Lefty would put the money up for Taylor to take them on in bank pool fifteen ball rack. The winner was the first shooter to drop eight off a bank shot. The game required much more skill than the white hot frenetic nine ball game required. Taylor became Lefty's "house shooter".

All the hustlers around town would make a trip to Lefty's to seek out the seventeen-year- old phenom.

Taylor's reign as the big gun at Lefty's didn't last long. He joined the Navy the following summer, and only four years later returned to south Louisville. He'd play at Lefty's every now and then, but had a full time job and wife to take up most of his time. The years went by quickly. He raised a family and was sad to get the news one day around 1995 that Lefty was diagnosed with Hodgkins disease, and the word was that he would have to sell the pool hall. Taylor went to see Lefty, and they worked out a deal. Taylor would run the shop with an option to own it should Lefty pass away.

That is what eventually happened. It was 1998 when Lefty died. Taylor quit his twenty-six year factory job and began operating Lefty's Pool Hall which he now owned.

One day in the summer of 2005 a sixteen year old named Chris Remington walked into Lefty's. It was slow, only two tables in the back being used, low key recreational eight ball, nothing like the fast paced nine ball fever that was these days being played for ten or twenty dollars a rack. Taylor was sitting on the stool behind the counter, the same position Lefty had occupied for many years. "Hi, you're new around here I take it."

"Yes sir, well, sort of new. We moved in a mile away last fall. I've always heard you had a nice pool hall, but this is the first chance I've had to come by. I played golf at school, and I've been in several tournaments this summer."

"Well, come on in. Let me treat you to your first game. I'm Taylor."

"Nice to meet you, Mr. Spaid. I've heard a lot about you. I'm Chris."

"I hope it was all good." Taylor handed Chris a cue stick and said, "Go ahead and break."

Chris checked the true in his stick and the balance. He rubbed a little powder up and down the stick, chalked it, and placed the cue ball a couple inches right of center, just behind the scratch line. He cued high and placed a couple of smooth preliminary strokes just short of the cue ball, then he let it rip. The clean CRACK of the cue ball on the one ball lifted the calm of the almost empty pool hall. Two balls were headed for pockets, one in the near right corner and another back in the far left corner. At the same time, the cue ball was just starting to dig in on the spin the high cue had put on it. When it got its steam up, it kissed the nine ball perfectly at about 140 degrees and sent it home to the near left pocket.

"Nice shot," Taylor said and went for the rack.

Chris dropped the nine again on the second break and almost on the third break. Taylor didn't get a shot 'til the fourth game and ran out. There wasn't much talking, and there wasn't any money put up on the rail. Just two good shooters matching skill.

A half hour later Chris said he had to go. Taylor said it had been fun and Chris didn't owe him anything for the pool.

Chris was looking at Taylor's cue stick and said, "Can I see your stick?"

"Sure," Taylor handed it to him.

Chris was looking closely at the hand carving on the handle end of the custom pool stick. "Yeah, it's just as nice as I always heard it was."

Taylor's face lit up in a big smile. He didn't know what Chris was going to say next, but he could have made a pretty accurate guess.

"My granddaddy made this stick for Lefty, back around 1948 they tell me. They told me Lefty gave it to you, but this is the first time I've ever seen it."

Taylor was amazed! He only knew the man's name that had hand crafted Lefty's personal stick. "Your granddaddy was Douglas Remington?"

"Sure was," Chris looked closer at the intricate carvings on the stick and pointed to the initials D.R. carved right below the unique cross that was part of the design. There looked to be a big cat, maybe a cheetah, or a cougar, and mountain land-scape, and somehow the unique cross fit perfectly into the flow of the design.

"You should have told me when you came in."

"I just wanted to see you shoot with it. You're every bit as good as they all said you were."

"You're not too shabby yourself."

Chris Remington and Taylor Spaid became good friends. Whenever Chris could find a few free hours from his hectic high school athletic schedule of cross country and golf, he'd be at Lefty's.

Taylor thought Chris hung the moon. Taylor had children of his own, but they had married and moved away. His wife loved him, but she was fairly well entrenched in church activities and the women's bowling league. She didn't think much of Taylor's quitting a solid factory job in order to own a pool hall. She'd never stepped a foot inside it.

There was something Taylor saw in Chris that was ... well it was all-American. Chris was a hard worker. He had natural athletic talent to be sure, but a lot of his success was the result of hours and hours and hours of practice and preparation. His father had started him running at birth. After the delivery the proud first time daddy started stretching Chris' little legs and massaging them. He gave him a pretty good aerobic workout less than an hour after his birth. Then at about three years his dad entered Chris into his first competition. It was a one mile fun run. It was anything but fun to his father; it was the beginning of a running program that would make Chris a premier distance runner by junior high school. In fact, ninth grade was the year Chris was fifteen years old and was in the top three in his age group in the state of Kentucky for a cross country runner. It was the year his performance was at its peak. His tenth, eleventh, and twelfth grade cross country times only got just a little better than his ninth grade times. His father had brought him along too quickly, or maybe that year, the ninth grade, was his body's natural peak. But Chris worked just as hard the last three years as he had early on. In fact, he worked harder. He increased his mileage, started earlier in the morning so he could do five miles before school started. He was dedicated, gave it all he had, and never flinched from injury or the damage he might have been doing to his young body. After Taylor and Chris had become friends, the story of Chris' cross country history became clear to Taylor, and that was the main reason he gave Chris such high marks.

As for the golf, well, Chris' father had enough gumption to lighten up on the running expectations and had begun taking Chris golfing as early as the eighth grade. It was the perfect stress reliever for Chris, and he was good at it. He had a natural "baby hook" in his swing the first time he hit a ball. By the time he was a senior, he was playing scratch golf. He'd even gotten Taylor to play a few rounds with him that fall after they'd met.

Chris' father had been ex-Navy and Taylor was always telling Chris all of his old Navy stories as well. It was no surprise to anyone that Chris joined the Navy soon after high school graduation. The surprise was going to be the experience that third class quartermaster Chris Remington had waiting for him off the coast of Isla de la Lejania three years later.

CHAPTER ELEVEN

The mid-day sun showed no mercy. Most of Coon Dog's face was being blistered by the burning rays. Only the narrow band crossing both eyes was protected. *Thank God for the beard. That helps.* In an effort to protect his face, three times he'd rolled over to his stomach and floated, but that was more energy sapping than it was worth.

He'd been second guessing his decision for most of the morning, and he still had at least eight hours to go. That's as soon as he dared start his swim to the shoreline. Also, he knew it would be useless to swim laterally up or down the coast until darkness arrived. Toros would see that. Toros could probably see him now. Coon Dog could see Toros or others in the gang. Every now and then Coon Dog would be riding the top of a high swell, and he could easily make out human forms up above the boulders, up near the jungle tree line. And he also noticed he'd drifted eastward a couple of miles. At this rate he'd probably be seven miles down the coast from where he'd evaded the cannibals this morning. And when the time finally arrived, when it was dark, would he swim right into the gang of cannibals? Unlikely. They would be as they were now, scattered an eighth of a mile apart. They would cover much more ground by doing so and decrease Coon Dog's chances of slipping through them into the safety of the jungle. Much would depend on the cloud cover and the moon tonight. A full moon and a clear night would mean probable death. Heavy cloud cover and a quarter moon, or no moon at all meant Coon Dog would have a good chance.

But all of that was eight hours away. There was no sense in Coon Dog's fretting over circumstances he couldn't control. He had to focus on simply swimming in the open ocean for now. He rolled off his back and swam the crawl stroke and did a little dog paddling to loosen up a bit and keep the circulation going strong. The water back in his private swimming hole near Jabez Junction was much warmer than the open ocean water, and he knew that if he had to stay out in the ocean overnight, he'd have been in real trouble maintaining his core body temperature. He recalled the time in the Bering Sea. He nearly died from hypothermia. The mission was for four SEALS to be bait to draw a Russian submarine up to the surface. Only in that way could the CIA gather critical ELINT, electronic intelligence on the sub that was the newest and most sophisticated to ever come out of Vladivostok. The SEALS arrived in the Bering Sea after their aircraft just happened to crash in the sea. All was going to plan until the IBS (inflatable boat small) inflated with carbon dioxide cartridges sprang a leak and left the SEALS in the freezing ocean with only wetsuits and flotation devices. Four hours later, after the brass realized the Ruskies didn't fall for the trickery, did the Navy send out two choppers from Adak, Alaska to pick up the nearly frozen SEALS.

The afternoon was dragging on way too slowly for Coon Dog's comfort. He was getting mighty hungry. He was sure that the pemmican he kept at Jabez Junction was gone by now, as well as the buckskins and tools and weapons that he kept there. *Do they know where my other two primary camps are? Will the huge stores of pemmican I've got buried in the jungle still be there when I get back, if I get back? My raft, only partially built, will it be where I had it hidden? And my new panther skin, will it be up high in the jungle canopy where I left it?*

A couple of hours later the sun was getting lower in the western sky. There was medium cloud cover, most of which was a band of gray that seemed to be thickening. That gave Coon Dog some hope that later on, the moon would be obscured, or better yet, blotted out.

But the hope that all factors would work in his favor as the afternoon wound down to sunset didn't last long. He spotted a flock of sea birds a mile away feeding on a school of fish. If they were feeding from the top, what might be feeding from the bottom? His thoughts quickly turned from anticipation of his next food to how to make sure he wouldn't be the food for any sharks prowling close by. Unfortunately there wasn't a thing he could do to prevent that very thing from happening. He was continuing to drift eastward toward the feeding birds and, God forbid, he realized he'd been picked up by a strong current heading out even deeper into the open sea. Decision time. *Should I start my swim in now, before dark? Or wait as originally planned?*

He didn't have to make the decision. Shark dorsal fins were a hundred yards away heading right for him. There would be no swimming now. He'd have to stay on his back, breathe slowly, and try not to move a muscle. There looked to be three or four. *Good,* Coon Dog thought. He'd always heard that the larger species, like Great Whites, were solo predators and didn't operate as a school. But how would these coming toward him operate?

Oh, no! They've dropped down under the surface. It wouldn't be so bad if they attack on the surface, go after my head, chest, shoulders, and arms. I can deal with that. They attack, I try to fight them off, I lose, I die, they eat me. I can deal with that. But down below me, I can't see them. I don't want no part of that. How long will they stay down there, sizing me up. How close will they be? When will they make a move. No, I don't want no part of that.

The darker part of his imagination was working overtime, and the ocean continued rocking his cold and naked body, taking no account of his nakedness or vulnerability. The sharks were circling down under him, not agitated, but certainly hungry and interested, very interested in the object floating above them.

CHAPTER TWELVE

Chris Remington and Frank Demarco were on the fantail of the *USS Nolin River*. Many times crew members would gather near the tail end of the ship when they had a break between duty shifts.

"How many you think are on the island?" Demarco was twenty-two years old and like Chris was planning on going to college when he got out of the Navy.

"I overheard the XO the other day. He said seven hundred and thirty-six have been put on Isla de la Lejania." Chris was privy to a lot of hot skinny. His eight hour watch shifts up on the bridge and pilot house allowed him to catch a good deal of operational information.

"Yeah, but I wonder how many are still alive?"

"Who knows? Probably not very many. I know that the Marines who drop them off don't think *any* of them survive for very long. I've heard them talk about seeing human skeletons from hell on the beach when they take the new guys in, but these skeletons were alive. Corporal James said that he and Sergeant Trusky were shot at about a month ago."

"Shot at? What are you talking about?"

Demarco had been assigned to the Nolin River only a month ago and wasn't aware of the stories that had been coming from the banishment island for over two years now.

Chris had been aboard the ship for about six months and had a pretty good inventory of stories, some of them thoroughly overladen with hype and unfounded innuendo. Some of them accurate down to every minute detail. "Bow and arrows.

Some of those monsters shot at them with bow and arrows. But James and Trusky said they quit going in that close. Now they dump the banished out in the bay a quarter of a mile. They either swim in or they don't."

"Man, I can't imagine. Can you? Just think. You are dumped out there in the bay knowing that if you make it ashore, you got cannibals waiting to eat you."

"They should have thought of that when they did their crime back in the world."

"I guess," Demarco said.

They were sitting in a couple of chairs the deck apes kept in a paint locker and were looking to the north toward the island. It was difficult to tell if the gray cloud bank moving in from the west was actually that, a cloud bank. It could have been the low hills in the middle of the island. Many times the cloud features and the island low hills were indistinguishable.

"You got the eve watch?" Chris asked.

"Yeah. What time is it? I guess I better get some chow before they secure it." Demarco was a radioman and would stay on duty from 17:00 until 23:30.

"You're cool man. It's only 16:00. I've got a question for you."

"What?"

"Do you ever dream about the island?"

"No, all I dream about is Lori back in Brooklyn. I'm going to ask her to marry me the next time I'm home on leave. Now, why would I want to be dreaming about that stupid island?"

"I don't know. Maybe it's because I've been out here longer. I dream about it a lot."

"You're kidding. Maybe you ought to see a shrink. That doesn't sound too cool to me."

"No, no. There's nothing weird about it. I just keep having these dreams. I'm not sure they are about the island, but I think they are because they started when I first came out here. When we rotate back into port at San Diego I don't have them. I only have them out here."

"Man, that is weird. You ought to see a shrink. What kind of dreams are you talking about?"

"Well, I actually see trucks. Lot's of big trucks, and they are driving around. Sometimes I think they are over there on the island and sometimes I think they are driving around back in the world."

"Trucks? Driving around on the island? You gotta' be crazy man."

"Trucks are not the main part of the dreams."

"Oh really. Well dreams can be complicated. That's for sure. Sometimes when I'm dreaming about Lori, she takes on different faces, uh, I mean ... I guess different identities. Sometimes she's my own mother, sometimes she's a dancer, you name it. Once she was a mountain bike. So what is the main part of these truck dreams?"

"Well, you see this tattoo?" Chris held his left arm out. The short sleeved chambray Navy work shirt did not interfere with the view of the tattoo. "This tattoo keeps popping up in the dreams. I've got a friend back in Kentucky who runs a pool hall. He's got a cue stick with a custom hand- carved handle. This tattoo is taken from that carving. It's identical. Anyway, that image keeps showing up in the truck dreams."

Demarco swung his gaze away from the gathering cloud bank over toward the island, back toward Chris. "Oh heck, that's not all that weird. Maybe you don't need a shrink after all."

The two young sailors continued talking for awhile. Eventually Demarco headed for the chow line, and Chris headed for his rack to catch a three or four hour nap. He was off duty until 24:00 when he would pull a mid-watch up in the pilot house. The *Nolin River* continued its southern sweep of Isla de la Lejania , holding at a steady twelve knots. It would be several hours before she came up alongside the *Rutherford County* . Both C.O.'s had planned a brief two hour training mission for the deck crews to practice a little NUNREP (night underway replenishment exercise). When that was completed, the *Nolin River* would turn back toward the west and retrace the same patrol route she'd been doing most of that day.

CHAPTER THIRTEEN

One of the sharks couldn't contain its curiosity any longer. It was an hour before sunset and after having spent most of the afternoon cruising between this floating object and the school of fish, it made a run at Coon Dog's legs. On the first pass it touched a foot with its nose. There was no movement from the object. On the second pass, the five foot long tiger shark came slowly. It opened its mouth and actually gripped Coon Dog's foot just tight enough to produce tearing of the skin and bleeding if Coon Dog would have tried to jerk his foot free. There was no movement from the object in the shark's mouth. The shark released the foot and headed off toward the island. Maybe it would have better luck there, cruising the bays and reefs. Occasionally a thrashing animal would be found there, very near the beach. Not often, just every now and then, a meal could be found. The tiger shark's companions had given up on Coon Dog way earlier in the afternoon. They were content to follow the fish and snatch as many of them as they could.

Coon Dog had nearly been asleep when the tiger shark had come in to test his foot out. He'd been saying to himself over and over and over. *Do not jump or make a move if one of them gets onto me. And do not pee in your pants or cut gas.* He had to laugh at himself when he thought about that. He didn't have any pants on. The old Navy SEAL passed the shark test well. If he hadn't, he'd been on his way to where all old dead Navy SEALS go to. As some SEALS were want to put it, he'd be crossing the bar.

But as troublesome and stressful as the shark encounter had been, Coon Dog was equally concerned with the miles he had continued to be pulled out into the sea. He guessed he was some eight or nine miles out by now. With sunset a half hour away, he didn't know if he had the strength and energy to swim back. He knew for sure he wouldn't attempt it until the sun went down completely. The sharks very possibly were still in the neighborhood. No sense pushing his luck. The last thing you want to be doing when sharks are nearby is swimming. After dark he'd stand a much better chance of not attracting them.

He began planning for the swim. He was thinking that an overcast night would be the best for when he came out of the water and made his dash from the beach to the jungle. But then he realized that if it were totally starless and moonless night he would have nothing to take a bearing on, nothing for a navigation aid. Why, he could easily get off course and be swimming toward South America or Hawaii, not toward the southern shoreline of Isla de la Lejania . Then he realized that if he didn't start now, he would have no clue as to what direction to swim if it did in fact turn out to be a starless and moonless night.

He rolled off his back and scanned a 360 degree arc around him. He didn't see any dorsal fins, or anything else; only barely could he make out the island's highlands. *I might be nine miles out,* he thought, *maybe more. Oh well, it's the only shot I got.* He let his raggedy head band wash away behind him as he started a slow, unhurried swim toward the island.

He looked up between every ten or twelve strokes to make sure he was on course and to notice the ever thickening gray cloud cover was now in total control. He knew that in fifteen more minutes it would be pitch dark and after a minute or so of continued swimming, he would have no clue what direction he was going. Did it make any difference? He didn't think so because he didn't think he was making any progress toward the island anyway. He knew better than to swim against an outgoing current, but what choice did he have?

After an hour of darkness, and with no navigational help from the stars or a moon that he could see, he realized he was probably done for. He stopped swimming and went back to the survival float on his back, and he started his final accounting and his final goodbyes.

"Heavenly Father, you've been mighty good to me all these years. I didn't deserve none of it. The good days with me and Daddy, huntin' in the rabbit fields, the squirrel hunts on ol' man Granger's ridgeline. The days I'd go with Uncle Marvin. He'd sit us down up on top the ridge. I can see him now cutting him off a plug of Mailman. And Daddy teachin' me to fish the creek with the crawdads. Yessir, I bet me and Daddy took more bass outa' that creek with crawdads than the rest of that county did with anything else. And the first time with Missy. Oh Lord forgive me, but I ain't never forgot it. We was under that old bridge, half in the water and half out, nary a thread was on us Lord. A hot day in the summer, and Lord … oh lordy … I just …well, I ain't never forgot it Lord. And Lord, let my brothers from the Nam know I'm comin' to see em' Lord. And Lord that NVA guard I put that shank through his throat. Just let him know Lord, it wasn't anything personal against him. I was, you know Lord, I was just trying to get away. And Lord, thank you for seeing me through that terrible time and getting' me back home. And Lord, thank you for Myrna, Katherine, and Janey. They tried to help me, you know that they did Lord. But I pushed them all three away and drank all the time. I'm awful sorry for it Lord. I shoulda' done better I know. And

Lord, thank you for Larry, the hitchhiking preacher. Lord, was he an angel, or was he a real man? You know he sort of aimed me at the JETS. Oh Lord, I wonder what them fellers is up to right about now. Jabez, Toby, Steve, Windjammer, Dinky, Daffy, Doolittle, Turbo, Lugnut, and the rest of them. Lord, I'd be grateful if you'd let 'em know I'm gonna' miss 'em. And Lord, I don't know how to say this Lord, I just want to ask … will you please look after Red Man? I don't know if I ever did truly understand his ways, you know his bein' a shaman and all and saying at the same time his was a Christian. I don't know Lord, maybe it's what I heard a preacher saying one time. I believe it was a scripture from Revelations, Lord. Something about the throne room judgment, or was it the second judgment? I'm sorry Lord. You know I ain't studied your book enough. Anyway, I believe this ol' preacher was saying that all those who never truly asked the Lamb to take 'em while they's still on this Earth, that they'll get one last chance at the throne room judgment, the second judgment. Is that right Lord? Well, if it is, I just ask you to keep a close eye on ol' Red Man and see that he makes the right choice."

"Well Father, I reckon I'm about done down here. Either the old sharkies will be a gettin' me or I'll run out'a body heat directly, and I'll be a comin' on home to see you. I love you Father, I love you Jesus, I love you Holy Spirit. In Jesus' name I pray. Amen."

Then he heard something big cutting through the water. He rolled off of his back and could see the running lights of the *Nolin River* a quarter mile away. If he didn't swim hard and fast, the ship was going to run right over him.

CHAPTER FOURTEEN

The starboard lookout on the flying bridge, Seaman "Spy" Everist from Port Orchard, Washington had scanned a wide arc of the ocean a hundred and fifty yards from the *Nolin River* with his powerful searchlight. It was SOP to scan both the port and starboard sides at all times of darkness. In two years this night time scan had only discovered two dead bodies from the banishment island. They had never once come across any evidence of live escapees. The planners of the security of the island had been accurate in their original procedures. Two Navy destroyers patrolling 24-7 was all that was necessary to ensure the security of the island.

Seaman Everist, manning the starboard searchlight, thought he saw something in the water. He retraced the arc he'd just scanned, but he didn't see anything. He worked the powerful beam of the light in a circular manner closest to where he thought he might have seen something. No, nothing there. He prepared to swing the arc out to two hundred and fifty yards, but no, one more time here for good measure.

"No way! No way!" Everist couldn't believe what he was seeing. He settled himself and then passed his report on to the O.O.D. in the pilot house via the headset/microphone he wore. "Sir, we've got a live one off the starboard bow, at about 30 degrees!"

Lieutenant Terry Fitzgerald put aside the copy of *Navy Times* he'd been thumbing through. He had been getting ready to send a seaman down to the crew's mess to bring him up a pot of coffee. Maybe the black mud from down there would be more tolerable than the acid from the wardroom. *What did the starboard lookout just say? A live one? I bet.* "What do you have seaman?" Lt. Fitzgerald asked on the microphone attached to the headset he just now put on, switching from the intercom in the pilot house.

"Sir, you better come out here and take a look. I've got a man in the water. He's alive!"

"All back to one quarter," Fitzgerald ordered, and then on the way out the hatch to the starboard lookout position he glanced over at the messenger of the watch. "Notify the Captain, the starboard lookout reports a live man in the water. And have the deck crew prepare a launch."

"Aye, aye sir."

"Fitzgerald was out on the starboard flying bridge in no time. "Show me what you've got."

Everist had the searchlight dead on a man in the water, now only a hundred yards away. It was easy to fix the man with the light. The seas weren't rough, and of course, the *Nolin River* was now slowing down.

Fitzgerald took Everist's headset from him and gave four quick succinct orders to the crew in the pilot house. "Initiate man overboard procedures, all engines stop, get a marker buoy put out starboard, and get two flares up on the starboard side." A moment later he added, "Get a marine security detail aboard the recovery launch."

Quartermaster third class Chris Remington was lying in his rack reading when all the commotion got started. The time was 21:39 (9:39 p.m.). He got dressed and headed out of the berthing quarters and up two ladders to the main deck. Flood lights had the deck lit up as if it were high noon, and already Chris could see a launch pulling away from the starboard side of the *Nolin River* and heading out to a nearby patch of water flooded in searchlight beams and illumination flares from above.

Remington spotted a couple of his buddies nearby. "What's going on?" he asked.

"They got a guy in the water. He's alive. See him?"

"I'll be dogged. Would you look at that. I never would have thought."

Then the jokes started. "I wouldn't get too close to him when they bring him aboard. He might try to eat us."

"No, they say there's plenty of good eating on the island ... if you like mud fritters and insects a la mode."

A half hour later three marines were bringing the lone swimmer up the sea ladder that had been hung from the starboard side of the *Nolin River*. When all four were safely up and standing on the main deck washed in all the flood lights most of the off-duty crew were milling around hoping to catch a glimpse of this wannabe escapee from the banishment island. Those that could actually get a peek at him couldn't believe their eyes. This was no wild eyed bare-ribbed, starving cannibal. This guy was a picture of health, firm, lean musculature with definition in his abs, chest, and shoulders. He looked like he hadn't missed a meal in a long time. It was easy to tell – the man was totally naked.

One of the marines found a blanket and covered him up, then Sergeant Trusky bellowed out, "Gangway, make a hole swabbies. You've seen enough; make a hole!"

They led Coon Dog toward an open hatch that would lead to the 01 level where he would be locked into the same cell he'd been in two years ago.

On the way to the hatch, Coon Dog glanced off to his left where several young sailors stood gawking. For some reason his eyes went to the tattoo on the forearm of a young clean-cut sailor standing close to the hatch. "I've seen that. I know what it means," Coon Dog said. Then looking up directly in Chris Remington's eyes, he said, "I know what your dreams mean."

The marines had him through the hatch before he could say anything else. The sailors standing with Chris weren't sure what the prisoner had said or to whom he had directed his words. Chris knew exactly what the prisoner said and for whom the words were intended.

CHAPTER FIFTEEN

"Okay Sergeant Trusky, get the prisoner and escort him down to the crew's mess deck." Captain Frank Weller then turned back to the four men assembled in the wardroom. "We'll have a chat with our prisoner while he's getting some good navy chow."

The executive officer (XO) Lieutenant Commander Robert Trent gave a questioning look at Captain Weller.

"Yes, I know. We're drifting off normal prisoner procedures a little, but in this case, I think it will be worth it."

The four men the captain was talking to were the XO, the operations officer, the chief master-at-arms, and the commander of the twenty man marine security detail, Lt. Joe Bellinger.

Captain Weller didn't know if the four men had studied this prisoner's file as closely as he had. He doubted it. They probably sized up this prisoner as just another grotesque psychopath who was getting his due justice now that banishment was a reality in the United States. Not only the XO, but the other three as well, were all inwardly questioning the captain's kid gloves approach to handling this newly captured prisoner. The crew's mess deck? Good navy chow? The captain knew they were skeptical, so he shared with them his rationale for a softer approach at handling the prisoner.

"Gentlemen, let's face it. This escapee, this Ronnie Matlock, is not your typical banishment island criminal. You all saw him. Why, he looks like he's been enjoying two years at an upscale health spa, not two years of starvation and staying one step ahead of a band of cannibals."

They all had to agree with that, but where was the Captain going with this?

"It's my belief that we may be able to extract some useful information from Mr. Matlock. Yes, we all know that satellite surveillance tells the legal eagles and congress what was predicted all along. Eighty percent of the banished die relatively quickly, many by cannibalism. But does the spy in the sky tell the whole story? Is there something we've all been missing? I don't know. But now, here tonight, we have a one time opportunity to take a look. That's all we're going to do here. We're just going to talk with him. We are just going fishing to see if we catch anything useful. When we get down there, I encourage all of you to ask the prisoner anything you want. Who knows what he can tell us? Maybe nothing. On the other hand, maybe something very useful. Are there any questions?"

They were still skeptical. Only the marine officer Lt. Bellinger piped up, "Sir, is it still your intention to return the prisoner to the island in the morning at first light?"

The question was asked as if they all expected the Captain to respond with "Negative, Lieutenant. We'll take him back to the world with us and release his poor misunderstood soul back to mainstream America."

The captain understood the underlying sarcasm and the lieutenant's attempt to discredit him. "Lieutenant, it's not necessary for you to question my motives. This may seem lenient to you, what we're about to do. Does it, Lieutenant?"

"Yes sir, it sure does. I didn't read anywhere in the SOP that we are to coddle an escapee and treat him to the crew's mess."

"Point well taken, Lieutenant. What do you know about the prisoner's background, Lieutenant?"

"Well sir, I know he is a sadistic rapist and murderer. I know we should have shot him. He never should have had an opportunity at even a banishment island."

"Is that all you know about him, Lieutenant?'

"Yes, Sir."

"Just for the record Lieutenant, I'm going to give you a little more background intel on Ronnie Matlock, not that I'm saying that the intel alone would justify treating him differently from any other escapee. I just want you to hear this, Lieutenant, loud and clear. Is that understood?"

"Yes, Sir."

Captain Weller turned sideways for a brief moment. He looked as if he were making sure he would say what he had to say exactly the way it should be said. He would be choosing his words very carefully.

"Gentlemen, I've read every word in Ronnie Matlock's file. I think the police call it a 'jacket'. The only problem, he doesn't have a 'jacket'. Other than the two rape murders that got him a ticket here, there is no other criminal record on the man. In fact, there are some that might describe Matlock as a model citizen, that is of course prior to his conviction of the two rape murders."

The captain paused and noticed Lt. Bellinger shaking his head incredulously, but the lieutenant kept his mouth shut. "How many of you know that Matlock is ex-Navy SEAL?"

Only the chief master-at-arms, Senior Chief Petty Officer Bill "Tug" Showalter responded. "Yes sir Cap'n. I know about him being a SEAL." Senior Chief Showalter was as tough as nails, true navy salt. Of his twenty-six years in the navy, he'd spent over eighteen of those years at sea, most of the time in a critical hot spot somewhere around the globe.

"Tell us, Senior Chief, what you know about him and how you came to acquire that information." Weller stood aside and motioned Tug Showalter to stand up.

The senior chief got to his feet, his khakis perfectly starched and creased, his salt and pepper hair and mustache perfectly trimmed and cut close. The shine on his brass belt buckle was blinding as it radiated out from his flat stomach. The USN anchor tattoo on his left forearm and the machine gun and K-bar tattoo on his right forearm had faded considerably over the years into his deeply tanned arms.

"Cap'n, when I accepted my duty rotation on the *Nolin River* two years ago, I didn't think much of the new banishment law. I didn't have strong feelings one way or the other about it. But now, well, how could anyone argue against it? We've got rid of most of the really dangerous psychos who want to hurt people. And the deterrent is so great, well, it seems that nowadays we just don't see too many that are willing to take the risk. Anyway Cap'n, when I first came aboard the *Nolin River*, I made it a point to read up, you know, the background on some of these animals we transported to this island. When I saw that Ronnie Matlock had been convicted of two rape murders and he was going to be on his way to the banishment island, it wasn't necessary for me to read up on his background. Sir, Matlock was a legend in the SEALS. Three tours in Vietnam, and he escaped from a North Vietnamese POW camp. Sir, I know men who served with Matlock after all of that. He was a top notch trooper, sir, one of the best. Of course, he was said to be a loner, and he baffled everybody when he walked out of the navy after nineteen and a half years. I always wondered how a man like that, a record like that, could have turned bad and get convicted of rape and murder. But it must have happened. They had DNA evidence." Showalter sat down.

"Thank you Senior Chief. You said pretty much what I would have said myself. The only thing I would add is the reason he walked away from the Navy forfeiting his pension. His father was dying back in the states, and the navy refused to transfer him his last six months so that Matlock would be closer to his father. Needless to say, the Navy screwed up, but the point is this. We've got an escaped prisoner waiting for us down there in the crew's mess who at least at one point in his life had the ability to see through pure bullshit and at great sacrifice, no ... I should say at tremendous sacrifice to his own well being, Matlock chose to remain loyal to a very high principal – love and unity to his family. So, gentlemen, don't you think we could show this man just a little compassion, just a hot meal and a little conversation. I think he's earned it. And don't forget, he just may share some intel about the state of affairs over on the island that could improve our mission procedures." He looked around at the faces and noticed the skeptical looks were gone; gone that is from all of them except the marine, Lieutenant Bellinger.

"Let's go down and meet Ronnie Matlock."

Coon Dog had snapped back from his eighteen hour ordeal in the ocean. He'd been in his cell on the 01 level for almost an hour. The only provisions made for him were a jug of water and a dungaree outfit to wear. After donning the navy work clothes, Coon Dog sat on the folding rack that came out from the bulkhead. There were two marine sentries posted outside the hatch that opened to his cell. None of the marines had talked to him other than the orders to wear the dungarees.

The thing going through Coon Dog's mind was the tattoo on the young sailor's arm. The big cat, the cross, the mountains, the exact same design he'd crafted into his own black panther skin. How could it be? How could it be the same?

He didn't know, and he sure didn't know why he had said to the sailor, "I know what it means, and I know what your dreams mean." He sat there thinking about it, but he couldn't come up with any plausible explanation.

The hatch door to his cell opened, and the burly marine sergeant who had locked him up an hour ago was barking orders at him. "Let's go prisoner, move it outa' there."

Coon Dog was surprised. He didn't figure they would bounce him back to the island til' first light which was at least four hours away.

Coon Dog stumbled to his feet. He was chained at the feet and handcuffed. He was hoping they would let him keep the new pair of navy issue work shoes. That would be something positive he'd take with him back to the island. But no, they didn't take him to the side rail and lower him into a waiting boat. The six man marine security detail, led by Sergeant Trusky, was walking him down into the bowels of the ship.

In a moment he was led into the crew's mess area. There were ten or twelve large metal tables with rails on them to keep trays from sliding around. Off to the side of the compartment was the actual chow line, vacated at the moment. Coon Dog could see two or three cooks milling around. They were looking out, trying to get a glimpse at the escapee – him.

The Marines sat him down at a table. Sergeant Trusky looked at a young Marine corporal and said, "Okay, get him a big old plate of chow and a pot of coffee."

Coon Dog was shocked. *What are they up to?* But he wasn't about to complain. The smell of hot food had ambushed him fifty feet before he was brought in and before he sat down at the table. And now the Marine corporal was about to set a metal tray in front of him, and another Marine had a metal coffee pot and a mug leaking steamy hot coffee vapors. Coon Dog didn't notice any silverware. He wouldn't have used it anyway.

"Take his handcuffs off," Trusky ordered. When that was done by one of the corporals, they got away from him and formed a perimeter around him from fifteen feet away. They were surprised at the manner he went at the food. He ate slowly, almost picking at the eggs, hash browns, sausage, gravy and biscuits. There was also corned beef hash and chilled fruit. Coon Dog ate it all and was really getting off on the hot coffee. He looked up toward Trusky when the pot was empty, but Trusky said, "No, that's all for now. You've got some visitors on the way down to see you."

A minute later Captain Frank Weller strode into the crew's mess deck, the four man committee close in tow.

"Attention on deck," Trusky barked out.

"As you were. Has the prisoner been served chow, Sergeant?"

"Yes sir, he has," Trusky barked out again.

"Coffee?"

"Yes sir!"

"Very well Sergeant. That will be all. You can secure the detail. Wait outside in the passageway."

"Aye, aye sir!"

As they were leaving the captain beckoned one of the marine corporals over to him. "Son, go back there and get Cookie to bring us out fresh coffee pots and mugs, and then tell Cookie to secure the galley. Don't worry; we'll get them back in plenty of time for breakfast."

"Aye, aye sir!"

Coon Dog was taking all of this in as the five men settled in around him. *They want something from me. I see that as clear as day.*

The captain opened up the show. "Do the dungarees fit okay?"

"They ain't as snug as my buckskins."

"We didn't notice any buckskins when we brought you aboard."

This guy thinks he's mighty slick. Gettin' me down here, hot chow, nice clothes. Whatever it is he's awantin', he ain't gonna get it. Coon Dog had no response.

"What were you doing out here ten and a half miles from shore?"

Typical Navy, Coon Dog thought. *Always the mission. He's looking for intel on how I could have got out here. How his ships could stop somebody like me from making it this far the next time. Old Coon Dog the truck driver, almost done turned over in the grave, swam out here ten miles. He don't care a flip about me, only about how he can tweak his precious mission.* Coon Dog never answered the captain's question.

The corporal and a mess worker from the galley showed up with fresh coffee all around. The captain directed the men to put a full pot and a full mug in front of Coon Dog. He might have been tight lipped, but not so tight that he couldn't slurp that hot coffee around his mouth until it cooled enough to swallow it down.

"You got any sugar?" Coon Dog asked nobody in particular. The captain himself got up and went back toward the galley and returned quickly with a handful of sugar cubes and a spoon. He put it down in front of Coon Dog and resumed his sitting across the metal table from him.

"The way I see it is you were running from the cannibals and got cornered between the sea and the jungle. You had no choice. You had to swim out. You got caught in a riptide, then caught in the easterly current and were dragged all the way out here. Did I miss anything?"

He thinks he's cool as a cucumber. Did I miss anything? "You got any cream?"

The captain looked over at Tug Showalter. The senior chief got to his feet and headed back to the galley. In a minute he was back with not only real dairy cream, but he also had a can of whipped cream. A moment later he returned with half a chocolate cake, a fork, and napkins. All were placed in front of Coon Dog, and Showalter sat back down without him or anyone else saying a word.

Finally, Marine Lieutenant Joe Bellinger couldn't contain his frustration any longer. His face had gone tight, and red, and began twitching a minute ago. If there were any valves in it, they'd be leaking by now. He jumped to his feet and shouted, "This is an outrage! This is a sacrilege! Captain, I demand this idiotic interrogation be stopped immediately and the prisoner be removed to the cell he belongs in." His hand went to his service 45 side arm, but stopped there, just resting on it.

Frank Weller met this opposition the only way he could. He got to his feet and advanced to within five feet of the Marine. "Bellinger, if you don't want to ruin a perfectly good career you've got going, you will remove your hand from your weapon, NOW, Marine."

Bellinger let his right hand drop away from the 45. "Now, remove your gun belt Lieutenant, and hand it to me."

Bellinger reluctantly undid the fastener on the gun belt and handed it over to Weller.

"Sit down Marine and listen up."

Coon Dog took a big bite of the chocolate cake and was sipping coffee as if he were the only person in the room. He hadn't even looked up at the two men as the confrontation played out.

But now Captain Weller's patience with Lieutenant Bellinger and with Coon Dog was running out.

The captain sat back down across the table from Coon Dog. "You are about to run out of options, Matlock. I think I've demonstrated my willingness to meet you halfway. Now it's your turn, and if you don't do some talking ... consider this. When we stick you back on the island, we can do it in such a way that you would not be seen by the cannibals. On the other hand, we can make a big show out of it in broad daylight, and of course, I think you know how that would turn out."

This time Coon Dog looked up at the captain. The captain made a good point – a real good point.

"What do you want to know?" He crammed the last of the cake into his mouth and poured more coffee into his mug.

"Let's start with my original question. What were you doing out here, ten miles from shore?"

"You already talked that one through. I thought I could stay closer to the shore. I was going to swim in after dark. I misjudged the rip and the current and ended up out here."

"Was there anything else pertinent regarding how you drifted so far out? Did you have a raft, any type of flotation devices?"

Now the other Navy men and even Lieutenant Bellinger perked their ears up. Maybe the Old Man hadn't gone rickety after all.

Coon Dog was starting to loosen up. All the caffeine was part of it. Another part of it was the fact that he had not been around normal human beings for two years, and of course, as the captain put it so well, he was out of options. He'd have to run his mouth a little if he wanted to stay alive.

"No, I didn't have anything to help me. Then the sharks paid me a visit. I had to wait til they got tired of testing me before I could start my swim in. By then, it was too late; it was dark. I figured I was screwed by then. But that's when I looked up and seen your running lights."

"Very good, Matlock. Now I'm going to have my staff ask you a few questions."

Captain Weller looked over at Lt. Commander Robert Trent. "XO," he said.

The executive officer could now see the brilliance of this talk with the prisoner. There could be a lot of useful information to be gained. He got up and sat a little closer to Coon Dog. "Matlock, let's go back a little further than your struggle in the ocean. The captain speculated you had nearly been caught by the cannibals. Is that what happened?"

"Yeah, they found one of my camps. It was a little after sunup. I had to make a beeline to the ocean."

"How many men were after you?"

"Four or five, maybe more."

"Did you know these men?"

"Yes, I knew who they were, the Toros Gang."

"How many gangs are on the island?"

"Probably six or eight. Maybe more."

"Are any of these gangs capable of mounting a credible escape attempt?"

"I don't think so. About the only thing they are capable of doing is killing and eating."

The executive officer didn't have an immediate question. He seemed to be pondering over what the prisoner just said. Finally, he asked another question. "How many individuals, not gangs, individuals, have survived?"

"I don't know. Not many. I've seen signs where maybe a lone wolf still might be alive."

"You mean yourself?"

"No, there might be one or two others."

"That's all?"

"That would be my guess."

"Do the gangs have any tools or any ability to build a craft of any kind, say a raft, a canoe, or anything bigger?"

"I imagine your satellite intel could tell you that."

"Not if the construction of such a craft were concealed under the jungle canopy. Anyway, I'm askin *you* the question, not any satellite we may or may not be using." The XO looked over at the captain who immediately trained a hard stare at Coon Dog and lowered his eyebrows in warning.

Coon Dog got the message. "They ain't got no tools to build anything like a decent craft."

"And what about you, Matlock? Do you have such tools?"

"No," Coon Dog lied.

The XO looked satisfied and sat down.

The captain could see that the operations officer wanted to take a shot. "Go ahead, Jerry."

Lieutenant Jerry Cissell was a wizard at electronics and was the division officer of operations. Not only was he by far the most gifted of any officer or crew at running herd on all the ship's sophisticated computers, communications and electronic paraphernalia, but he was also a keen student of psychology. At one point in his career he'd been snatched out of fleet operations to work in the pentagon on "Black Ops", the less than savory operations the military and the CIA sometimes ran in order to sway an enemy's civilians toward a certain political persuasion.

If there were one individual present at this unlikely gathering whom Coon Dog's lie would not have been accepted or believed, it was Cissel. "No? You have no tools?"

Oops, Coon Dog sensed he better be careful. "I didn't say I didn't have any tools. I said I didn't have any to build a craft with."

"I see. Then, tell us exactly what kind of tools you do have." Cissell was looking directly at Coon Dog.

"Just a few crude weapons to hunt and fish with. That's all."

Cissell was shaking his head slightly as if in the midst of deep consideration. His eyes were unfixed, moving around, as if they were trying to see what it might be like to exist, attempt to survive, on the island. Finally he shifted his gaze back toward Coon Dog.

"Just a few crude weapons ... please be more specific. Tell us about these weapons in detail."

Coon Dog noticed that the captain had raised his eyebrows at him again.

"Nothing any good boy scout couldn't make. I got a flint-stone knife, tomahawk, a spear, a bow and arrows, and a few small tools to work animal skins with, an awl, a rock hammer, and the like. Oh yeah, I got me a pretty good fishing net if I don't say so myself. Ya'll like good fresh aku. They's some mighty good aku around these parts. Make real good sashimi. A little dried sea weed, some wild onions on the side. It ain't bad fellers. Ya'll come pay me a visit sometimes; I'll get a mess of it ready. Add some crustaceans, you know, them little critters that lives on the rocks by the ocean. We'd be eatin' in a big way fellers. If you give me enough advance notice you was comin', I'd get a little turtle stew ready for you. I tell you what fellers, or should I say shipmates, us all being here together you know, ya'll bring a few girls with you, and we'll really have us a party. I come across a patch of wild strawberries here back aways. It makes a pretty fair homemade wine. Yessir, I'd be proud to serve it to you. I hear tell the modern Navy's got women aboard ship these days. All of that was just startin' when I left the Navy back in 87."

Coon Dog would have continued, but Cissell cut him off; he'd heard enough. And what he heard, he knew was not the effects of a coffee high swangdoogling the prisoner. No, he figured it was the prisoner attempting to swangdoogle *him.*

"All right Matlock, enough of the party invitations." Cissell would have continued, but he was cut off by the Marine, Lieutenant Bellinger.

"You're damn right it's enough. Captain, it's time to stop this nonsense and put this animal back on the island. I can't believe what I'm seeing here. I ..."

The captain cut off Bellinger. "You are right Lieutenant. It is time to secure here." Then he turned his gaze back upon Coon Dog. "Matlock, we appreciate your candid responses to our questions. We know you had a spotless record and performed nineteen and a half years of honorable service in the Navy. And just so there is no question about what took place here tonight, that is the *only* reason you've been treated leniently. No, not leniently, respectfully. I'm afraid we'll have to pass on the thoughtful dinner party invitation. We'll get you back ashore before sunup, and don't worry; the cannibals won't know a thing."

The captain paused and placed his hand on his chin and added, "But now hear this, Matlock, if you don't want your position compromised when we put you ashore, you've got one more question to answer."

The captain paused again and was looking hard into the prisoner's eyes. Coon Dog nodded in the affirmative.

"What was it you said to a crew member when they brought you aboard? He says he didn't hear you, nor did the others. What was it you said to him?"

"All I said was I liked the tattoo on his arm."

CHAPTER SIXTEEN

Captain Weller, the XO, and Jerry Cissell the operations officer were in the ward room. It was only twenty minutes after they oversaw the launch departing the *Nolin River* with the prisoner.

"Well, he did pretty much confirm what we've been thinking. There doesn't seem to be a credible threat at an escape attempt by any of them." The XO yawned. "I think I'll try to get a few winks before the day watch starts. Good night gentlemen."

The operations officer was sitting with the captain. "Sir, I've still got mixed feelings about how the questioning of the prisoner turned out."

"I know you do. I expect that from you."

"The XO is right. Matlock didn't shed any new light on what the satellites have been telling us all along. There's nothing to suggest we have to worry about one of the gangs building something substantial enough to mount an escape attempt.

"I concur, Ron, but it's not the cannibals you're thinking about is it?"

"No sir. It's Matlock. You saw him, sir. Is that guy unbelievable or what? Swims out here ten miles or was carried by the current. I'm not sure which. I don't have any doubt he had an encounter with sharks. And how do you suppose he survived that? Sir, what if he planned it all? You know it's possible that he's been keeping a record of our patrol routine. Let's say that he knew where we'd be tonight, so, he swims out with the intention of being picked up."

Cissell stopped and thought about it for a moment. "No, that wouldn't make any sense. If that were the case, he probably would have made a move. You know, grab a hostage, make some demands. No, he was genuinely surprised to see us come up on him. He didn't plan a thing. I just don't understand, Captain. There's something missing here."

The captain felt compelled to lay out his thinking. "Jerry, lest we get carried away with some very bizarre fantasy scenarios, let's just assume he told us the truth. We know from the satellites that there is one individual on the island who moves around quite a bit. He's the only one, evidently, who isn't ganged up. After tonight, I think we know who that individual is. Matlock even said it himself. He said something about seeing signs of one or two; I think he called them lone wolves. I believe he is the only lone wolf out there. It makes perfect sense. He is ex-SEAL. In the past, he survived some last ditch missions that were just as tough as the banishment island. No, I don't see a mystery here. Matlock is one tough hombre. But there is one question I have. Maybe it's crossed your mind, too. The tattoo on the quartermaster's arm. Matlock said he liked it. Doesn't that seem odd to you?"

Jerry Cissell said, "Yes, sir. I was going to ask you the same thing. Very odd indeed."

....

The launch had made phony insertions into two separate bays. They had kept their running lights on wanting to be totally announced and exposed. They maneuvered to within three hundred yards of the beach, then pulled away. The third insertion they made with no lights and cut the motors and paddled to about one hundred and fifty yards off the coast. Marine

Sergeant Trusky didn't feel one way or the other about the prisoner. He was simply carrying out the specific orders of Captain Weller. "Make sure the prisoner is not compromised when you put him ashore, Sergeant."

"Aye, aye sir," was Trusky's response. Now the sergeant had a few words for Coon Dog. "All right Matlock, here's where you get off. We've given them two phony inserts. You ought to be good to go."

Coon Dog went immediately over the side of the launch and was swimming for the boulder strewn shoreline. He didn't want to linger in the bay a second more than necessary. The swimming wasn't that easy with the Navy clothing and shoes they let him keep.

In five minutes he was scrambling around the boulders, working his way northwest where he thought the boulders would play out to a sandy beach. He had a pretty good idea where he was because one of the Marines had picked up on the scuttlebutt that Coon Dog was ex-SEAL, and so what would it hurt? He gave Coon Dog their location in relation to several landmarks Coon Dog knew very well.

A half hour later Coon Dog was in the jungle working his way toward a camp he'd hidden in many times over the past two years. The camp had a water source nearby, a plentiful supply of buried pemmican, and tools and weapons that had been stored there for an emergency, for tonight.

An hour later Coon Dog stopped to rest and to give the new morning an opportunity to get organized. Predawn was emerging from infinity and Coon Dog was alert to the fact that he had nearly merged with infinity last night. As whispers of gray-pink and silver-gray-pink oozed around the corner of the earth, Coon Dog found himself on his knees. "Father, I love you," is what he said, his forehead on the ground between his hands. He stayed like that for a long time, not saying much, but getting through to the IT, THE SPIRIT, THE CREATOR, THE ONE, THE ALMIGHTY. Yes! Getting through in a big way.

It was twenty minutes, and when Coon Dog got to his feet, there was enough light for him to recognize several landmarks he'd been hoping would be nearby. Thick, heavy vegetation controlled everything to his right, and a dry streambed curved through low scrub to his left. Coon Dog used the morning dew to mix with dirt to apply a mud paste to his face, hands, and arms. He stayed in the heavy jungle to his right. Would the Toros gang or others be waiting for him at the camp? If so, they hadn't come in by the same route Coon Dog was now on. He was an expert tracker. He would notice even the hint of a game track or a human trail. He moved through the jungle slowly, cautiously, and noiselessly. He was on point again. Bellar, Jones, Romanski, Lt. Findley, Thompson, and Pluta weren't behind him this time. He didn't carry a sawed off twelve gauge and a CAR-15 this time. And Coon Dog and his SEAL buddies he remembered so well weren't patrolling the Rung Sat near Saigon preparing to set up an ambush on the skinny little river at night. It was only thirty meters wide. That night they destroyed two sampans. It was close to sunup. They'd been waiting all night, fighting the mosquitoes, ants, snakes, leeches, the hunger in their belly, and then they heard voices on the far bank. They waited. Two sampans showed up a minute later carrying weapons, ammo, and supplies. The SEALS waited until the unloading started, then they opened up. They got return fire immediately, but unlike most ambushes, this time Victor Charles had placed a machine gun thirty meters on each side of the sampan landing site. The SEAL team's ambush had been turned upside down. *They* were the recipients of a murderous cross fire. Two of Coon Dog's buddies were hit bad. Bellar was dead by the time Coon Dog got to him, and Romanski died in his arms as helicopter gunships finally arrived to drive away the enemy across the river. It was just breaking sunup, like now, here on this God forsaken island off Mexico. Coon Dog was screaming at Romanski to stay alive. "Don't die on me Romanski! You hear me trooper? You *will not* die on me!"

"Where are we Matlock? I'm cold. I'm cold. I'm going …I'm going … I'm …"

And Coon Dog stopped again and ran his hands down his flanks and then brought them back to his face as he dropped again to his knees and wept.

Coon Dog had entered his hidden camp early in the morning. He drank some water and removed his new Navy work clothes to try to let them dry thoroughly. He had put on some buckskins and moccasins and put his backup flintstone knife at his side as he rested. At noon he emerged from the heavy thicket where the camp was hidden . He took the pemmican with him to the tiny spring nearby that leaked a tiny rivulet and mixed the water and pemmican. As he ate, he began making plans to complete his getaway raft in order to get back aboard the *Nolin River*, this time unannounced. That would seem to be impossible, but he had a plan, actually a very good plan. The only question was, would it work?

CHAPTER SEVENTEEN

The Burlington, Colorado Truck Stop and Café was nearly full. Pete Thompson, Jabez to those who know him well, was drinking his third cup of coffee and finishing off his red-eye gravy with a biscuit, sopping it as they say down south.

Toby Etheridge, another truck driver and Coon Dog's cousin was sitting with Jabez. "Yeah, I've been feeling it too. Something is about ready to happen down there. You're right. We need to intensify our prayers, but how can we? We are already praying for him most of the time."

Jabez's eternally patient eyes had deep understanding in them. "We just need to pray harder and to pray all the time. Has The Father ever forsaken us when we've poured our hearts out to Him?"

Toby was considering the question. *He's done it again. He's gone straight to the heart of the issue and hit the bull's-eye. Why can't I see things as clearly as Jabez? Because I'm not an angel, that's why.*

Toby had been back on the angel theory for a couple of months now. He'd been wavering back and forth for …. *let's see, how long have I known Jabez now? Five years, six years?* Just about every time Toby had come to his senses and said to himself, *No, he can't be an angel. Angels don't laugh, and tell jokes, and drive trucks, do they?* Every time that happened, Jabez would do something that left little doubt as to his status in the pecking order of creation.

There were other times when neither the label of angel nor human attached to Jabez would satisfy Toby. Sometimes he was sure that Jabez fit into an entirely different reality. He might be a unique spirit, not unlike The Holy Spirit. But no, how could that be? God only used angels to come to earth in human form to perform heavenly duties. Or did He? Not only that, but isn't The Holy Spirit a third of the Trinity? Toby got so confused considering the possibilities that sometimes he'd want to tear his hair out.

Toby noticed Jabez giving him a peculiar look, so Toby asked him, "Are you reading my mind right now?"

Jabez was perfectly capable of doing it, but all he said was, "It's time we quit jabbering. Let's go outside."

The two truck drivers paid their bills and left a good tip. Outside, Jabez didn't walk to his truck. He was headed out to the open prairie on the southwest side of the café. Toby was right with him.

After about a ten minute walk, the two men, well ... the one man and the other spirit, maybe angel, and possibly a man after all, they went to their knees in prayer for Coon Dog.

Later they were walking back to their trucks. "You gonna run twenty-five with me up to Cheyenne?" Jabez asked.

"Yep, then I'll turn west to Salt Lake." Toby was hauling a large retailer's load to a distribution center.

"Ten- four. I'm going on up to Deer Lodge and pay Big Montana a visit. My load delivers pretty close to there." Deer Lodge is a small town thirty-eight miles north of Butte where the Montana State Prison is located.

It was three and a half years ago the Christian truck driver group, the JETS had helped pull serial rapist Grady Johnson (Big Montana) out of more trouble than he was already in, and the trouble he was already in was plenty. He got an extremely lenient eight year sentence for the rapes he'd committed. That was before the banishment law was put into effect. Despite his background and the brutality associated with the rapes, he came to Jesus one night in a country beer joint parking lot. He had a little help from Jabez and particularly from Jabez's born again pit bull, Nicodemus.

Ever since then Jabez would swing by Deer Lodge when he was in the neighborhood and spend an hour or two with Big Montana on visiting day.

Jabez and Toby swung their rigs out on 70 west, and two hours later they were approaching Denver. An hour later they were on 25 north of Denver heading for Cheyenne. They'd been praying for Coon Dog a good deal of the time down on CB channel seven. Jabez was just ending a ten minute prayer, "So, again we've come to you, Heavenly Father, asking Your will be done. Asking You to bring Coon Dog back to us if it fits in Your grand plan. We will continue our prayer vigil, Father. We put it all in Your hands. In the name of The Holy Lamb of God, Christ Jesus, we pray. Amen."

Jabez heard Toby key his mike, "Amen." Then the two of them heard a third voice appear on channel seven, "Amen and Amen. That were a fine piece of prayer Mr. Jabez."

"Yessir Mr. Jabez, mighty fine prayin'," a second new voice said.

And then a third, "Ah reckon it were bout as good a prayin' that's ever tickled these old flaps stickin' off the side of my head."

"How long have you three been sneakin' around our back door?"

The leader of the threesome, Dinky, spoke up. "About the time you started in on your prayin'. We was prayin' for Coon Dog on seven, too, but when we heard you, Jabez, we settled down to listen in."

Dinky, Daffy, and Doolittle were JETS and three company drivers that ran together all the time. Wherever you'd find one of them, you'd find the other two.

Toby keyed his mike, "Hey fellers, how ya' doing?"

Daffy jumped in, "Toby, it's good to hear you. We just missed you back in Memphis a couple of days ago."

"Yeah, I know. Where you three headed?"

Doolittle came back, "Got loads up to Seattle. Thought we might pay Big Montana a visit on the way."

"That's where I'm headed," Jabez said.

"Ten four. We'll tag along back here on the back door. Sure is good to sneak up on ya'," Dinky said.

"We'll stop just outside Cheyenne. They say ol' Wyoming Slim is still grillin' the best 20 oz. T-bone anywhere." Jabez might be from another reality, he might *be* another reality, but he loved to eat just as well as any truck driver on this earth.

Wyoming Slim's was a rip- roaring hoot of a western steak house. Truckers, bikers, ranchers, tourists, locals – all swam in its authentic good time, good eating, raucous flowing excitement as if they might never get another chance to come back. The five truckers ate their fill. All except Doolittle had attacked the 20 oz. T-bone with all the trimmings. Doolittle surprised everyone when it came time to order. He raised his voice to the highest feminine pitch he could get it (which wasn't very high), looked up at his waitress and said, "Let me see, maybe the house salad with vinaigrette and tuna on one piece of lightly toasted rice wafer."

After everyone laughed merrily, he actually stayed with the salad and tuna. Then when the food came he'd only pick lackadaisically at the salad and tuna and try to steal chunks of T-bone from the others. It was an act he'd put on every now and then. The other four were used to it, and always said Doolittle was the worst comedian in the JETS, but he tried the hardest.

Toby and Jabez were outside Wyoming Slims. Dinky, Daffy, and Doolittle had cranked it up and were headed north ten minutes ago. Jabez had told them he'd catch back up with them. Not one of the three doubted *that* was possible. There was only enough twilight left to make out subtle facial features, and Jabez noticed a look of questioning on Toby's face.

"I've been having some strange dreams lately," Toby said.

"I thought that might be the case." Jabez was looking off to the west, his eyes holding onto the last whisper of twilight.

There he goes. He's been reading my mind all day. "Okay, tell me what you know," Toby said.

"Well, earlier today we were talking about something about to happen on the banishment island."

"Right."

"I think your dreams have something to do with it. Tell me about the dreams."

Toby looked over at Jabez in the last of the twilight. *An old man. How old? Might have been 55, might have been 80. Eternal ... no doubt. Cosmic ... no doubt. Human? Must be. He eats, sleeps, drinks coffee like we all do (to survive).* Toby realized for the second time today it was wasted time when he tried to pigeonhole Jabez into anything specific except goodness. That was easy. Somebody once described Jabez's face as a good place you'd been to a long time ago and always wanted to return. "I've been getting them for awhile now. There's an Indian, and there's an old timey trucker goes by "Old Soft Shoe". I'm not exactly sure what they are doing, but the Indian is just sort of floating around, kinda' like he's only an observer. And

sometimes I see Coon Dog. He's sitting at a school desk. He's
a student. And most of the time, but not always, a sailor shows
up. He's got a really nice tattoo on his arm. A mountain scene
with a panther, and a ..."

"A cross," Jabez said.

CHAPTER EIGHTEEN

It was four days after Coon Dog had been returned to the island. In that time he'd made considerable progress on his escape raft. It didn't need to be a large craft. He wasn't going very far on it. The first thing he did was disassemble what little part of it he'd already put together. He moved the disassembled parts about two and a half miles from where he'd been hiding them. His worry that Toros would continue to lurk around Jabez Junction proved valid. He reconned the area his second day back, and there they were, all six of them. As he sat motionless in the jungle above the boulders that led down to the cave, Coon Dog saw two of the cannibals wearing his buckskins, and on down at the edge of the sea, he saw two more casting his fishing net into the sea. He was sure they'd gone through the little amount of dried meat and pemmican he kept in the cave. Most of his stored food around Jabez Junction was buried up in the edge of the jungle, the same way Indians used to do it, wrapped tightly in dried skins.

That night after he'd seen all he needed to see, he climbed the tree where he'd had the panther skin drying and recovered it. He hauled the panther skin and the buried food he'd recovered back to his current camp.

Today he was working on the raft again. If he didn't have to maintain secrecy and silence and stealth, he could easily have built what he needed in two days. But he had to be careful. He couldn't chop down what he needed. That would have produced too much noise. He had to use downed timber as close as possible to the specs he wanted and work from there. And he couldn't put the craft together and try to drag it a mile to the sea. He had to have prefab sections already built and only do the final assembly the night he intended to escape.

So today he was transporting prefab sections through the jungle, getting them closer to the sea. The work was brutal. He was carrying a three piece section of eight-foot long, eight-inch diameter logs that were lashed at both ends to two foot cross sections with tough vines.

He got three sections moved, and had them hidden about a hundred fifty yards apart, and two hundred yards deep in the jungle. A rocky area met the water where he intended to slip the raft in, not the big boulders but much smaller rocks. A small channel ran out seaward from these rocks, and Coon Dog had checked it at high and low tides. It would provide him access to the deep.

He returned to camp nearly exhausted. He drank a lot of water and mixed some with pemmican. He also cracked open three bird eggs he'd climbed a tree after. He let the gooey protein slide down his throat. He was missing the crustaceans and fish he'd been able to eat at Jabez Junction. *Oh well ,*he thought, *if all goes well, I should be ready to hightail it outa here in about three more days.*

His muscles ached, and he wanted to lie down to rest. He estimated maybe two hours of daylight remaining. *No, can't rest. I gotta' work on the panther skin.* As he worked he sensed some of the same flowing, thoughtless design and shaping of the panther skin that he'd experienced before. But this time, he also noticed a definite purpose to his crafting the piece, and when he started on the detailed carving he noticed that the design did indeed look exactly like the tattoo on the young sailor's arm on the destroyer. How this could be, he didn't have a clue. He was too tired to worry about or try to figure out what was going on.

He worked until it got too dark to continue. He mixed more pemmican with water and put down as much as he could. He wanted to eat as much as possible the next three or four days. He figured that if things went wrong on his escape attempt, the extra fat he was storing might come in very handy.

Finally, he prayed asking God for the strength to complete his preparations, and to execute a successful escape, and for God to be with the JETS, his Vietnam buddies, and Red Man. He lay down and was almost asleep, and then he got back to his knees and prayed again. "And Father please be with that young sailor with the tattoo. He must be the one. Protect him from evil. Lead him and guide him in all that he does. I pray his heart is open to Jesus and that he will help me when I need him. In Jesus' name I pray. Amen."

He was asleep the moment he laid his worn out old body down in the jungle. It didn't take long. The truck dreams were underway.

* * *

The wreck was just in front of him, maybe three hundred yards. He saw the dust it stirred up first, then the brake lights of several vehicles between him and the cars involved in the wreck. You always see the dust first he was thinking. He began braking, bringing his eighteen wheeler to a crawl. As he approached the scene, he could see that only one other vehicle had stopped to render assistance to the victims in the two wrecked four wheelers. He pulled over on the shoulder on the right and set his four way blinkers. He darted between the rubber neckers who were inching by to get a good look at the carnage, but didn't stop. As he approached the two stricken four wheelers in the median, he saw a body in the grass. She had been tossed aside like yesterday's trash. In the closest vehicle which was upside down, steam vapor was escaping the cooling system in a light cloud, and he could see another body pinned between a half-opened door, one of its hinges completely torn off. He went to the second car which had butted a tree, head first. The only part of it that still looked like a car was the back wheels and trunk area. He saw a baby blanket in the grass close to that car, but he walked on toward it. Two, maybe three bodies were pancaked in the car. It was impossible to tell exactly how many. He walked around the car looking in the grass. A baby moved in the grass. The truck driver picked it up and held it in his big arms. The baby was a little girl. She looked up into the truck driver's eyes, she smiled, and then she died.

Another truck driver was a thousand miles away. He had been bullied as a child. It was terrible. He'd never felt accepted or loved, and he was always bullied by those bigger and stronger than he. He was a naturalized American citizen. He was from Central Europe and had only been in the United States for a couple of years. He was young, and because of the bullying as a child, he had a poor self image. In fact, he had no self image at all. It all came to a head one day at a truck stop. He'd closed the curtain to the sleeper birth and lay down on the lower bunk. He wound a piece of co-ax cable around his neck and tugged on both ends as hard as he could. In a couple of minutes he sensed his body was stiff and cold, but his mind was still conscious. Five angels came to him. Two were on his left and three were on his right. They were very thin, and they wore white robes and sandals. They had no faces. There was a bright light where their faces would have been, and indeed all around them. Their voices were very delicate, pleasant, and high pitched. "Why are you doing this? You don't have to be doing this. God has something bigger planned for you." The angels went away. Then he could feel his body moving again, and he noticed the co-ax cable had been loosened. He was totally awake.

Another truck driver was driving eastbound on Interstate 10 in New Mexico, and he was like all other men - imperfect. His personal and family life was disintegrating because of his sinful nature. Satan saw an opportunity to claim totally the driver's soul. Satan's demons entered the cab while the truck driver was driving. A day and a half later the truck driver woke up and found himself driving on Interstate 40 in Oklahoma, some seven hundred miles northeast of the location on Interstate 10 where Satan's demons had entered the cab and he had blacked out. The truck driver knew that somehow his entire life had just changed. He couldn't account for the lost time or how, when he woke up, he was seven hundred miles away. For some period of time he pondered the strange event. There was nothing he could remember about any of it. All he had was the unmistakable feeling that everything had changed. Then a few weeks later God revealed to him what had taken place. There had been a spiritual battle for his soul right there in his truck. Twenty angels defeated ten demons. God explained each sequence of the battle and how each sequence pertained to some part of the truck driver's past history. When the truck driver would tell his story to others, there were many who did not believe that such a thing could have happened. But there were others who not only believed, but who confided in the truck driver that similar things had happened to them.

The baby had lived until it died. The bullied driver wanted to die but had lived. The other driver could now live freely.

Old Soft Shoe smiled. The wheel was firmly in his hand. He wished the little wheel- chaired boy at church could come out with him sometime. He'd like to take him on a tour of the west. *The mountains would be splendid for the little guy. And we could camp at a beautiful lakeside cove. Catch a couple of trout to grill. The little guy would like that. He's got such a good heart. He's got a pure heart. Why can't we all be like that.*

Old Soft Shoe could drive for hours and hours with nothing but good thoughts and good questions. When ordinary thoughts and questions tried to sneak into his thinking – *my wife wants that back porch repaired, the insurance premium is going up again, I better check on that, the graveyard cleaning is next week, can I make it home on time?* Old Soft shoe could whisk it all aside and go back to what he was best at. *How can I make it a special week for the little boy? How can I make a difference in my little town? What would it be like to go on a motorcycle trip with Jesus? With Paul? Would he wear shades? With Moses? Would he wear sandals and a robe? And the little baby – why had she smiled up at the truck driver before she died? Was it because she was happy to have had a chance to live even a short time? Probably. Was it because she was glad she wasn't dying alone in the grass? Probably.*

Old Soft Shoe stretched a bit, and he scanned all the gauges in front of him. How long would he continue to drive? Oh, a couple more years he hoped. He was seventy-nine years old now and had no trouble passing the DOT physicals. Yes, it had been a big ride all the way – over eleven million miles. He got his license when he was eleven. That would be 1941. He missed the war, but went in the Navy in 1948. A couple of years later his ship pulled out of port at a town on the China coast. Old Soft Shoe missed the ship. He was still with his girlfriend. The ship never came back for him, so he did what he had to do – he went to work. His girlfriend's grandfather was wealthy and had a business in another town up the coast. Old Soft Shoe went to work for him driving a truck. The girl's grandfather liked him a lot and offered him a million dollars to marry his granddaughter and take her back to America. Old Soft Shoe never told anyone if that's what he had done. He always liked to tell the story up to that point and stop.

Old Soft Shoe felt like it was time to fill his thermos. He knew a little place up ahead a few miles where the coffee was better than most. And tonight he would splurge a little and add some of that sugary English vanilla cappuccino to it. He pulled in, climbed down from his truck and dragged his long body in the door. There were a few familiar faces he said hello to, but he didn't know their names. They said, "Evening Soft Shoe, you headed north?"

"Yeah."

"I guess you've heard. They've really got it coming down."

"Yeah, and I expected it tonight. Just seems like that kind of night."

He paid for his coffee and headed back out. He didn't tell them this was the kind of night he lived for. Hard snow, little visibility. Hunkered down in his little private world. Everybody slowing down, him too. Slowed down to where he really had to *drive* the truck, not just set the cruise on seventy and let it roll on aimlessly. No, now he'd feel every little bump. Now he'd anticipate every inch ahead of him. And the snow was beautiful. Why not enjoy it? He'd miss nights like this after he quit driving. What would he do then? Sure, it was lonely out on the highway all the time, but you were moving. You always had a destination. Always moving. That was it.

What would he do when he quit? What would he do? He put the thought out of his mind and settled into the long, the lonely, and the beautiful night of driving. Maybe he'd pick up a hitchhiker. He'd do that every now and then. Maybe he'd cell phone his brother just to say hi. No, they had stopped with the phone calls a few years ago when his brother retired. Before that, they were regulars with the calls to each other. His brother had been a truck driver too. Now, he was what? Now he was an old man, that's all.

Old Soft Shoe was having a tough time tonight shaking the blues, the grays, the blacks, whatever. He wasn't a singer, a comedian, or an entertainer, but he picked up his CB mike and keyed it.

"Howdy fellers, I'm just an old-timey truck driver getting ready to sing me a song. You're welcome to join right in, and sing right along."

And then he started singing, making up the words as he went:

> This ol' truck was made for truckin'
> And that's just what she'll do
> One of these sorry nights my friend
> She's agonna' roll right over you.
>   Yee Ha!
> Now listen to me, and hear my words
> That's what you need to do.
> We'll roll these trucks all night long
> Six hundred miles before we're through.
>   Hot Dang!
> We'll run the Rockies, and we'll run the coast
> We'll run 'til the wheels come off

We're Jesus Truckers every one
And we're a lookin' for the cross.
    Yes Sir!
Now listen to me all you men
And listen to me good
We'll drive as long as the fuel holds out
Cause that's just what we should.
    Hoo Yah!
I thought this night was gonna' be sad
And I thought that I might cry
But now I know, and I always did
I'll be a driving 'til I die
    All Right!

Soft Shoe let the key on the mike slip, but another driver
kept that song going. Didn't miss a beat:

Yeah, they say Soft Shoe is a big old wuss,
But really that ain't true
I seen him drive on pins and needles
I seen him drive right through.
    Yah Hoo!
He can drive in the weather and drive in the snow
He can drive like the blinding rain
He got no fear, he got no pause
And ain't that a dog gone shame
    Look Out!
Cause we'd all like to be like him
Everybody knows it's true
His mind is set on a higher plain
Even when he's got the blues.
    Yah Hoodle Doodle!

They were rippin' and roarin' now. Ten drivers all jumped in. They were singing and shouting. Sure you got it, they were all friends. They didn't need the CB no more. Their voices whipped through the wind, bounced off the mountain sides and came right back again:

Now truckin' ain't what you heard it is
No, it ain't just fun and games
It's a lot of worry and a lotta heart ache
But that is why we came.
    You Got It!
Yessir, we drive like fire all the time
Just to get the freight on through
You spend just a day or two with us
And you'd know that it is true.
    Zippity Doo Dah!
We'll run the Rockies, and we'll run the coast
We'll run 'til the wheels come off
We're Jesus Truckers every one
And we're a lookin' for the cross.

The song seemed to go on and on and finally there was nothing but static and crackle from Old Soft Shoe's CB. He relaxed. What a hoot – all the singing. Where did the others go? He didn't know. *They are just like me,* he thought. *What would they do without trucking? What am I going to do?* There was so much about it that he really liked. But he remembered back a few years when he was a trainer. He didn't tell the trainees all. There were some things, a lot of things, they'd have to learn on their own. Change was one of those things. He could have warned them to get ready for it, expect it, and accept it.

But there was no use. Some drivers can handle it, some can't. He did instruct them on how to handle a bad day – *once a really bad day gets started, it won't end quickly. One bad thing would lead right into another. It will go on and on.* The good drivers will hold fast and deal with one problem at a time, and they will expect things to get worse. But they will ignite an inner flame. They'll set their jaw tight and keep the hammer down. Bears, bad weather, no sleep, hunger, three hours behind, can't stop, gotta' roll, road construction, shifting load, damaged freight, claims, problems back home, low on fuel, you stink in your four day jeans and shirt, can't drink any beer 'til your break in four days, no parking holes to sleep in and the CB went out. They'll set their jaw tight and keep the hammer down. They won't sleep. They will keep drinking coffee. They will keep driving. They will run a scale and hope the bears don't chase them and slap a seven hundred dollar fine on them. They will talk dirty on the CB and ignore the others who are always saying to them, "Shut up stupid." They will degrade rookies and make jokes about flatbed drivers, and they will look important and command attention when they back their rig into an impossible hole at an overcrowded truck stop at three in the morning when everyone else is too exhausted to attempt it. They will drink coffee and when they try to sleep, it won't come easy.

No, Old Soft Shoe was thinking, there was no point in telling the trainees everything. A lot they'd just have to learn the hard way.

He thought back to an incident that had happened to him thirty years ago. He was still young enough to allow certain people to rile him up and get him fighting mad. He'd pulled into a receiver's dock about two in the morning in South Bend, Indiana. The grocery warehouse was closed and there was another trucker who had just backed up to the dock also. The two men climbed down from each truck and Old Soft Shoe could see that the other driver was friendly and the other driver offered his hand for a shake. "I'm Calvin."

"They call me Soft Shoe." A friendly handshake took place. "What time is your appointment?" Soft Shoe asked.

"Six a.m. How about you?"

"Seven," Soft Shoe replied.

"Well … we should be okay here tonight. I like to bump the dock until they open. Ain't no way a crook could get back there and mess with the load."

Soft Shoe could see in the dim light that the security lights proved that the driver was right. The warehouse sat on the edge of a run-down neighborhood, and having the trucks backed up to the dock would be the safest way to wait 'til the warehouse opened up in another four hours.

"You been here before I take it?" It was more of a statement than a question.

Calvin said, "No, but we'll be all right. We got the first two appointments. Won't nobody need these docks 'til they open."

"Hey, if I'm not up by seven, knock on my door. Okay?"

"Sure," Calvin said, and the two truck drivers went back to their trucks to try to steal a few hours of sleep.

Soft Shoe's alarm went off at five minutes to seven. He was dressed and out of the truck and walking into the warehouse at exactly seven o'clock. He saw Calvin being handed his paperwork by a big burly tough looking Irish dock foreman. Soft Shoe said to the man, "I'm your seven o'clock. My truck is on the dock sitting right next to his." He looked over at Calvin.

"I know where your truck is. You tied my dock up. You ever try to do that again, I'll throw you outta' here."

"Yes sir!" Soft Shoe knew the sarcasm laden response was wrong when he said it. He thought the tough Irishman was going to swing at him, but he didn't. Instead, he barked out his orders as if he'd been the Gestapo pushing around Jews at Bergen Belsen. "Get your tandems back and open the doors." That was all he said. There were no other instructions that most dock foremen would have given a driver.

Calvin felt bad. He and Soft Shoe were outside in front of their trucks. "He didn't need to talk like that."

Soft Shoe only responded with catty remarks about the probability that the Irishman's sex life had not materialized last night.

An hour later Soft Shoe knew that his trailer was unloaded. The noise and the shaking of the truck by the fork lift had ceased. He'd been getting madder and madder thinking about the uncalled for treatment he'd received from the Irishman. He'd made up his mind that if the big bully said anything else to him, there was going to be a fight, and he was going to throw the first punch. When he got inside the warehouse he saw his paperwork on the desk, but it had not been signed. There was no sign of the Irishman. Instinctively, Soft Shoe knew what was going on. This was the Irishman's payback. Make him wait, try to ruin his day, don't get him out of there on time. Old Soft Shoe knew for a certainty that was what was happening.

As he settled in to serve his time in the payback prison the Irishman had built for him, his anger and hatred was growing by the second. He stood there alone. Was the Irishman watching him, maybe from behind a two -way mirror or a peephole. Old Soft Shoe stood there and began looking around the warehouse. He couldn't believe what he was seeing. The place was immaculate. Not a spec of dust or dirt anywhere. No trash, no broken pallets or splintered wood from pallets. Everything was spotless. He'd never seen a warehouse like it. Even the concrete floor was waxed and buffed – it shone. Pallets were stacked with goods in perfect order, perfectly square, not a morsel of product was out of line anywhere. Then it struck him, what the big Irish dock foreman had said. "My dock." Ah, yeah, *his* dock. Now it was all coming clear. *His* dock. The guy was married to this place. Look at the way he kept it. This place was his life. He'd been right in guessing the guy struck out in his sex life last night. He'd struck out every night. His lover was right here, this place! Still that was no reason to have treated Soft Shoe the way he'd been treated.

He stood there in the silence, looking around at this spotless sanctuary for the poor Irishman's love affair with order and cleanliness and control. And he was getting madder and madder as each minute ticked off. *Why should I have to pay the price for this guy's hatred of the normal world, a world where things weren't always clean, things weren't always in place, a world where truck drivers do get a bad piece of advice and the door is opened to a lie that the Irishman's dock had been tied up? Why should I pay the price?* The question kept coming back. He couldn't shake it.

Pay the price, pay the price, pay the price – something was running through his mind. What was it? There it is. It hit him over the head and square in the middle of his heart. Who actually paid the price, the ultimate price? Who paid it two thousand years ago? Who paid the price for the Irishman's misbehavior, for Soft Shoe's hate in response to it, and indeed for each and every weak moment every human being had ever had? Who paid *that* price? Soft Shoe knew who it was. He stood there thinking about it. Easter Sunday was just a few days away. When the Irishman finally came out, Soft Shoe silently and meekly accepted his signed paperwork and walked quietly back to his truck.

CHAPTER NINETEEN

Coon Dog was awakened from the truck dream. He didn't have an opportunity to savor the afterglow as sometimes folks are apt to do. There was something moving in the jungle twenty feet away. His hand was on the flintstone instantly. Were the claymores set? It took him a second or two to dismiss that possibility and get his bearing back. It was a man, no cat this time. And evidently the man cared nothing about making noise; he was making plenty of it. Was there more than one? That was the only thing Coon Dog was trying to figure out. A quarter moon and about half the sky was scattered with thin clouds. Very little of the moonlight was allowed to leak through the canopy overhead. If Coon Dog remained motionless the intruder was likely to stumble on through the jungle and miss his camp altogether. *Probably one of Toro's cannibals. Must have gotten lost out here by himself. Has to be. They never travel alone at night.*

"Christian, Christian, where are you?" The voice called out in a normal conversational volume, loud enough to hear nearby, but not far away. "Christian, I need to talk to you."

Coon Dog heard the words, but they left no impression on him. All he was thinking was, *I've got a cannibal close to me. I need to put him down quickly. We'll see about what he's got to say after that.* He was moving now, slow and silent, picking up the back trail of the cannibal. It was easy; he moved when the cannibal moved. There he was, eight feet in front of Coon Dog, not even stopping to check his back trail. Idiot, still jabbering something about wanting to talk. Coon Dog closed on the man. Four feet away he jumped him from behind. His left hand went in the cannibal's mouth and simultaneously his right hand brought the flintstone to the man's throat. The man wasn't talking now.

Coon Dog said, "Put your hands behind you." He kept the flintstone on the man's throat. His left hand was busy wrapping wrists and hands loosely with buckskin ties. Finally he slipped the flintstone in a sheath on the side of the buckskins and went to work with both hands tightening and knotting the ties on the man's wrists.

"Get on your knees." He tied up his feet and took another tie to pull them tight toward his hands. The cannibal would not be going anywhere for awhile. Coon Dog hadn't brought anything for a mouth gag. If there were going to be any talking, he would control it.

"I ask the questions, you give the answers. You go any other way, I'll put your lights out." Coon Dog could see the man trembling in the limited moonlight. He didn't look to be much of a threat – skinny and ragged looking.

"How many more are with you?"

"None, I came by myself." He squirmed on the ground a little, still trembling, still lying sideways the way Coon Dog had hog-tied him from behind.

"Alright. Just to make sure that ain't a lie, we're both going to just sit here a spell and see if anything else comes diddy bopping down the trail."

He waited a half hour, fairly certain the man had come alone. Coon Dog figured it was the middle of the night and that sunup was still four hours away.

"Okay partner, you said you wanted to do some talkin'. I said you only talk when I ask a question. Here's your first question. Who are you and what are you doing out here?"

The man didn't have to be told to keep his voice low. He was now under Coon Dog's control. Whatever happened to Coon Dog would happen to him also.

"My name is Hector. I was in Toros' gang. I was one of two Toros sent out five nights ago to find your hiding place by the sea. The next morning when you swam into the sea, Toros was very angry. He started yakking about why had we not taken you in the night. He was working himself up to kill. We ate the man you killed, but that was not enough. Toros wanted more. I knew it would be me or the Sergeant. When the gang gets the meat lust, nothing will stop them. And Toros provoked it. I knew they would take me or the Sergeant, or both of us. I ran away. I suspected you had another camp nearby. I've been looking for you since then."

Coon Dog considered the man's story. It was plausible enough. He had no doubt Toros was capable of eating two or three of his own men.

"How many of you?"

"Five or six are still at your cave. It depends on whether they ate the Sergeant. The others are on the way there."

"The others?"

"Yes. When the eight of us set out to find your hiding place, he instructed the other ten to follow in four days." The cannibal continued to squirm on his side, very uncomfortable in the knot Coon Dog had put on him. "The other ten?" Coon dog was thinking the lies had just started.

"Yes. Our gang has grown. We picked up three new arrivals to the island. They looked like good fighters. Toros did not want them to be eaten. And seven others we captured after a fight with one of the north shore gangs. But Toros was convinced you had a good place down here. He decided we were all going to relocate down here."

"Why did he split you up, have eight come first, and then the other ten?" Maybe it wasn't a lie.

"I'm not sure. Possibly it was to test the man he'd left in charge of the ten. He was one of the three Toros decided not to kill and eat."

Coon Dog decided to let that go, but he'd better find out more about this cannibal right here in front of him. He looked at him squirming around in the muck of the jungle floor, and realized the man was being devoured by a swarm of mosquitoes. He was enduring pure torture as he was unable to swat them away. Coon Dog dabbed his fingers in the repellant pouch he carried with him.

"Hold still. I've got something that will keep them off." He smeared a lot of the repellant on the cannibal's exposed skin and immediately the squirming and torture ceased.

"Okay, so what about you? Why did you want to find me?"

"That's easy. I'm going to die if I don't learn some of your ways. I knew you would be back. When you swam away the other day, I had a feeling that somehow you knew what you were doing, that you'd be back. I had no choice. Toros would have eaten me, and I was sure you had another camp somewhere down here on the south side. I made up my mind to search the jungle until I either found you or died trying."

Oh great, Coon Dog was thinking. *Now I've got a basket case on my hands. Three days from getting outta' here and I've got a basket case. Why couldn't I have kept those nice dreams going? They were great.* And then he thought about Old Soft Shoe's Easter dilemma. Fight with all the hate and anger you can muster, or do the right thing – give up your violent nature, *your* will, and submit to God's will. That's what he started thinking.

CHAPTER TWENTY

Toby Etheridge loved truck driving as much as any driver out there. He'd only been doing it for seven or eight years, but he was pretty much addicted already. When he went home he had a hard time sleeping in the big bed he shared with his wife Sarah. There was no diesel engine noise in his bedroom and as a result he rolled around all night expecting to hear a diesel start up. And when he'd get up in the morning, he didn't know what to do. There was no map book by his bed, no CB, no qual-com satellite to tell him what direction his five hundred miles would take him today.

Every new trip he'd read off the qual-com satellite computer gave him a thrill and anticipation that nothing else could do. Will it be a new town I've never been to before? He felt like a child thinking about it. Where will I go on this trip? It was like magic. The hope of a new adventure, a new place he'd not been before.

Once settled into a trip, why sure, some of the trips could be boring. But when a new trip was starting, there was always excitement. Anything could happen on a trip. You never know. Anything is possible. And the thing about Toby was, he always *looked* for the unusual, the new adventure, the interesting person he might meet. Another thing about Toby was that he usually found those things.

There was one time he was supposed to pick up a load in Shahan, New York. It was a small town maybe a hundred miles from New York City, and ten miles from Woodstock. The shipping office was small; the whole place was small. Toby parked his truck in a tight muddy lot that fronted four shipping docks that had seen better days. He walked in the office at one end of the docks, but no one was there. He took a quick peek out in the warehouse. Same thing, nothing moving, no one out there. Back in the office, he called loudly, "Anyone home?"

A woman's voice from somewhere at the top of a stairway said, "Yes, come on up."

Toby climbed the stairs and saw an attractive woman lifting herself out of a swivel chair in a small office. He looked around but didn't see anyone else and remembered noticing when he pulled in the lot, there was only one car.

He stated his business, "I have a load to pick up going to Minnesota." He looked around the office and noticed a lot of Woodstock souvenirs and particularly some tie-dyed peace sign T-shirts and other sixties stuff. The lady was much younger than Toby, probably around forty. She was very open and friendly, something you don't always see in shipping office clerks.

She smiled as she walked toward him, "There's no one here except me.' She was still smiling, then, "Our warehouse man won't be back for another hour." She was walking closer to Toby and he stood his ground. She lightly brushed him as she went to a coffee pot and said, "Would you like some coffee?"

"Yes 'ma'am."

She poured him coffee in a cup and handed it to him.

"Thank you."

"Sure." She was still smiling but giving up on him at this point.

"I could load the trailer myself."

"Okay, why don't you do that." She'd given up completely.

Yes, anything could happen on a trip. You just never know.

After his meeting with Jabez a few days ago at Wyoming Slim's Steak House, Toby had delivered in Salt Lake City, and then picked up a load out of Provo and was heading east to deliver in Atlanta. He stopped up high in the Rockies around 10 p.m., at a truck pull-over at the 11,990 foot Loveland Pass. It was twenty-five degrees in the middle of the summer. He remembered a very bad night at this same place eight years ago when he was a rookie driver. He and another rookie were westbound in a snow storm and had made just about every mistake you could make in mountain snow. But eventually they brought the truck down and were rolling through Glenwood Springs Canyon by four in the morning. They were lucky, very lucky.

This night, on his way east, Toby fixed a salad and broke out a tin of sardines and a box of cheese crackers. After eating, he read from a favorite gumshoe detective series he enjoyed, and then he opened his Bible and with his eyes closed, he leafed through the pages and randomly stopped. He opend his eyes to see where he had stopped. He was in the book of Exodus and he was looking at the 22nd chapter. He liked to do this every now and then, just to see where God would have him read from His Word.

The 22nd chapter was a list of laws God had given to Moses who would in turn give them to the children of Israel. Toby studied the chapter carefully. He'd read it many times over the years and nothing in it had ever really got his attention. Tonight he noticed there was one of the laws that he looked at very carefully, because like so many passages in the Bible, it confused him. The law said, "You shall not permit a sorceress to live." Toby was wondering, what about a sorcerer? But it didn't deal with a sorcerer at all, only a sorceress. Toby didn't dwell on it. He skipped around randomly again, and this time, found he had stopped in the book of Chronicles, chapter 6. Solomon asks the question, "Will God indeed dwell with men on the Earth?"

Toby assumed this was a direct reference to the coming of Jesus, and didn't give it any more thought. He continued thumbing through the pages, stopping now and then to look at a passage very closely and realizing that although there were many passages that confused him, there weren't as many as there had been thirty years ago when he first began reading the Bible.

Eventually he tired of reading. He turned the light off and rolled over on his side with three pillows under his head and shoulders. He was doing the same thing he'd taught Coon Dog to do – he was conjuring up a dream. He started by thinking about golf. He'd played since his early thirties, and the process of seeing a lush open fairway in front of him, stepping into the tee box, and making solid contact on the ball with his driver – thinking through that sequence several times is all it took for him to drop off to sleep.

On this night it was impossible to tell when the dreams actually started but there was no denying that the golfing thoughts had carried over to the dream state. He was still on the tee, but his target wasn't the middle of a fairway. He was trying to hit a procession of big trucks that were speeding around the golf course. He'd lead each truck by aiming thirty yards or so in front of them then snap off a perfect swing and watch the trajectory of the shot as it rifled down the path, then a solid "crack"! as it smacked the center of the 53-foot trailer. Oh, this was fun! What a dream! Then the target became the banishment island. The golf balls became bubbles being blown toward the island. Some presence, some good energy source was blowing the bubbles and there were copies of the Holy Bible in each bubble. The bubbles were over the sea and getting closer and closer to the island. When the bubbles reached the island, they burst, and thousands of Holy Bibles drifted slowly and softly toward the ground. Before they landed, the

Bibles were picked from the air by the men on the island. And then, not unlike other recent dreams Toby was having, Coon Dog showed up in the dream. Coon Dog was sitting at a school desk studying – not from a book. He was thinking, contemplating. And then, like before, an Indian was in the scene. He was sort of floating around back behind Coon Dog, not menacing but maybe he was a shield, a protective force for Coon Dog. Then Toby's dream had him back on the tee taking more shots at the trucks. Up and down the tee there were others. They were swinging their drivers and striking the golf balls solidly, watching them sail off to bang against the trucks. One of the golfers was a young sailor. It was the same young man as before. The same tattoo was on his arm – mountains and a black panther, and a cross. The young sailor was a very good golfer. He could direct his golf ball anywhere he wanted. He had perfect control. He hit high shots, low shots, hooks, slices, or anything he wanted. They all found the truck targets. Then Toby noticed there was one big old truck driving around out there on the golf course that was the primary target. It was being hit much more than the other trucks. The driver was not familiar to Coon Dog, but somehow Coon Dog felt like he should know him. The driver's CB handle was on his door, "Old Soft Shoe", and he was telling the golfers they couldn't hit his truck, but every time a ball hit it brought a roaring laugh and a big smile from Old Soft Shoe. Then all of the truck trailers became sign boards for scripture. Toby couldn't make out the exact words, but he knew the scripture was from all the various books of the Bible. Every time a new golf ball found the scripture and smacked up against it, he saw that Old Soft Shoe wasn't roaring with laughter anymore. He was still smiling though, even bigger, and brighter, and warmer than before.

The dream ended. Toby was up at dawn, still tingling with the aftertaste of the dream. He put on a pot of coffee, dressed and climbed down out of the cab. The cold, thin Rocky Mountain air hit him solid. He walked away from the truck moving his arms up and around trying to pump some blood to warm things up a bit. *My, my! What a beautiful place! What a beautiful morning! The air is so crisp you almost need a glass of water to go down with it.* The trees were as dark, sheer green as anything he'd ever seen. They were thinner here than down around Golden and Denver, and they were non existent just a couple of thousand feet above. Here, at almost 12,000 feet, he could see snow- covered peaks close by and in the distance as well.

He walked slowly for ten minutes and stopped. He hit the preset on his cell phone for Jabez. He didn't know whether he'd have a signal up that high, but he did.

"Yes lad, and good morning to you. How's the view from up near the top of the world?"

Toby gave up. To try to understand how Jabez could do things like know where he was; it was impossible.

"Splendid. Enchanting. No, I think it's better than that. Ask me again."

"How's the view?"

"It might be described as the likeness of God's breath into a newborn's lungs. But that's not really a view is it? It is a feeling. Yes, a feeling. It also feels like, as Windjammer has described to me, like you might feel while dropping down the face of a thirty-footer. As if creation itself was the board under your feet and you were cutting wakes through endless spectrums of resplendent light. Yes, that might be the feeling. The view, it's better than that."

Many times, on mornings like this, they would go on and on. Jabez started, "And as Windjammer described to me, the feeling of cutting a wake through a thirty-footer is like experiencing your own birth again, only magnified by speed, crystalline sunlight off the water, and the knowledge that God is there in it. That it *is* God; that He wants us to sail through it and for us to know it is Him we are in."

"I wish I could be as sure about the purpose of these dreams I'm having. Last night's was a doozie."

"Yes, I'm sure it was."

"It sounds like maybe you already know the details."

"No, I don't know any details other than I suspect the young sailor with the tattoo was in it again."

"Yes, he sure was. Come on now.... What else do you know about it?"

"Nothing. Really. But I do know there are others having the same or very similar dreams."

"Who?"

"Coon Dog, myself, and a young sailor who is somewhere very near the banishment island."

"Does he have a tattoo with a black panther, mountains, and a cross?"

"He shore'nuf got all of that."

CHAPTER TWENTY-ONE

"What is it?"

"Pemmican. Dried meat mixed with berries."

"We haven't killed a deer in months. Are there any left?"

"Very few."

"Is what we are eating deer meat?"

"Yes."

"Did you kill it recently?"

"No."

"How do you preserve it?"

"You pound it into a powder, mix it with fat and dried berries, and then you wrap it tightly in dried skins and bury it. Done properly, you can eat it two years later."

"How much of it do you have?"

"Oh, I reckon I could eat off of it for four or five months."

Hector was astonished. "My God! If Toros knew that, he would not kill you. He would torture you and try to get you to show him where it is buried." He continued eating the pemmican that Coon Dog had given him.

Coon Dog had finished his portion of pemmican and was working on a handful of wild berries. "Well Mr. Hector, let me tell you something. First off, Toros ain't never gonna' get his hands on me to do any torturing. And secondly, if he did, you would already be dead. You get my drift?"

"Look Christian, you must believe me. I know who's in charge here. I keep telling you. That's why I came. I knew you could have killed me. That's why I took the risk. I can't go back. I either learn how to survive from you, or you kill me. It's not easy for me to say this.... I am totally under your control. I will do anything you say – anything. I want to live. I want to survive."

"What did you do to get sent here?"

"I smuggled cocaine. I was one of three main suppliers to the Miami buyers." Hector had finished off the pemmican. Coon Dog got him some more.

"What do you feel about all of that now? Do you have any remorse?"

"I know my life is in your hands, and I think you would see the lies I might tell. I think it is wise for me to answer that question truthfully. Remorse? No, I don't think so. I killed ten maybe twelve men. I bought politicians and judges and cops as a child might buy candy. I did what I wanted with women. I was what you might say.... ruthless. I was cold, and I suppose empty. No amount of money or power would satisfy me. To say I am remorseful for all of that would be a lie. I don't know what I am now. The obvious I suppose – starving, and afraid to die. Remorse, no. But I do know that if I were not on this island, I would not go back to my old livelihood. There are other ways of living I think I would seek out. What is the word they use? Deterrent? It is real."

"You say you are afraid to die. Why?"

"I don't know. Maybe seeing all I've seen here. Maybe something else."

"What else?"

"I don't know. There was an Indian that came into our camp. Toros killed him. We ate him. He wasn't afraid to die. You could tell he was not afraid. He was reading from the Bible. He knew he was going to be killed and eaten. He came right in and read from the Bible. I think he had a strength inside him. He did not fear death. I have no such strength."

Neither man said anything. Coon Dog thought back to the first time he'd dealt with Big Montana, the serial rapist turned JET, back when Big Montana was running out of time in a spiritual warfare battle. Satan was tugging at him from one side and Jesus was waiting for him on the other side. Coon Dog, having known about such problems from his own sordid history, asked Big Montana a simple question: "Who do you trust? Jesus or Satan?"

Now, he looked at the scrawny, pitiful Hector, once powerful, now probably doomed, "Mister I ain't no preacher, and you can believe me when I say this: I ain't got very much figured out in this world. But I do have this much figured out: If you killed ten or twelve men while you were running drugs, and you got no remorse about it .... Well, I'd say your chances of survival don't amount to much.... No matter what you might learn from me."

"What do you mean?"

"Just what I said. You could learn every survival skill in the book. You could be the toughest Rambo anybody ever seen, but if you don't get right with God about what you done, you won't make it on this island and you won't make it in eternity."

Ah, so this is why they call him Christian. He really believes it all. He's like the Indian. I'll play along. His brand of Bible thumping will probably be different than all that crap the Catholic priest and nuns used to throw at me. And, I've already got a good meal out of him. I better not make any moves for awhile. Just play along.

Hector was not in a move-making status at the moment. Coon Dog had released him from the hog tie, but now his back was tied tight to a tree. His hands were free so he could eat.

Coon Dog had also brought him water in a wooden cup, and Hector drank the last of it. Then he broke the silence of the last couple of minutes. "Eternity? I'm not sure I can continue living another week. If you had not fed me tonight, I don't know what would have happened." Hector might have wanted to plan some moves to make on Coon Dog, but when he spoke, only the truth came out.

Coon Dog got to his feet and walked forty feet away in the dark. He was gone four or five minutes. Hector could hear him working away at something. He heard brush moving and he heard trees being manipulated in some way.

Coon Dog came back and said, "We've talked enough tonight. I've got your bed all made for you."

He untied Hector and walked him over to the spot he'd been working. "Okay, you can lie down right here."

Hector lay down on a cleared out area, but it was too dark to see much of the surroundings. Coon Dog tied a vine rope around each wrist, then went into the darkness for a moment and came back. Hector could feel a tension on the vine rope that tugged slightly on his wrist and Coon Dog said, "Don't move your arms."

Coon Dog put a noose around Hector's neck. "Hector, you're in something of a fix. Now I plan on getting some more sleep before the sun comes up, but I don't want to worry about you. You feel them ropes pulling on your arms just a teeny bit? Well, if you move them to take the noose off your neck, a tree I got about half bent over is gonna' jerk you off the ground about as quick as a cottonmouth can swallow a tadpole. And I don't reckon you'd have much fun dangling around up there fifteen feet off the ground, you know, just a hangin' and your arms torn out of your shoulder sockets."

"I reckon we can talk more about eternity and you know.... remorse.... and all that sort of stuff manana. Sleep tight." Coon Dog walked away in the darkness and Hector couldn't see him or hear him anymore, but Hector knew in his heart of hearts that his thinking about making any moves on the Christian had just come to an end.

CHAPTER TWENTY-TWO

Coon Dog slept four hours. His dreams had no truck adventures in them, but he could sense the presence of Red Man in them. Or was it Red Man's Bible? Dreams don't always reveal identities or objects. Sometimes they only leave clues about who or what was in them. As he rubbed sleep from his jungle eyes he thought about Hector and what he would do with him. He couldn't kill him, unless Hector surprised him and tried to do something stupid. So, what *could* he do with him?

Hector was a shell of a man, down about as low as a man could go. Coon Dog wondered if this once mighty criminal could be salvaged as a good human being? He went to his knees in prayer. "Father, here I am again, seeking your mercy, your strength, your wisdom, and seeking to do your will, not mine. It's Hector, Father. I don't know if he's sincere, but I'm getting the feeling You want me to work with him as best I can. Is that right Father? I'll do it. I'll do the best I can. And I'll look for signs You might send me. And I'll love You Father. I'll love You 'til the day I leave this earth, and then I'll keep loving You. Be with all those I need to pray for Father. All of the JETS, Red Man, my buddies from Nam, all the lost. the homeless, the sick, the hungry, and Father please be with Hector. I pray his heart would be open and that he'll ask Jesus to come in and take control of his life. Thank You Father. Thank You for this day and for all the days You've given me. In Jesus name I pray. Amen."

The morning was crisp and a little cooler than ordinary. Coon Dog got to his feet and peered through the jungle's shadows that were hiding from the sunlight oozing in through the cracks. He was thinking, *How to salvage a broken man? Was he really broken? Am I being set up? Is he here as a spy? Will he get intel on me and my camps, and my hidden food stores, then return to Toros? Or is he really broken and being honest saying that I am the only way for him to survive? Will any of this change my plans for escape?* He thought he knew a way to find some answers.

He approached Hector's bedroom and found Hector in miserable shape. Hector was babbling and sounded as if he might be going mad. "All right Mr. Hector, we are going to get you loose from this. You won't have to spend another night like this."

Coon Dog took the noose off Hector's neck first and when he removed the vine ropes from his wrist, a half-bent over fourteen foot high tree sliced straight up through the air whipping the noose up ten feet off the ground.

Hector's babbling changed to a bawling cry that lasted five minutes. When he was through crying, he got to his feet and seemed to regain a good deal of his composure.

Coon Dog waited for him to say something.

"I thought I would die. I thought I *was* dead, but I did not move my arms. After a while it all seemed so useless – living. I started to put my arms up to my neck, but I didn't. Then I guess I lost it."

"Hector, the Lord, I think, has shined His light on you. If you're going to be a survivor, we got work to do. Come on."

Coon Dog walked sixty yards or so to the center of his camp, which never would have been ID'd as a camp. Everything was hidden or buried. The untrained eye would not have picked up on the trip cords which would have planted an arrow in a man's chest. Coon Dog had to be careful with Hector so that Hector wouldn't be killed on the short walk.

"Sit down."

Hector sat and Coon Dog went to a cluster of huge ferns fifteen feet away and emerged with dried fish, pemmican, and honeycomb.

"Start on this. We've got to get some meat on you if you're going to survive."

Hector didn't argue. He sat and ate. Coon Dog disappeared again, came back shortly, and gave Hector a dried skin with more food, and the wooden cup of water.

Hector looked in the skin. "What is it?"

"Dried seaweed, and dried insects. Eat all you can. It's good for you."

Hector didn't argue. He gobbled up everything in short order.

"That's enough for now. A lot of that will run right through you til you get used to it. When you go, make sure you are five minutes away from camp, and take this with you." Coon Dog handed him a small digging tool. Coon Dog also produced the club he'd taken from Hector last night. "Here's this back, and I got something else for you." He handed Hector a master-crafted flintstone knife, not any less perfect than his own. "I reckon you know how to use one of these."

Hector was like a little boy. He was no stranger to knives and guns and the like, but this piece he was just handed simply astounded him. Perfect balance, perfect weight and size for killing, a cord grip that bonded to your hand like cement. *My God! What is this Christian not capable of doing?* He just looked at Coon Dog with an expression of wonder and amazement. He didn't say anything. He just worked the flintstone from hand to hand, loving its feel.

Coon Dog was still on his feet. "I've got some things to do. I'll be back around noon. If you leave camp, go out that way. There are no booby traps." Coon Dog was pointing to the thickest, hardest part of the jungle – the northeast. Before he left he showed Hector the route to a nearby spring and said, "Get some rest. There will be plenty for you to do manana. Tonight we will talk." Coon Dog set out for the area of the raft. He'd move a few more logs and do a little more planning.

CHAPTER TWENTY-THREE

It was past noon when Coon Dog got back to camp. Hector was asleep, curled up under the ferns. In the daylight he looked even smaller and weaker than earlier that morning in the shadows and emerging light.

Coon Dog sat down ten feet away, watching him. *He could have found a lot of food and been long gone, but no, there he lies. On the other hand, he still could be just biding his time, gathering more intel until he makes his move.* Deep down inside Coon Dog was reading Hector's continued presence in camp as one of the signs he'd prayed for.

In a moment or so Hector rolled over and saw Coon Dog sitting there. He sat up and for the first time was able to take in the full measure of the Christian. If he didn't know before, he knew now, he would have been crazy to challenge this man physically. Maybe to the sailors Coon Dog was tough- looking and physically fit, but to a starving cannibal he might be Superman. He had real muscles, not the skinny appendages most of the cannibals had. He had confidence. He had clear eyes, and to Hector's amazement, he even had a smile.

"Sleep better than last night?" Coon Dog asked.

"Much better, but I'm not sure I moved my arms very much."

"Well, like I said this morning, you won't have to spend any more nights like that."

Coon Dog opened a skin bag he had and produced two good sized grilled rabbits. He tossed one over to Hector and started eating the other one for himself.

A few minutes later he resumed the conversation. " I cooked them over a fire about two miles from here. Don't ever build a fire any closer than that. Got it?"

"Got it."

"I got 'em on my snares. You ever use a snare to trap game?"

"No."

"I'll show you how. It's similar to the noose rig I had you in last night, only the rabbit has to nibble on the bait to spring it. Ain't many rabbits left around here. Any of your people know how to trap game?"

"No. And they…. ah …. they are not my people."

Maybe another sign, Coon Dog was thinking.

"Well, somebody's been killing 'em besides me."

"Maybe one of the north coast gangs."

"How did Toros' people kill deer?"

"We'd run them toward four or five men with crude bows and arrows. Every now and then one of them would get lucky and wound one. We'd follow the blood trail 'til it died."

No one talked while they finished the rabbits, then Coon Dog laid out his plan to get some answers to the questions he still had about Hector.

"Okay Hector, here's the plan. The way I see it, you actually got some potential. I give you a B-minus on how you handled last night. And today, you could have run off with a good knife and a lot of my food, but you didn't. You got a long way to go on the spiritual side, but you know what? Most men do. A drug king-pin who's killed ten men troubles me a whole lot. If you ever have remorse and want deliverance from your past sins, …. well, that's between you and God. If you ever want my help with that process, I'd be glad to do what I can. I ain't a preacher, so I don't really know the exact way something like that could be done. But I could tell you how it worked for me.

We call it a testimony, sometimes called witnessing. If you ever want to hear mine, I'd be glad to do it. But here's the kicker. I *want* to trust you, but at this point in time I can't. I'm going to need to see a sign from you, actually something a whole lot more than a sign. I'm going to need to see you go out on a limb and take a big risk in order to prove to me you're on my side."

Hector's eyes looked strained and listless. He didn't say anything. "You told me the Indian that came into your camp was reading from the Bible. Is that right?"

"Yes."

"What happened to his Bible?"

"One of Toros' men kept it. When new arrivals from the world arrived and Toros would snap them up, he always burned their Bibles. The Indian's Bible was picked up by Terry Wagner, a mass murderer back in the world. He hid it away. Toros never knew what happened to the Indian's Bible. He was too excited about eating the Indian. He was worked up into one of his frenzies."

"Yes, I know. I was hiding nearby that day. I saw Toros kill the Indian. He was my friend. Is Wagner still alive?"

"He was a few days ago."

Coon Dog was looking hard, right into Hector's eyes. He didn't say anything for a moment, then, "Okay, you are .... you are going to pay him a visit. I want you to retrieve Red Man's Bible and bring it back to me."

"Red Man?"

"Yes. That was my name for the Indian. You will find Wagner and get the Bible. I don't care how you do it. You can take food with you and trade it for the Bible. You can simply steal it, or you can do it in any other way you think might work. But if you don't bring back Red Man's Bible, I'm through with you."

There was no response from Hector. He looked deflated.

"I know it won't be easy, but I will help you get prepared for your mission. You do this .... I will help you survive. I'll teach you everything I know."

CHAPTER TWENTY-FOUR

Hector Estrada was selling marijuana by the time he was fourteen. As he graduated from simple thirty and forty dollar a bag sales of weed on up to multi-million dollar sales of cocaine, he had developed a reputation which any serious smuggler would have been proud of. His product was always the highest grade cocaine that money could buy. But the thing his competitors were most envious of was his ability to see through a scam, a set-up, a rip-off, a deal about to go bad. It was like a sixth sense he possessed. No one ever recalled stories of Hector Estrada having been ripped off in a drug deal, or any other kind of a deal. And if something like that almost happened, the perpetrators were never seen again. The talk was Estrada himself handled those situations. He didn't use his own thugs or hire outside muscle. He did it himself.

Growing up in his uncle's home in Sarasota, Florida, Estrada had gone to Catholic schools and was expected to be a good Catholic boy. His father had been killed in the fighting in Cuba in the late fifties. His mother was able to get him out with her and go to live with her brother in Florida. But Estrada wanted no part of the Catholic Church, especially after he'd witnessed two priests have their way with an altar boy – Estrada's cousin. Estrada was hiding when the incident took place, and he'd always had a feeling of guilt. He hadn't done anything to stop the evil. He just watched from the keyhole in a closet in the rectory as he shook almost uncontrollably. He was twelve. Two years later, he started his criminal drug career.

When Coon Dog had first laid out Hector Estrada's mission, Hector didn't think he could do it. He asked Coon Dog if he could think about it over night, and Coon Dog said, "Sure". The actual thinking he did didn't have anything to do with the mission. It was more a review of his life. Where had it all gone wrong? Oh, there were years when he was at the top of his game in the narcotic wars. He took some pride in it. That was the reason h e'd been honest with Coon Dog when he said he didn't think he had remorse. Where *did* his life really go wrong? The death of his father? Hector had been told by his family that his father had died a hero. Would things have been different if he'd lived? What about the two priests? Were they responsible for his ruination? Was it the neighborhood gangs in Sarasota? Was it the tough Sarasota cops? Was it.... was it.... and finally he asked the question – was it me?

The morning Coon Dog expected Hector's decision, he happened upon a sight he did not expect to see. It was dawn. Hector was up before Coon Dog doing push ups and sit ups.

"I'd say, by the looks of things, you've decided to take the mission on."

"Yes. Yes I have. I think I should be ready to carry the mission out in three days. Will that be satisfactory?"

"I reckon so."

The next three days were a whirlwind of activity for both men. Coon Dog took Hector on a foraging hike in the jungle. They came back with edible roots, plants, insects, and two dead snakes. Coon Dog also showed Hector how to mix the wild vegetables with the pemmican to produce an appetizing stew. Dandelion root, wild parsnip, pine nuts, daylily roots, cattail heads, and bulrush root were particularly effective in making a hearty stew.

Coon Dog gave Hector two hours a day of PT and close quarter physical combat, and another two hours a day on weapon and tool manufacturing. Another two hours a day were instructions on resistance and evasion. Coon Dog's vernacular for the military tactics was Jungle Truckin'. His pupil was making progress, and about midway into the third day, Hector said, "Come out here, there's something I want to show you." Coon Dog followed him out into the jungle about five minutes, and Hector proudly said, "Look." He was pointing to a beautiful solid eight inch turd he'd deposited. "You were right. The food quit running through me."

"Don't forget to bury it." The instructor was all business.

That night Hector Estrada left camp about midnight. His plan was to make it back to Jabez Junction by first light in the morning and stay hidden in the jungle above the cave. He would observe the activity, and most importantly, watch to see if Terry Wagner was still alive. Coon Dog had insisted that Hector be well armed, well fed, and that he use the jungle camo concoction on his skin. Also, Hector carried a skin full of pemmican to use as a trade for the Bible.

The sun came up and Hector was settled into a good hiding place. He had a jungle spear with him as well as his prized flintstone knife. He knew the cannibals weren't early risers so he spent some time reflecting on the last four days. There was no doubt about it. Coon Dog was making a big impression on him. He had to admit that at first all he really wanted to do was figure out Coon Dog's primary food source and then, if circumstances afforded him a good opportunity, he would kill the Christian. But then, he'd seen in the strong jungle man something he'd not seen in a long time, maybe never. He saw a strength of character not based on gangland one upmanship, on

ruthless turf wars, on single-minded greed. He saw a man who
was plenty tough, but who lived with an honest sense of fair
play and even forgiveness. He didn't judge others. If an enemy
threatened his life, he could strike swiftly and lethally, and have
no guilt about it. But until someone made a move against him,
Coon Dog reserved judgment and action agains that person.
That's the way Coon Dog had treated Hector.

The spiritual side of Coon Dog was similar. He obviously
was a man of faith, *whatever that was,* Hector thought. But he
didn't beat you up with it. He was nothing like the Catholic
priest, or at least the ones Hector had seen operate. Other than
the offer Coon Dog had made to share his testimony, he had
not mentioned anything else to him about God, remorse, eternity, or being saved. True, Coon Dog would many times make
references to those things, but it was for his own ears, not anyone else. It was the way he lived. Hector grew to respect Coon
Dog's ways.

The heat began to take its toll. The sun was cooking the
island and anything on it that was trying to live. Hector made
his way carefully to the spring in the jungle above the cave.
Coon Dog had told him about a place where the spring bubbled
up above ground but was concealed enough not to get caught if
you wanted to refresh yourself. That's just what Hector did. He
stripped off his ragged dungarees and the wonderful moccasins
Coon Dog had made for him. He sat in the cool spring deep
in the shadows and well below the thick jungle canopy. He
bathed, drank his fill, dressed, and dabbed fresh camo and mosquito repellant on himself. He was back at his hidden observation post in twenty minutes.

A little while later he noticed two cannibals emerge from
the boulders below him. One they called Ringo, and the other
one must have been from the ten back in the center of the island

who were to travel to the seaside cave. There was no sign of Terry Wagoner. The two headed east up above the boulders. Soon three more cannibals appeared down by the sea. They began casting the net, hoping to catch some breakfast.

Hector waited. He couldn't do anything until Wagner showed himself. Two more cannibals climbed the boulders and emerged on top. They headed off toward the west. One of them looked like Wagner. Then two more showed up and took positions in the edge of the jungle, not a hundred yards from Hector's hiding place. Hector realized that the ten new cannibals were here. And the leader of that bunch must be influencing Toros a great deal. The six sentries he'd just seen spread out was something he'd never seen Toros order. The new guy must be behind that.

Hector backtracked deep into the jungle to skirt the two sentries nearest him. His spear was in one hand, his flintstone in the scabbard, and the skin pouch of pemmican hanging from the shoulder strap. Hector moved a quarter mile westward. He turned back toward the sea and approached slowly. When he got up close enough to risk a peek up and down the coast, he could see the two sentries to his right, maybe sixty yards away. They appeared to settle down at the edge of the jungle. Hector settled himself into a good hiding and observation location. His camo blended in smoothly with the vegetation. The sentries never would have noticed him if they'd walked right by.

Hector waited. In a few minutes one of the cannibal sentries got to his feet, walked to the boulders and then continued on down into a sea-filled inlet. It was Terry Wagner. He stripped off the rags that served as clothing and swam in the relatively calm waters of the inlet. A half hour passed and finally Wagner had dressed and climbed back up the boulders to sit back where the other sentry was still posted. Hector watched as the second sentry got up and started down the same trail to the same inlet.

It's now or never, Hector thought to himself. He backtracked thirty yards into the jungle and then went the sixty yards toward Wagner. Coon Dog's instructions on silent jungle maneuvering really came in handy. He got within ten yards of Wagner, who was facing the sea, his back to Hector.

"Wagner, I've got food for you."

Wagner bolted upright, and turned to see who had sneaked up on him. His club was up and ready to sling. He recognized the voice but not the camo face of Hector.

"Hector? Is that you? Are you crazy?"

"Yes, it's me. I've got food for you." He held the skin pouch out toward him.

"You must be crazy. You know what Toros will do if he finds you."

"Yes, I know. You must listen. You must hear me out."

Wagner looked back toward the sea. His fellow sentry had just waded into the inlet down below. "You better make it fast. He will be back up here soon." He lowered the club.

Hector approached him slowly, pushing vines and jungle growth aside. Wagner could see that Hector looked much better, much stronger, than the last time he'd seen him, some nine or ten days ago. He also noticed the best jungle spear he'd ever seen, and of course the menacing flintstone, still in the scabbard.

Hector was close to Wagner now. He opened the pouch, took a handful of pemmican and handed it toward Wagner. "Eat this. It is good. It is deer meat."

Wagner took the pemmican and didn't hesitate. It was gone in an instant. Hector gave him some more. It didn't last long either.

"This pouch contains maybe twenty-five pounds. I have brought it for you. But there is something I must have in return." Hector could see immediately Wagner was about to make a move on him. His hand went to the flintstone. "I won't give it up without a fight. But it is yours without fighting. Just listen to me."

Wagner stopped and let the words sink in. Also he sensed this wasn't the same Hector that had fled ten days ago. Wagner wasn't sure at all that he could kill him now.

"What do you want from me?"

"Do you still have the Indian's Bible?"

"Yes."

"That is what I want."

"You are crazy. Where did you get this food?"

"Listen to me. This food is yours. I think I can get more for you. I'm not sure. Certain things must happen. All I want from you is the Indian's Bible."

"You've been with the Christian. He came back didn't he?"

"Where I've been and who I've been with is none of your business. I've brought you a two month supply of the best food you've seen in two years. It's possible I will be able to continue bringing you food. Take the deal or leave it. All I want is that Bible. I will be here tonight one hour after the sun goes down. Come alone. If anyone is with you, you will be the first to die." Hector turned and disappeared into the jungle. He worried over his pitch being too strong. He needn't have worried. Wagner had already decided he would return one hour after dark with the Bible.

CHAPTER TWENTY-FIVE

The night that Hector was exchanging the food for the Bible with Wagner, Coon Dog was into another truck dream. There was a conversation taking place among four truck drivers, and Coon Dog sensed that his cousin Toby Etheridge was one of the drivers. There was an ornery Tex-Mex Latino, there was another Latino, and the fourth driver Coon Dog felt for sure was Old Soft Shoe, the dream figure who had been popping up lately.

The Tex-Mex Latino was running off at the mouth, "You redneck hillbilly gringos go on back to your shacks and your single wides. Your wives and daughters are waiting there. But you won't be able to do it to them. Your son is into them. Yeah, that tongue tied kid of yours is tapping them out. Go on back! Get in line. Yeah, get in line behind him and the neighbor men, the other retarded gringos. We coming back gringo. We coming back. We take Texas back, California, and the rest. And we wouldn't touch that white trash women of yours. Your donkeys and dogs already got them."

Toby was listening. A few years back he would have called the Tex-Mex Latino out. Now days he was more inclined to simply turn the CB off and not listen. But today Toby continued to listen. Then another Latino voice keyed his microphone and spoke up, "Meesta, you don't know what you talking about. You got a green card? I bet you don't. You talk good English, but I bet you a Tijuana gangbanger on de run. You don't know nothing about this country. Me, I come here in 1960, then I go to Vietnam and fight for this country. I love this country. I lost daughter in Iraq. She was Air Force Lieutenant on a hospital plane. Iraqis shoot it down. Filthy animals shoot down hospital plane. Fifty-eight died. I know about this country. America good. But I think she may fall. Terrorist come in, but we no stop them. Politicians no back bone. They all politically correct. We gonna' loose the country."

Tex-Mex Latino came back, "No man. You don't know your history. America always run over the little man – Indians, blacks, Muslims, you name it. American pigs always hurt the little man. You look at your history, man, you don't know."

"I do know! I fought for this country. This country is worth fighting for, but I worried we gonna loose it. Most blacks and Latinos vote for Obama. Not me. I saw right through his lies. He promised free health care. Now it is a law. Everyone *must* buy it. What is that? Everyone *must* buy it. He bails out big business and promises tax cuts. What is that? I see no tax cuts to anyone. I see the opposite. I think we lose the country. It never be what it was before."

Toby finally jumped in the conversation. Angry Tex-Mex Latino's CB signal got too weak to hear, so Toby assumed only the second Latino voice might still be listening. "Mister, I'm a Vietnam vet also. I agree with everything you said. And your daughter, I'm .... I'm not sure what to say." He couldn't quite get the words out but finally he said, "I will pray for her soul and for you and your family."

"Thank you, driver."

Another trucker's voice keyed up. It was Old Soft Shoe. "I too will pray for your daughter . That other guy was nuts. He just doesn't understand what Americans are. Me, I understand. And I know God is there looking out for all of us, not just Americans. Two weeks ago I just about bought the farm.

God saved me. It was a bad wreck, but God saved me. He had to have done it. No other way I would have lived through it."

"I heard that driver," Toby said. "One day we will all be together in heaven. We will all be with the Heavenly Father, that is, all that love Him and want to be with Him. You know drivers, …. I don't know if you've ever thought about this or not, but what about the ones who never believed, the atheists, what will happen to them? I've heard preachers say they will have one last chance to accept Jesus. The throne room judgement they call it, or the second judgment. Read Revelations, chapter twenty. Just think about it. All the unsaved here on earth will still have an opportunity to be saved. It makes sense to me. Don't you know some really good people who have never accepted Jesus as the only way to eternal life in heaven? I do. I have them in my family. I pray for them. Even though they don't know the truth here on earth, they will have the opportunity to know it and accept it at the second judgment. What an awesome God we have."

"Amen, driver. I know that without God I'd be a lost soul." Old Soft Shoe was feeling real good. "Let's go boys. Let's keep on truckin'! I'll run the front door. We got a load of hope and love to deliver! Hammer down fellers, let's roll!"

A thousand trucks headed out; Old Soft Shoe was leading the way. They were just north of Philadelphia on I-476. Old Soft Shoe led them right into downtown Philly. Air horns blasting, a thousand Peterbuilts, K-Ws, Freight Shakers, Internationals, Macks, Western Stars, Volvos, and all the rest, rolling through Old Philadelphia. People lined the streets to see them roll through. Bands played, flags waved. The drivers waved at the crowds and kept on rolling. They turned north to New York City, Newark, Providence, Boston, Concord, Burlington, and Bangor. Baltimore and Washington D. C. were next, then

Dover. The crowds grew bigger and happier to see the trucks
rolling through. Then down to Richmond and Charleston. On
to Jacksonville, Miami, Orlando, Tampa, Atlanta, Charlotte,
Charleston W. Va., Pittsburgh, Cleveland, Detroit, Cincinnati,
Knoxville, Nashville, Louisville, Indy, Chicago, Milwaukee,
St. Louis, Memphis, Birmingham, New Orleans, Jackson,
Little rock, Kansas city, Des Moines, Minneapolis, Bismarck,
Sioux Falls, Grand Island, Wichita, Oklahoma City, Dallas, Ft.
Worth, Houston, Albuquerque, Denver, Cheyenne, Billings,
Boise, Salt Lake City, Phoenix, Las Vegas, Portland, and Seattle.

Then they came to Hollywood, but there were no people
there. The streets were empty. There was only a high cold wind
jostling through the streets. Neon lights were being shattered,
and a million souls were being lost every day. Old Soft Shoe
brought the thousand truck caravan to a halt. "Let's get out and
find the children."

The truck drivers all left their cabs and searched the city
for the children. They found them hiding in every conceivable
small, dark, hiding place. The children were alone and weeping and hiding. The truck drivers picked them all up and took
them back to their trucks. Then the trucks left Hollywood. The
children were with them.

Coon Dog awoke from the dream. His mind was dizzy with
the waves of implication the dream produced. And there was
his cousin Toby, right in the middle of the dream. And the
new guy, Old Soft Shoe, *now he is a piece of work.* But oh! Would
Coon Dog like the dream to be real, and if only he could just
be back, driving through all of those cities again. If he could
just wake up again to look out the window of his cab and see
the pink sunlight breaking the eastern horizon, sitting up high

in the Blue Ridge at Afton, or Fancy Gap and looking down on the farms that looked like toys so far below, like he was in an airplane, seeing the square patches of turned sod, corn, beans, hay, wheat, seeing it all from above, and the forest in the Appalachians behind him. Ah! To once again take a walk on the trail, see a bobcat, a fox, deer, and bear cub and its momma. He'd done it all before. To do it again would be… it would be …

Well, there's only one way *that's* going to happen.

It was still an hour before sunup, but Coon Dog checked the camp. Hector was still out on his mission. *No sense hanging around here fretting about dreams or about Hector.* He grabbed his weapons, tools, and a pouch of pemmican and headed out through the jungle, toward the building area of his raft.

By the time he arrived the sun was well up in the east and he had eaten insects and frog legs on the way. Four of the frogs had been on or near the trail. Coon Dog had no trouble catching them, cleaning them, and he even built a quick fire to cook the legs.

After an hour's work he had all of the pieces of the raft down close to the sea. They were hidden in the jungle in what he thought was the roughest area on the entire western coast. He'd only seen cannibals in the area two times in the last two years, and they didn't stay for long. Unlike other coastal areas of Isla de la Lejania the jungle here almost came right up to the water. The beach was narrow, maybe twenty-five yards from the water to the jungle.

Coon Dog sat down and mentally went over the steps he'd take for the final construction of the raft. He rehearsed not only the construction and launching of the raft, but also the grand plan to get aboard the *USS Nolin River* undetected, and then to stow away until the ship arrived back in San Diego on its thirty

day rotation. Just like the old days in the SEALS. Always a
pre-mission briefing. Go over every detail. Think it through –
objectives, locations, weapons, insertion, extraction, personnel, timing, evaluation and debriefing, and now, prayer, which
wasn't something he did much of forty years ago in the SEALS.
Tools and equipment would be the key to his current mission.
There should not, if all goes well, be any need for weapons. But
the equipment was crucial. The raft itself had to get him ten
miles out and to sit high enough in the water to keep the fire
platform well above the water. When the fire was lit, it had to
burn brightly and not be smothered by encroaching waves, no
matter how rough the seas might be on the night of his escape.
The fire was the key to the plan. It would draw the destroyer
to the raft. As it approached Coon Dog would be submerged
and breathing through a reed on the other side of the destroyer.
By the time the destroyer realized it had been duped, by the
time they realized there were no escapees on the raft, Coon Dog
would already have climbed the far side of the destroyer and
gotten himself hidden away in the paint locker on the starboard
side. It was a long shot, but it was possible, and Coon Dog kept
telling himself that with God all things are possible.

CHAPTER TWENTY-SIX

Chris Remington, third class quartermaster aboard the *Nolin River* was laughing with his shipmate Frank Demarco. They were playing cards in the crew's lounge.

"Tonk!" Demarco roared. That hand put him up thirty bucks.

"No way. You cheated." Remington laughed it off, "Anyway, I'm done. That'll make us even. Remember the poker game the other night? The thirty bucks?"

"Yeah, you're right." They both laughed again.

"How about the dreams? You still seeing the trucks?"

"Oh yeah. In fact, last night was one of the best I've had."

"Really. Tell me about it."

"Well, like all of them, it was pretty weird. First there were a couple of Latinos arguing. Then a couple of rednecks show up preaching or talking about God and the Bible. Then one of them, some old codger is leading a thousand trucks all over the country. Everywhere they go, people are waving and cheering them on. You sense that somehow the truckers are saving the people. It's nuts. So anyway, they finally get to California and they come into Hollywood. There isn't anyone there. A cold wind is blowing, neon lights are being shattered, and something big time is wrong. I couldn't understand what it was. Then the old trucker says, "Let's get out and find the children." They find little kids hiding. They are scared and crying. The truckers go through the city and get all the kids and take the kids with them." Remington stopped, and a wonderful warm smile came upon his face. His head was tilted up a little and his eyes were closed.

"Is that it? It was over?"

"No, it wasn't over." Remington's gaze might have been aimed at a zillion twinkling stars. He had opened his eyes, and they were still aimed somewhere above. He wasn't seeing the overhead in the crew's lounge. He was seeing something altogether different, something that had him mesmerized.

"So what else was there?"

"I'm sorry Demarco. I can't tell you."

CHAPTER TWENTY-SEVEN

Jabez, Dinky, Daffy, and Doolittle were happy to see Big Montana again. This would be the fourth visitation trip for each of them. The first two visits had been conducted with the plexi glass between them and Big Montana, and conversation was via the phone on each side of the thick plexiglass. The third visit was in the family visitation area. Big Montana had been a model prisoner, therefore the privilege of seeing visitors in the family room had been granted to him. It was a large room and most Sunday afternoons it was full of prisoners and their families.

He walked to the table where the four truckers were and sat down with them.

"Hi guys, thanks for coming."

Jabez had a big smile as did the other three, "It's good to see you. How are they treating you?"

"Not too bad. I've got just under four more years to do. I think I'll be able to make it."

"We all pray for you Big Montana. We pray every day. We're anxious to see you get out of here. And we'll keep it up." Dinky wasn't all that comfortable in these sorts of situations, so that's about all he would say on this visit.

But Daffy and Doolittle talked Montana's ears off. They told him all their latest adventures, filled him in on how all of the JETS were doing and seemed excited to tell him about their prayer vigil over Coon Dog, and that they all thought something big was about to happen down on the banishment island.

Big Montana responded to that with, "I owe him a lot, and all the rest of you. I'd hate to think what might have happened if you hadn't all showed up that day."

Jabez spoke up, "Anybody would of done it for you. We're glad we were there. And you've already proved it. You are worth it."

"Anything I can do to help with Coon Dog?" Montana was a different man than he'd been before going to prison. He'd not only been saved but his new life in Christ had taken on a certain maturity that even the JETS didn't see. They had no idea that Montana had started up the most successful prison ministry this particular institution had ever witnessed. In his four years at Deer Lodge, Big Montana had prevented four suicides, held weekly Bible studies for fifty inmates, led at least twelve more to accept Christ, and he had commanded two separate demons to get out of two possessed inmates, and they did. These were giant spiritual steps for anyone to take. For Montana to have accomplished all of that in just three years, well, it was nothing short of a miracle.

"All the prayer you can mount up would be real good," Jabez said.

"I'll see what I can do." Montana said.

They had no idea that within the next twelve hours that Ronnie Coon Dog Matlock would have a new four thousand four hundred and eighty-three prisoners and inmates throughout the state of Montana praying for him. Not just the Deer Lodge prison, but Christians in all the other prisons and all the jails throughout the state would be praying for something good to happen to Coon Dog.

CHAPTER TWENTY-EIGHT

Hector Estrada and Terry Wagner were in the same place in the jungle they'd been earlier that day. It was dark now, but silvery shafts of moonlight leaked through the overhead canopy. The exchange of the pemmican for the Bible had just taken place.

"You must get me more food. I can be your eyes on Toros. I'll tell you everything."

"I will do what I can. If I can come back with more, I will. I could find you again just like today."

"Yes. The two man sentries are posted everyday."

Whoosh-thud! The arrow went through Wagner's heart but stopped short of coming out the other side.

Whoosh-thud! The second arrow went just under Hector's left clavicle and the arrowhead came out a half inch on the other side. Hector turned to make a run for it, then turned back to tear the pemmican pouch from Wagner's dying grasp. He stuffed the Bible in it, then turned again to run. A figure jumped in front of him, club ready to be planted in Hector's head. Hector started to try a jabbing move with the spear but at the last second he remembered Coon Dog's instructions – in very close quarters, always go with the knife. He dropped the spear, grabbed the knife and hit home with it, just under the dark figure's sternum. He ripped upward and waited a second for the cannibal to fall. He picked the pouch back up with his good hand and half stumbled and half ran thirty yards through the jungle. He had to force himself not to scream out every time the shaft of the arrow caught on brush or a vine or a limb.

He stopped and with his right hand broke the arrow shaft at the front where it had entered. He heard the commotion on his trail. At least three of them were in pursuit. He had to think quickly. Coon Dog had told him that with practice, survival would come instinctively – if you practiced doing the right things over and over again, they would be automatic when you needed them. Hector wasn't there yet. He had to waste time to think it through. *One more burst, go as far as I can in a minute, then hunker down, get lower than the piss on the ground if I don't want to be found.*

He ran as hard as he could. He ran through the pain that was tearing his shoulder absolutely apart. And he ran for a minute and a half. That's all. That's all he could do. Get down. Get in the mud. Get *under* the mud if possible. He didn't hear them yet, but he would. *Try to get your breathing under control.* Coon Dog had even taught him how to do it. Three belly- deep breaths, all you can take in, then quick rapid breathing like birthing women do in Lamaze for fifteen seconds, pause seven seconds and repeat. Here they come. Thirty yards and closing.

"Where are you Estrada! You know what we are going to do with you don't you? You know. Come on. You wanted the Bible for the Christian didn't you? He's back isn't he? We might even let you live a couple of days before we eat you. Come on out." Toros was in rare form. "Wagner is being cleaned up already, and the one you killed. Come on out. I will let you have one of his legs. You can eat on it for at least a couple of days. Come on out."

Hector was glad Toros continued to run his mouth. It reduced the chance they might hear him breathing. The three were spread out maybe fifteen yards apart. Toros was in the middle and very near Hector. But Hector knew that if they didn't get him in the next few minutes they would give up.

They didn't much like the jungle at night. They much preferred blazing campfires. Plus, they already had two men to eat tonight.

Hector had gotten his breath back, and not any too soon. Toros was six yards away. He'd quit running his mouth. Did he smell Hector? Toros was motionless. The other two were still moving slowly. What was he doing? He was pissing. Hector smelled it. Toros moved on. A few minutes later Hector heard them turn back toward the east. Toros picked up the stupid threats, "We going to eat you Hector, come on out."

The threats died out, and Hector was finally able to examine the wound. It was a mess. He was soaked in blood from his left shoulder down to his leg, and it was still running out. Already he was light headed, dizzy and barely conscious. He removed the rag he wore for a shirt and tried to apply pressure to the front side. When he did it, the back side poured blood even quicker. He passed out. He lay there most of the night before he came to. All he could think about was when the sun came up they would be back for him. The bleeding had almost stopped. He tried to think. He had to move. He couldn't stay there. He struggled to his feet and the dizziness returned. He mustered up everything he had left and pushed slowly away. He at least felt like he was going in the correct direction. But that's all he felt he was doing correctly. He knew he was dying. He made it a half mile and fell in his tracks. It was a half hour before sunup.

Coon Dog had been restless most of the night. Even though he'd tried not to worry about Hector, the worry came anyway. Finally, about three hours before sunup, he arose, grabbed his weapons, and headed out in the direction of Jabez Junction.

At sunup Coon Dog picked up the trail Hector had left on his way toward the coast. A little later he found the first hiding spot Hector had used. He then followed another trail to the place Hector had met Wagner. He came up on what was left of two men – their heads and entrails. Even for Coon Dog, a man who'd seen similar things many times, the reflex to gag and dry heave overcame him. Then he spotted a blood trail leading out of the death area. Whoever this trail belonged to wouldn't last long. The blood trail led out a couple of hundred yards to a worn down place where the victim had dropped. There was a large pool of blood drying up.

The rest of the way he could plainly see that if it were Hector, he had given up all attempts at trail security. No effort had been made at all to cover the beaten down trail of a dead man stumbling along. Then he found him and immediately he recognized the shoulder wound and arrow head protruding from Hector's backside.

"Aw Hector, no, no." He sat down and put Hector's head on his lap. Hector's eyes opened slightly and a weak smile opened up. He was trying to say something. Coon Dog put his ear down to Hector's lips. "I got it for you," Hector whispered. Coon Dog looked around and spotted the skin pouch full of pemmican and noticed a bulge in it. He pulled the Bible out.

"Aw Hector, I'm sorry."

"No," Hector whispered, "You did good. Now give me your witness."

Coon Dog said, "I simply asked Jesus to take me."

Hector's weak smile grew, and he said, "Jesus please take me." And He did.

CHAPTER TWENTY-NINE

When Coon Dog got back to camp he retrieved the panther skin from its hiding place and spread it out. He placed Red Man's Bible on it and Hector's flintstone knife, then he stepped back a ways and sat down and looked at them for a long time.

He kept seeing the flames and watching Hector burn. He wouldn't leave the corpse for Toros to find. Even if he'd buried it, he knew what would have happened. He built the pile of brush, sticks, and downed limbs up to five feet tall. He placed Hector on top and lit the fire.

Now, back in camp, he kept seeing the flames. He sat there and let it all play out. It took a while, and then he was through with it.

He got to his feet, and finally, he decided. Tonight would be the night. He had to make his move. If he were ever going to get off the island it would be tonight.

He thought it through. He knew what time the *Nolin River* should be making its southward patrol – 04:00 on the button. He also knew there would be a half moon tonight. Perfect for the vision he would need to assemble the raft. The vine cord was ready, the oar was ready, the message for the skipper of the *Nolin River* was ready, the weight belt he would wear and the bamboo breathing tube were ready, the grapple and throw line were ready, the fuel for the fire was ready, the panther skin was ready, and he was ready. Well, he was as ready as he would ever be. He knew he would not be able to sleep today. He would be too keyed up. But he knew he could get plenty of rest.

Before lying down to rest he stuffed as much food into his stomach as he could, and he reminded himself to do the same one more time, late this afternoon, before he left camp. He drank water from a skin, and lay under some thick ferns to rest.

Distant thunder rumbled. The sky was darkening. A storm was trying to get organized to the southwest. Would a heavy rain accompany the storm? If so, Coon Dog knew his plans for escape tonight might be in jeopardy. It was nothing he had any control over. He turned his back to the approaching storm and surprisingly he fell asleep.

It was fitting, perhaps, that the last sleep he might possibly get on the island produced one last dream.

* * *

There was a truck driver sitting at a truck stop, backed in on the last row – what a lot of truck drivers call "party row". But he wasn't interested in drinking or inviting a working girl up into his truck. He was doing what all drivers do when they pull into a truck stop – catching up his log, planning the route and fuel stops for tomorrow's run, and thinking would he put something together to eat from his truck or would he go inside and wolf down some greasy, fat laden slop from the fast food counter? What he wouldn't give for a home cooked meal!

The driver noticed a truck backing in next to him. A memorial was neatly painted on the outside of the sleeper – "In loving memory of Alice Crenshaw, died Oct. 17, 2008. My life partner, my wife, my best friend, my co-driver."

The driver continued his routine – checking the qualcom messages, some map reading, and touching up his logs. Eventually he glanced over to his right at the truck that had just pulled in with the memorial painted on it. He saw a male driver behind the wheel, and the man was reading a book. The first driver could see the cover of the book and it looked like the same cover of a popular book he himself had recently read. He was curious to find out what the driver thought about the book, so he got out of his truck and walked over . The second driver rolled his window down and looked at the first driver. The first driver said, "I noticed the book you're reading. I finished it a couple of weeks ago. How do you like it so far?"

"I like it a lot. This guy is one of my favorite authors."

"Yeah, I've read a couple of his books. He's pretty good."

About then the first driver noticed there was a woman in the passenger seat. All three of them introduced themselves, and the second driver said the lady was his girlfriend. The three of them talked for a couple of minutes about nothing in particular. The first driver noticed that the two of them smiled a lot and seemed very happy. The first driver went on into the truck stop to take care of a few things, and for several days he would continue to think about the two he had just met.

In a while he returned to his truck and an hour before sundown he noticed that heavy traffic into the truck stop was peaking. The mad scramble to find a parking spot for drivers who had been working all day was underway. Many of the drivers who had their hole staked out, claimed, and occupied already, enjoyed watching the battle for what few parking holes might still remain. A lot of nights it would be about the only entertainment they could expect to enjoy. The competition for one last empty space was fierce, and usually the last few spaces were not choice spaces. They were always the tighest, the hardest to back a big truck into. It was fun watching an experienced driver make it look easy, and equally as fun to watch a couple of rookie co-drivers work for twenty minutes to attempt a difficult back-in, only to give up on it.

As the dream progressed, Coon Dog was aware of his suspicions that the driver in the dream was actually himself. He couldn't be sure it was himself, but that's what he suspected. You know how it is when you are aware that you are dreaming and that as things are moving along in the dream, how very much you want to influence the flow of events – you want to be the director? Well, that's the way Coon Dog was feeling . But, as is usually the case, he just had to be a passive viewer of this, what might be his last dream on the banishment island.

Whoever the driver in the dream was, he was no longer in the truck stop. He was rolling now. It had been raining hard for a couple of days. All the streams and rivers were flooding and the driver came up on a bridge with what appeared to be low water across it. There were three automobiles in front of him, all slowed down sufficiently to contemplate risking a crossing. They tried and all three were swept away. But the driver in the eighteen wheeler said, "I can do it," and he headed out across the bridge with the water across it. The truck became a raft and it was swept away by the fast running water. At this point in the dream, Coon Dog *knew* he was the driver, now the sailor, on the raft. Everything sped up; it all became a blur. He saw the raft approaching an armada of war ships. There were cannibals floating, heads floating, a black panther swimming, truckers up high in mountain passes, rice paddies, AK-47's ripping off short bursts, high school cheerleaders in yearbooks and scrapbooks, Paul of the Bible was preaching and crying, Coon Dog's father, Horace Matlock, appeared and then disappeared, and Coon Dog's heart went empty in the dream and in his real body.

Coon Dog was awake. The worst of the storm had stayed south of the island. It was a little wet. Only a light shower had touched the jungle. Coon Dog got to his feet. He wanted to get busy. He wanted to shake the emptiness the dream had left him with. He wanted to get off the banishment island tonight. He gathered up a few things and headed off toward the launching sight, eating more pemmican as he went out. There were maybe three hours of sunlight left.

As he approached the ocean, he did a little recon a half mile on both sides of his get-away inlet. There were no signs of any cannibal activity, but still he waited 'til dark to gather the timbers he'd hidden in the jungle, the vine cord, and everything else, and bring them down to the beach and start the construction.

Before he started, he built a small hidden fire twenty yards deep in the jungle. He didn't need the fire for constructing the raft, but he needed the coals the fire would produce. He'd take them with him when he launched the raft and would use them to ignite the diversionary fire.

The work went without difficulty. The half moon was rising, but Coon Dog could have done the work in total darkness. Each deck timber had been pre-notched to fit perfectly to the underlying cross timber pieces. The lashing down of all the timbers with the vine cord took the most time. The six foot high framework of the fire stand had also been prefabricated and only took a few minutes to mount and lash down tightly. Coon Dog then filled the four foot square fire box on top the frame, actually an open lattice work affair, with tender, quick, bright burning kindling. Heavier fire wood would not be needed.

He loaded the other things he needed, then he went to the fire in the jungle and loaded a couple scoops full of hot coals into a thick wood bucket with a rock inner lining which he had constructed. He even had a form fitting top for the bucket to ensure the coals wouldn't tumble out in choppy seas. He lashed the bucket to the framework of the fire stand. He dropped to his knees and said a quick prayer and didn't even look back over his shoulder as he dragged the raft to the water, pushed it in and climbed on board.

His plan was to paddle rapidly through the inlet to the open sea and then erect the mast with the small sail he'd made by weaving several layers of fern leaves. It took him longer to get out to the open sea than he had expected. He knew he'd have to get things moving quickly or he'd be late on his rendezvous with the *Nolin River.*

After he'd finally cleared the inlet and erected the sail, he still paddled hard. He only rested to utilize the paddle as a rudder every twenty minutes or so. After a while he slowed down because he felt like he'd made up the time he'd lost in the inlet.

He estimated the time to be about 03:00. He felt sure he was where he needed to be – ten miles out. While he waited for the *Nolin River* to show up, he did what all SEAL'S do in preparation for a mission – he checked, double checked, and triple checked his equipment. He slid into the water and with one hand on the raft forced his head a foot under water. The special fitting for the mouthpiece on the end of the six foot bamboo snorkel worked very well. It had taken him a month to carve it out and find a resin that allowed him to sun bake it tightly into the hollow bamboo breathing tube without any leaks.

He climbed back on board the raft, stripped and wrung out the new Navy issue dungarees he wore, the ones they had given him twelve days ago. When he'd gotten all the water that he could possibly get out of them, he put them back on. There was no sense shivering in the cool night air. He would need to conserve all the body heat he could. He checked the weight belt he would wear to keep him submerged – about twenty-five pounds of rocks sealed into a buckskin girdle. He double checked the airtight seal he had on a buckskin tote bag with a shoulder strap. In it were the hand- crafted panther skin, three or four day's worth of pemmican, a small sealed gourd with drinking water, Red Man's Bible, and Hector's flintstone knife. He wasn't sure that all the special work he'd done on the bag with bee's wax and a particularly tough species of plant leaf he'd discovered would keep the buckskin tote invulnerable and dry from the sea water. He'd just have to take his chances. He couldn't control everything.

He opened the lid to the hot coal bucket. There were still plenty of coals to start the fire. And, he wanted to make sure that the message he wanted to leave for Captain Weller was secure and in place. It was. A small buckskin pouch latched to a freestanding sapling contained the message. The words CAPTAIN WELLER were carved on the outside of the small pouch and the message inside was very legible. Coon Dog had dried eight inch leaves and used a wild berry extract to pen the message.

He'd done all he could do. It was now after 03:30. The running lights of the *Nolin River* should be coming out of the north any minute now. *Where is it? Come on! Come on! Just like the Rung Sat in Vietnam, he thought.* But instead of sitting in mud all night waiting to spring the ambush on the VC, he was on a raft waiting …. not to spring the ambush, but to escape the banishment island and try to make his way back to the hills and woods of Alabama.

He thought he saw a flicker of something from the north. It disappeared, then came back again, disappeared, then came back again. Finally he made out the running lights and then the sweep of the searchlights off each side. The ship was probably five miles away, but there was no doubt about it, it was headed his way.

Coon Dog jumped up, removed the lid from the fire bucket, and in his haste to light the tender and kindling, he tipped the fire bucket and the coals spilled out. Most hit the water spitting and steaming. One lodged between two deck timbers but was put out quickly enough by the water. Were the coals all gone? He still held the bucket and like the good Christian he was, Coon Dog said, "God, I know You are still with me." He brought the bucket up to the level of the tinder and kindling and turned the bucket over on the dry grass nook. One small red ember about the size of a raison came out and smoldered for a few seconds in the grass. Coon Dog could see a few tiny whiffs of smoke but they disappeared. He stepped up closer and blew at the spot. Nothing. "God, I know you are still with me." He blew again. A spark flew. He blew again. A tiny flicker started, then stopped. He blew again. The flicker returned and produced a tiny flame on two strands of dried grass. The flame caught on a tuft of grass and then began to spread. Coon Dog forgot about everything else for a moment. He went to his knees, "Heavenly Father thank You. I love You. I know You are still with me. Amen."

He donned the rock girdle, slung the watertight buckskin bag over his neck, the bag coming to rest under his left arm. He positioned the mast and sail the way he wanted them. He grabbed the bamboo snorkel and the grappling hook with the line, and finally he slid in the water and pushed the raft away from him. He could see that the wind was just about perfect. It was just a little onshore, and the raft was moving away from him very slowly – perfect.

CHAPTER THIRTY

The pilot house and bridge of the *USS Nolin River* were quiet. Quartermaster third class Chris Remington was at the helm. The Officer of the Deck, Lieutenant Terry Fitzgerald, was on the sound powered phones to the enlisted men down in the engine room, snipes, in Navy vernacular. They were talking about a new pressure valve's performance. Hourly checks were made for several days. It was nothing out of the ordinary.

Fitzgerald got up to stretch. It was 03:52. He went outside to the flying bridge for a little fresh air. Seaman "Spy" Everist was working the searchlight on the port side.

"Any swimmers tonight?" Lt. Fitzgerald asked.

"No sir. Not yet anyways."

"That was good work you did the night we picked up the cannibal."

"Thank you sir. I just try to keep my eyes open. Last night I spotted two whales three hundred yards off."

"Yeah, sonar was all over those two. Williams said he got a terrific acoustic on them. They were chatting away. Can you break whale code?"

"Yes sir I sure can. The male gives three long whiny hollers, two grunts, and a weird shrieking noise. I think it's his mating call."

"And what does the female answer with?"

"Well sir, she says, 'Henry, why do you always blow your snout three times, and wipe your butt twice, before you slip your condom on?'"

"Seaman, I think you better keep your day job while you work on the comedy."

"Yes sir."

Fitzgerald turned his gaze to the horizon beyond the moon-lit port bow.

"Seaman, dowse the searchlight. Do you see anything off the port bow, maybe four miles?"

Everist switched the searchlight off and strained his eyes to make anything out."No sir."

They both scanned the ocean for a few seconds.

"There it is again," Fitzgerald said.

This time Everist's eyes had adjusted and he saw something. "Yes sir, a little flicker out there. You're right. I'd say about four miles."

"Give me you headset."

"Yes sir."

"Bridge. O.O.D., bring her fifteen degrees port."

"Bridge aye. Fifteen port." Chris Remington said.

As the *Nolin River* was making a slight left steerage adjustment, the flicker in the ocean four miles away was coming closer to the bow straight away, but not quite head on. The flicker was also getting a little larger.

Lt. Fitzgerald issued another order. "Helmsman, send the messenger of the watch to Lt. Cissell's cabin. Wake him and tell him I'd like to see him on the bridge."

"Aye aye Lieutenant."

Four minutes later Ops Officer Lt. Jerry Cissell entered the pilot house rubbing the sleep out of his eyes.

Chris Remington said, "Sir, the O.O.D. is on the flying bridge."

As Cissell walked out, the O.O.D. was on his way in but saw Cissell and said, "Sorry to wake you Jerry. I wanted you to take a look at this before we may have to wake the Captain or the X.O."

"Sure. What do we have?"

Fitzgerald handed Cissell a pair of binoculars and walked him out on the flying bridge. He pointed just left of the bow.

What was a flicker five minutes ago was now a steady small fire in the ocean and only a mile away.

Cissell strained his eyes to make more of it. "Whew! It's got to be mounted on something. I can't make anything out."

"Right. Nor can I. Seaman Everist, I'm relieving you of your searchlight duties for a couple of minutes. Hustle down to the X.O.'s cabin and get him up here, then double time back here."

Everist was gone.

"I knew you were in the welcoming committee the night we fished Matlock out of the water," Fitzgerald said.

"Yeah. That guy is a piece of work. The captain and I talked about it afterward. There was a very strange thread running through that whole situation. This, whatever *this* is, smells like Matlock again."

"That's why I called you first. Maybe we won't have to wake the Captain."

"It's a raft I think. I can't make out a hull. There's a small sail. Don't see anybody on it," Cissell said.

"All back one half," Fitzgerald ordered the *Nolin River* to slow down.

The fire was clearly above the deck and beginning to illuminate the logs below it. A half mile now. No sign of human life.

The X.O. came up behind them. He could already see the fast approaching small fire very clearly. "Don't tell me. Matlock has come calling again."

"Not sure sir. We don't see anybody aboard. It looks like a raft," Fitzgerald said.

"Okay gentlemen, let's do the same thing. Get the flares up. Bring her alongside slowly. No launch yet. Let's see what we have."

"Aye aye sir."

Coon Dog had been staying underwater most of the time ever since the port side search light of the *Nolin River* began getting close to him. About once every minute and a half, he would kick hard and use his arms to get his head above water for a few seconds. He was doing that now and could see that the ship was close to the fire-lit raft. He realized that he'd be in big trouble if the ship decided not to pull up right along side the raft. He would be gobbled up by the destroyer's screws. But, as he had predicted, the brain trust on the *Nolin River* would not put a launch in the water unless absolutely necessary. They would simply ease the ship up close to see what might be aboard the fire-lit raft.

He went back under water for another minute or so, this time holding his breath. He didn't want to risk the starboard side lookout to see the bamboo snorkel sticking out of the water. When he came back up, he noticed that the searchlight beam was scanning a couple of hundred yards out behind him. He also noticed that the fire on the raft was about to be hidden from his view by the ship. *This is it! Jettison the snorkel. Tie it to the rock belt. They will go to the bottom. Swim underwater to the ship. Get on board! Now!*

He took in all the air his lungs could hold, went under, and started the forty yard swim toward the destroyer. Halfway there he came up for air again. Other than the search light, there didn't seem to be any other activity on this side of the ship. Understandably so. All the action was on the other side.

When he resurfaced again, he was alongside the *Nolin River*, perfectly amidships, right where he hoped he would be. The ship was dead in the water only rolling gently in the light seas. *Now!* He tossed the wood grappling hook above and felt it catch. It didn't make any noise. He'd covered it with a layer of buckskin. He didn't waste any time pulling himself up, up, and finally, he was aboard the destroyer – the destroyer whose specific job it was to keep him confined to the island.

He tossed the hook and line back into the sea and swiftly darted down the darkened deck toward the fantail, his water-tight buckskin pouch still hanging over his shoulder. There it was, the paint locker. He opened the watertight hatch and went inside. He closed the hatch. The room was dimly lit with two red night lights. There were two rows of unopened five- gallon paint pails in a steel shelving framework. The rows went five feet high. There were other paint pails and various paint equipment and deck equipment in lockers or secured against the bulkheads. The only thing loose on the deck were three folding chairs.

Coon Dog surveyed the small room quickly and placed the buckskin pouch behind the second row of five gallon paint pails. He stripped his dungarees, wrung them out, and mopped up the pools with rags he found hanging on a hook. He draped the wet dungaree pants and shirt over the two red lights. Otherwise they might never dry. There wouldn't be any sailors in here 'til 07:30. He knew enough about shipboard routine to figure pretty close on that. And it was possible nobody would come in for several days, but he couldn't count on it. The way he saw it now, the paint locker was a temporary home. He'd have to find another hiding place. Coon Dog sensed that to be successful, to remain undetected, would depend on the young sailor with the tattoo.

"Boats, you think we can yank it up here without tearing it up, and without putting a launch or divers in the water?" The X.O. was asking the question to chief boatswain's mate Ed Trindle. The entire foredeck was lit up brightly with flood lights, and all the lights bearing down on the raft allowed them to determine without a doubt there was no one on board and nothing posing any kind of a threat. They had doused the fire from the fire stand with a fire hose from above. It was not even smoldering.

"Yes sir, no problem. I'll rig an arm over the side. We can get four hooks into the corners and winch her on up without busting a splinter loose. Won't take twenty minutes." Chief Trindle got his crew moving quickly.

"Sir, do you see that, uh, what is it? A leather pouch?" The O.O.D. was looking over the rail at the raft fifteen feet below.

Lieutenant Commander Robert Trent had spotted the pouch already, "No, I don't think it's leather. It looks like buckskin, and it looks like something is stamped or carved on it."

Chief Trindle's estimate of twenty minutes was right on the money. "Bring it in easy now, that's it. Easy does it. That's it. Let her down."

The X.O. was the first to poke around the raft. Everyone else stayed back. He went to the buckskin pouch and removed it from the upright pole it had been lashed to, protecting it from the sea. The words CAPTAIN WELLER had been tooled in perfect script on the small pouch.

Lt. Commander Trent stood there shaking his head. "O.O.D. I think it's time to wake the captain up. Tell him I'll be in the ward room"

"Yes sir," and Lt. Fitzgerald headed off toward the Captain's cabin.

CHAPTER THIRTY-ONE

Third class petty officer Chris Remington was feeling a little strange. Already the buzz in the pilot house was that the prisoner they had dealt with ten days ago was somehow behind this empty raft with the fire. It was common knowledge by now that the buckskin pouch presumably had something inside it for Captain Weller. Already there were bets going down as to what it might be. Several deck apes put fifty dollars on it being a snake. One of them said he'd seen something moving inside it. Others bet it was some island grown marijuana that Matlock was gifting the Captain.

Remington made no bets, but somehow he had a feeling that he would soon be personally involved in the activity that was taking place on the *Nolin River*. Personally involved! He kept thinking back to ten nights ago when the prisoner said to him, "I've seen that. I know what it means. I know what your dreams mean."

The O.O.D. showed up in the pilot house a moment later and noticed Remington in a zombie like state. His eyes were open, but he seemed to be off somewhere daydreaming.

"Snap to quartermaster! Are you awake?" There was no mistaking the tone of the O.O.D.'s voice. You could be court marshalled for sleeping at the wheel.

"No sir. I'm not sleeping . Sorry sir, no excuse, just drifted away for a second."

"I'm glad to hear it. We will sweep this area with an expanding square search track. Bring her 90 degrees to port. All ahead three quarters. We want to see if there are any more surprises out here tonight."

Remington would be glad to come off duty at 07:30. He was sure in an emotional fix. He knew something was going to happen soon – something very personal was going to happen to him. He just knew it.

The X.O. and the captain were at the table in the ward room. They both sat there, looking at the pouch lying on the table.

"The raft looked like a squad of SEALS had worked on it for a month. It was perfect. He probably could have sailed it to California," the X.O. said.

They both continued to stare at the pouch. "Well, let's see what Matlock has for me." The captain ripped through the watertight seal with a pocket knife and flipped the flap back. Nothing seemed to be crawling out. He picked the pouch up and shook it. Two dried leaves floated out, and nothing more. They had some words on them. The captain brought the pouch closer and inspected inside. Nothing else. Only the leaves. He picked them up and began to read. When he finished, he had a bemused look on his face and maybe even a tiny twinkle in his eye. He handed the leaves to the X.O. for him to read:

Dear Captain Weller, I just wanted to thank you for the hospitality you extended me recently. It is only appropriate I should make the attempt to do the same for you. Should I notice your signalman flashing me your acceptance tonight around midnight, then I will know to expect you the following evening, let's say eightish? The strawberry wine really is very good, and I think you might enjoy my specialty dish – sashimi served around barbecued sea turtle. Hoping you will accept, and .... regretfully, I must run now – literally. I smell cannibals about a mile away.

Yours Truly, Ronnie Matlock.

The X.O. couldn't contain a little chuckle. Nor could the Captain, and he added, "You have to admit, he does have a certain flare. Sashimi served around barbecued sea turtle. That sounds awfully good."

They didn't say anything else for a moment. They both knew they would have to put aside the absurd lunacy of what Matlock had pulled off this time, and ask some hard questions about what he really might be up to.

"A diversion? Get us tangled up with this floating fire raft at this location, while he is sailing away on a bigger and swifter craft fifteen miles back?" The X.O. wasn't chuckling now.

Captain Weller said, "Could be, but wouldn't he need an accomplice to launch the raft here, if he indeed intended to sail away fifteen miles back?"

"Yes sir. That would make sense. Plus, we know, or at least we think that he's a solo operator."

"Right, it's got to be something else. What if he's sincere with the invite to dinner? If we were stupid enough to take him up on it, maybe he'd try to nab me for ransom or more likely a demand. Money wouldn't do him any good."

"Yes sir. Could be. But surely he wouldn't think that you would actually accept the invite," the X.O. said.

"Who knows? I imagine that a man stuck on that island for two years could conjure up just about anything in his mind."

"Yes sir. I agree."

They continued talking; trying to figure an angle that Matlock might be playing. They couldn't come up with anything. They got up to leave the wardroom and the X.O. asked Captain Weller, "What should we tell the crew about the pouch? There's scuttlebutt being thrown around. Half of them have placed bets on what it was."

"Tell them the truth that a prisoner on the island sent me a dinner invitation, and I turned him down."

As they were leaving, the captain scratched his head. There was one other angle that Matlock might be employing that they hadn't talked about. The captain knew that it was an extreme long shot, and he kept it to himself, but couldn't contain a good chuckle.

"What?" the X.O. asked.

"Oh, nothing."

CHAPTER THIRTY-TWO

Coon Dog didn't really feel like he was back in the Navy, but he did feel like he was back aboard a Navy ship. He had sometimes wondered how long it might take to get his sea legs back. He wouldn't find out tonight. The sea was very tranquil and the *Nolin River* swayed gently to the ocean's gentle waltz.

Coon Dog had settled down on the deck back behind the second row of five gallon point pails. He wasn't even trying to sleep, just get a little rest and stay mentally alert; try to figure out what his next step ought to be. Every twenty minutes or so he went to the two red night lights and turned the dungarees on them. By daybreak they would be dry. The problem of his wet clothing would be solved, but daybreak would bring another problem along with it. What if he were wrong about his figuring it wasn't likely anyone would come in the paint locker until later in the day, if at all?

He thought about moving now while it was still dark. As long as he stayed out of well lit spaces, he probably would not be detected. With his dungarees, he'd look like any other enlisted man moving about. But where to move? He had a couple of ideas, but he wasn't sure about them. He decided to stay put, at least for the time being.

He got up again and took a closer look at the room. *Did I see drop cloths folded and stored in one of those lockers on the deck?* He walked over to the bulkhead to the left of the entrance hatch. The eight- foot locker was open and must have had fifteen or twenty paint drop cloths folded and stored away, a testament to the old Navy adage, "If it moves, salute it. If it doesn't move, paint it." Coon Dog grabbed a drop cloth and took it back behind the second row of paint pails. In the daytime he could scrunch up in the corner with the drop cloth over him. The likelihood of anyone's even going back there behind that second row was not very good, and if they did, what would they see? A drop cloth crumpled up in a corner that some deck hand was too lazy to store properly. And as for the night time? He'd bet a lot of money, if he had any, that there would not be any sailors in the paint locker at night.

Just a little longer now, the dungarees would be dry. It would feel good to get them back on again. And his new boon-dockers (Navy work shoes) the good captain had been so kind to provide him? Well, they would not dry out completely for a day or two. But what did he need them for? He wasn't going anywhere.

CHAPTER THIRTY-THREE

Chris Remington hit the breakfast chow line at 07:38. He was secured from his watch at 07:30 by another third class quartermaster named Rafael Mazada, an ex East L.A. gang banger gone straight – real straight – he joined the Navy.

As Remington was walking off the bridge, Mazada said, "Man, you don't look so good."

"I'm fine. It was just a long night," Remington lied.

Well, it *was* a long night, but Chris wasn't fine. The feeling he had that something was about to happen to him had intensified. He loaded his tray with scrambled eggs, bacon, hash browns, toast, and coffee. He saw his buddy, Radioman Frank DeMarco, and sat across the metal table from him.

"I had my money on the weed. How about you?" Demarco was picking at corned beef hash and adding a lot of catsup to it.

"I didn't bet."

"Hey, are you okay? You look like you just pulled five mid watches, not one."

"Yeah, everybody's been saying I look fragged out."

"I guess you heard the X.O. pass the word, it was a dinner invitation. I don't believe it. That makes no sense at all. What? You kidding me? A banishment island cannibal invites a U.S. Navy Captain to dinner in the jungle? What are you talking about? I don't buy a word of it."

"Yeah, it sounds pretty fishy." Chris was poking around at his breakfast. He thought he was hungry, but now he didn't seem to be.

"The X.O. had me shoot off a couple of priority messages to any nearby ships, and the captain just a while ago had a couple of pri-ones go to group in Diego."

"That's no surprise. I suppose they had to let everyone know what happened."

"Yeah, I guess so. I'm gonna' hit the rack, catch some z's."

"See ya'," Chris said, and wondered what he would do the next couple of hours. He was in no mood to sleep. There was only one thing that could soothe him down a little, get his mind off the impending doom he anticipated. Was it doom? No, he knew it was something more complicated than that. He sensed it was something that was going to test him in a way he'd never been tested before. It was going to be a unique challenge that would test his spirit, his judgment, and his faith in all things good. As soon as he accepted the nature of what was coming at him, he felt much better, but he still wanted to get with the one thing he knew could help him. He left the remains of his breakfast on the tray, returned it to the receptacle and headed off to the workout room where he would get on the treadmill and do five hard miles.

He did the first mile at a seven and a half minute per mile pace, and bumped the second mile up to seven, and then bumped number three up to six and half, the next one at six, and finally he ran the fifth mile at a five and a half minute pace.

He flashed back to his glory days in high school. He thought about all the rugged training miles he put in back in those days. Recently he'd had a conversation with a low key recreational runner who said about the only training he himself had ever employed was LSD - long slow distance. Chris laughed and said they never heard of that kind of training at his high school. "The training we did was very competitive. Every workout you pushed hard to bring your times down. Training for cross country racing was nothing less than an exercise to determine the amount of pain you could endure." And Chris could endure enormous amounts of pain. Many times his teammates would have to hold him up and walk him off the course at the end of a race. He'd have nothing left to stand on his own. He was a gifted runner, his gait smoother than silk, no wasted motion, long strides, not heel to toe, or up on his toes, somewhere in the middle. He had plenty of talent, but he had the heart to go along with it. And not just his actual resting heart rate of 38, but that other part of the heart – the part that kept him fighting, kicking it, busting it, when the others were ready to cash it in.

After the five miles, he decided that wasn't enough. He busted three more at a five minute pace, and then the ninth mile he backed off and slowed down to a recovery pace of seven and a half minutes per mile.

He took his shower and slowly dressed into clean dungarees. He hustled back to the crew's mess where the breakfast grill and hot food had been secured, but he knew he could still get cereal, pastries, and fruit.

He was feeling much better. Running is a great way to clean up the troubling mental junk pile. He still knew something unusual was about to take aim at him, but he was relaxed now, prepared, even favorably anticipating whatever was about to happen.

He went topside and was greeted by a warm but not stifling sun. Some heavy gray clouds were forming up far off to the northwest. Broken light-gray cotton balls were overhead. The ship had resumed its normal patrol pattern, and a lot of the hubbub produced by the dinner invitation had died down. He headed back toward the fantail and saw a couple of deck apes come out of the paint locker with wire brushes and paint chippers. They closed the hatch behind them. Chris could see there weren't any sailors off duty back around the fantail, but still he decided to grab a chair and sit on the deck to catch a few rays. He opened the hatch and walked in. The three chairs were unfolded and just in front of the first row of five gallon paint pails.

Coon Dog had just been watching the deck apes through a tiny crack he had created in the two rows of paint pails. *Whew! That was close. I guess they'll be back later.* He was about to return to the corner, cover up with the drop cloth, and maybe catch a cat nap, but he noticed the hatch open up again. This time he saw only one sailor, and his attention perked up immediately. It was the same young man with the tattoo – the tattoo of the mountains, the panther, and the cross.

Remington grabbed a chair and was turning back toward the open hatch. He heard a voice and he stepped to the hatch to see who was outside. No one was there. He turned to look back inside.

"I know what your tattoo means." It was coming from behind the two rows of paint pails bunched tightly together in the steel shelving framework.

"Is that you Demarco?" He knew it wasn't when he asked the question.

"No."

"Who is it?"

"It's me." Coon Dog came around the end of the row of paint pails where Chris Remington could see him clearly.

"Before you go tell the captain, all I ask is you look at something I brought for you. I am not a killer or a rapist. The night you all pulled me in, remember what I said? 'I've seen that. I know what it means. I know what your dreams mean.' Remember?"

Remington couldn't think of anything to say, but now he knew what all the strange premonitions had been about. He just looked at Coon Dog, as if he weren't sure he was real.

"I can prove it. Let me show you what I brought for you. Don't go. Don't go. Just a second, I'll get it." Coon Dog stepped back behind the paint rows. He went to the pouch and removed the panther skin. He came back around the corner. Remington was still there.

"Here. Take a look. I made it for you." He handed the panther skin to Remington.

Chris took the Panther skin and slowly examined it, a black fur jacket put together in a way he'd never seen. It had full arms that were stitched at the shoulders with tanned leather straps, or was the stitching from another animal skin? Likewise, where buttons on the front would normally be, this jacket had thin tie offs on both sides to close the jacket at the front. The effect the tanned tie-offs and stitching had was stunning. The contrast they made with the luxurious black fur was an example of mature, rawboned crafting genius, using the highest quality fur.

But it was the tooled design that had Chris reeling in disbelief. The simple mountain scene, with a panther and a cross seemed to be more than it was. Maybe a story was being told by the craftsman who carved the images. There were three identical scenes in the work. Two small ones, one on each breast plate in the front, and the entire back of the jacket had the same scene.

"Put it on. See if it fits."

Whoa, whoa! What am I doing here? An escaped prisoner here in the paint locker. This is... "You saw my tattoo. Somehow you made this after you saw my tattoo. You think I'm young and dumb. You think I'll fall for this con."

"The truth is, I didn't know who I was making it for. I had already started on it before the night you all dragged me outa' the water. The design, it just came to me. I swear. And what I said to you that night, well the truth is, I really don't know what it means. You can see, it's identical to your tattoo, but I didn't know that when I was making it. And .... the dreams .... well I ain't going to tell you I really know exactly what they mean, but I do think I might have a few clues. I think I have the same or very similar dreams that you have. You see truck drivers in your dreams, don't you? And a few nights ago you saw an old trucker with a thousand more. They were in Hollywood saving children from evil."

Coon Dog stopped. They were both just standing there. Chris recalled the dream and the feeling he'd had at the end of the dream – the feeling that he couldn't tell Demarco about it because it was too good to share and because he didn't think it would have been wise. It was the same feeling he was having now.

Chris had an incredulous look on his face.

Coon Dog said, "Yeah, I know, that was great wasn't it? So okay, it's all in your hands. You do what you gotta' do. All I ask is you think it over. Give it a day. I'll be right here tomorrow morning. You can turn me in or not."

"I've already made my decision."

"What is it?"

"I'm going to help you."

CHAPTER THIRTY-FOUR

It was two days after Chris Remington had discovered Coon Dog in the paint locker. Chris had moved him to a safer hiding place the next night. It was a sea bag storage room down below decks, very near the crew's berthing quarters. Nobody ever went in there unless the ship was nearing or in port. Chris had pilfered some canned food and a few other items from the galley store room and also made sure Coon Dog had water and plastic bags for going to the bathroom. Coon Dog had thought he'd never see another roll of toilet paper in his life. He was very thankful for all Chris was doing and the huge risk he was taking. The two had not talked since that first morning in the paint locker. Chris thought it best to let things settle down completely before risking a meeting.

Chris walked down the narrow passageway which would have opened up to the berthing quarters. He made sure no one was coming in either direction and quickly slipped in the hatch behind which the crew's sea bags were stored.

He whispered, "Matlock, it's me." He heard something shuffling around in the back of the room.

"Come on back," Coon Dog whispered back.

Chris stumbled his way back. There was only one dim red night light in the room. "How you doing?" Chris was still using a barely audible whisper.

"Doing great. I'm off the island and alive," Coon Dog matched the turned down volume.

"It's pretty hot in here. You'll be fried in a couple more days, and I can smell you already. We'll have to sneak you into the showers in the middle of the night. I think I know how we can get away with it."

"Whatever you say. You are my lifeline. I trust you."

"Yeah, you know, that's why I didn't rat you out. I could tell you trusted me. And you didn't lie about anything. Man, this whole thing has really blown me away. But you know what? I knew it was coming. And when you knew what that dream was ..... that did it. I knew you were for real. Can I ask you something?"

"Sure."

"How were you framed for a double rape-murder? I mean, you know, that's what some of the guys said you were banished for, a double rape-murder."

"It's a long story, but what two bad guys did was they gassed me, took sperm out of me and planted it in the two girls."

"They must have wanted you awful bad."

"Ain't no doubt about that. These are two of the worst you'd ever find."

"Are you going to go after them when you get back?"

"No way. I just want to get back in the woods down in Alabama and live a quiet life. Maybe do a little truckin' if I can get a new identity and all of that."

"Trucking? So you are a truck driver?" Chris had never considered that particular angle.

"I been drivin' for four years before I was sent to the island."

"So, do you know some of the truck drivers in your dreams?"

"Yessir. One of them is my cousin. He's a JET. And some of the others are JETS too."

"What's a JET?"

"It stands for Jesus Express Truckers. There's a group of us. Was 'bout forty or fifty when I was shipped away."

"Man! This whole thing just gets deeper and deeper. So, maybe, since we are having some of the same dreams ....uh, maybe the truck drivers in my dreams are the JETS?"

"I would suspect that some are, for sure. Probably not all of them. In my dreams I'm not always sure who some of the drivers are."

Chris asked him, "Was there a truck driver in your dreams named Old Soft Shoe?"

"You bet. He ain't been around in my dreams too long. Only showed up recently. I never knew him in the JETS."

"He seems like he might be the Moses of the truck driving world."

"No, that would be a feller named Jabez, but I reckon Jabez could have a brother." Coon Dog had to chuckle at the implications of that.

They whispered for ten minutes, mostly comparing recent dreams. Many were either exactly the same, or very similar.

Chris said, "I'd better be going. We got four more days on station and two days steaming back to San Diego. You should be off this tin can in less than a week."

"Chris, I appreciate everything you're doing. I owe you."

"No sir Mr. Matlock, you don't owe me anything. I'm doing this because it *feels* like the right thing to do. Anyway, if you did owe me anything, I would say that panther skin jacket more than paid it off. It's unbelievable."

"Where did you hide it?"

"Right over there in my sea bag. I'm going to wear it everywhere when we get in. If anybody asks about it, I'll just tell them I had it made by a specialty leather shop. But after I wear it for awhile, I'm going to put it away and preserve it. It's way too nice to wear it out."

"Sounds like a plan."

CHAPTER THIRTY-FIVE

It was the day before the *Nolin River* was to slip into its berth at the Navy piers in San Diego. Coon Dog had just woke up. He'd had another dream. In it, Red Man had shown up . He was talking to Coon Dog, "I must tell you, Island Dog, how it ended. The day before I walked into the camp of the one they call Toros, I had been reading my Bible. You remember when I told you that God gave instructions to Moses to stay away from mediums and familiar spirits? I got to thinking about it, strong thinking, and studying other scripture which backed it up. I was responding to your doubts that I could thrive in both worlds. Well, Island Dog, you were right. One cannot live in both worlds and please the Great Father. No! The day I went into the cannibal camp, I was preaching strongly from both the Gospel of John and from Revelation. The Holy Spirit had taken over. All that morning I prayed and meditated on repentance, my own repentance from trying to live in both worlds. I cried out my desire to live only for the One True Father and to depart once and for all time, forever, from the other world of sorcery, lies, and entrapment by the evil one. Yes, the Holy Spirit led me right into the camp of Toros, the evil camp, and as I died I was proclaiming The Father, The Son, and The Holy Spirit. I am telling you this because I know it has worried you. Fear not my brother. I am in that place where the scripture tells us He has gone to prepare a place for us, that where He is, we may be also. And, Island Dog, the mystery of the mountains, the panther, and the cross will soon be no mystery."

The dream had left Coon Dog with a tingling sense of relief and well being. He looked around the cramped nest he'd been living in for nearly a week. He was sure going to be happy to get out of there! Chris had said he'd show up tonight to get him one more shower at 02:00 in the morning, "Can't go ashore as a new man smelling like a pole cat." Coon Dog was thinking about it when all of a sudden the hatch opened up and Chris jumped in quickly.

"Matlock, it's me," he whispered.

"Come on back."

"Did you just have a dream?"

"Yes, I sure did."

"Was it the Indian telling you about preaching to the cannibals before they killed him?"

"Yes, it sure was."

"Unbelievable. I've got to tell you. I do believe in God, but I've never read the Bible very much. You know, the Indian said the mystery of the mountains, the panther, and the cross would soon be no mystery. Do you think that was meant for me, too? And do you think the Bible will play a part in solving the mystery?"

"I don't know the answer to those questions. We'll just have to see how she goes. You know, do what we've been doing all along – follow the signs, keep an open mind, and never doubt the power and strength of God."

"Yeah, I guess." Chris didn't seem as convinced as Coon Dog.

He changed the subject, "Are you ready for the big day tomorrow? I think I've got a pretty good plan."

"Ready, willing, and able. What's the plan?"

"We'll be tied up on the pier by twelve hundred. Liberty call will go about fourteen hundred. I've got myself in charge of a work party that will be cleaning up some equipment and file cabinets and lockers in the ops compartment. Most of that stuff will be removed from the ship by two- wheeled hand carts. It's going over in a warehouse not far from the pier we'll be tied up to. After your shower tonight, I'm going to get you stuffed in one of the old beat up metal lockers we are taking off the ship. You'll have to gut it out in there for about twelve hours or so. Then when I get you down the gangplank and roll you over to the warehouse, you'll have to wait a couple of hours until the work party is secured. I'll get liberty around eighteen hundred, go get my car, stuff you in the trunk, and we will diddy bop right out the front gate."

"Sounds like a plan. Hold on, I've got something for you." Coon Dog put his hand in the skin pouch and removed Red Man's Bible. "Here."

Chris took it, but it was too dark to see what kind of a book it was.

"It was Red Man's Bible, the Indian in your dream."

"Wow!" is all Chris could whisper.

The next day the *Nolin River* was tied up at the San Diego pier by twelve noon. Coon Dog's cramped muscles were scream-ing for relief, and he was sweating like a stuck pig. He still had six hours to go before he'd be a free man, assuming that every-thing in Chris' plan worked to perfection. The metal locker he was in was plenty wide enough but was only five feet high. Chris had stuffed cardboard all around Coon Dog to prevent him from smashing around inside when the metal locker was moved. Chris had wanted to leave the equipment and metal lockers in the operations compartment until it was time to cart it ashore. Jerry Cissell, the ops officer, changed those plans,

"Remington I want to go ahead and get this stuff out of here. No need to wait until we're tied up. Move it down to the main deck and have it ready to go."

Chris didn't have any choice. He got his work party of five seamen to load the stuff on the two wheelers and strap them down good and tight. There was one five foot high metal locker he handled himself. When everything arrived down on the main deck it was only 10:45, and the sun and heat on this San Diego morning was vicious.

By the time liberty call was made at 14:00 Chris was plenty worried. He was standing in the shade with the work party just a few feet from all the stuff to be rolled off the ship. As soon as the first forty or so sailors headed out for liberty, his crew would be cleared to roll the equipment down the gangplank. Chris kept glancing down nervously at the five foot metal cabinet he was the most concerned about. *OH NO!* He saw a rivulet of liquid slowly escaping from the locker. At the pace it was running, it would produce a small pool in the next ten minutes. *OH NO! What have I done?* He got between the other members of the work party and the leaking locker, hoping no one would see the escaping fluid. *What was it? Sweat. Gotta' be sweat. He's dying in there.*

Just when he thought things couldn't get much worse, he noticed Captain Weller striding down the main deck, coming right at him.

"Attention on deck!" Chris barked. Everyone within ear shot snapped to attention.

"As you were," Captain Weller said. Then he walked up close to Chris and was looking around at the strapped down equipment. He eyeballed each piece, before coming to rest on the five footer next to Chris. You could see that he was looking directly at the lengthening rivulet of liquid. Then he shifted his gaze up at Chris. "Quartermaster Remington, I'd like to speak to you for a moment." The captain looked toward the group of young sailors in the work party, " Seamen, if you don't mind." The work party drifted down the deck forty feet or so.

When they were alone the captain looked back down at the leaking metal cabinet, "Looks like something was left inside this one doesn't it Remington?"

Chris didn't say anything.

"You know, I was casually taking a look at the duty rosters for today. I don't always do it. But I did today. No real reason. Nothing special about today, but I took a look. I was surprised to see that signalman, what's his name, the third class signalman, Carson? Yes, Carson. I was surprised to see his name crossed off and your name scratched in. I asked him about it. You know, I just like to know what's going on with the crew. You know what he said?"

"No sir." The sweat was starting to roll down Chris' neck.

"He said that you didn't want early liberty today, and that you offered to take over his work party out of the goodness of your heart. Remington, I must admit, that was a very noble gesture. Now tell me honestly, did you have another motive."

"Honestly sir?" Chris noticed that Captain Weller was stirring the growing pool of sweat with the tip of his spit shined brown oxfords.

"Absolute honesty, quartermaster. That's all we're talking here."

"Well sir, yes I did have another motive."

"You want to tell me what it was?"

"No sir, I sure don't."

"And why not, quartermaster?"

"It's personal sir, very personal."

"I see." The Captain took his toe out of the sweat pool and continued, his gaze now directly into Chris' eyes. "Son, you know sometimes when a man puts his neck out for another man there might be a speck of lingering doubt. I mean, he might say, 'Have I made a mistake? Is this other man worth the risk?' You know what I mean?"

"I think so sir. Yes, I do understand. I know what you mean."

"And of course it would be a real shame if, let's say in a particular situation that the guy sticking his neck out, and in this situation, I mean really sticking it way, way, out there. You know what I mean?"

"Yes sir, I *do* know what you mean."

"It would be a real shame if the guy never could gain a complete, total, one hundred percent certainty that the other man was worth the risk. Don't you agree, quartermaster?"

"Oh yes sir. I totally agree."

"Well good. I'm just rambling, that's all." He turned to walk away, but then as if in an afterthought he turned back to Chris, "Oh by the way Remington, I thought this might interest you. It has nothing to do with what we've just been talking about, nothing at all. And needless to say, this is confidential, just between you and me. Got it?"

"Yes sir."

"Do you remember the night we picked up the escapee, Matlock?"

"Yes sir, I sure do."

"Well, I called a little meeting with the group of officers whom I took with me to interview the prisoner. You know, just going over it a little bit – what we wanted to achieve in the interview. Prior to that we discussed Matlock's service record, some personal things that drove him out of the Navy, what kind of a man he was as a civilian and so on. You with me?"

"Yes sir."

"You see, I wasn't sure that the group of interviewers really understood that other than the conviction a jury gave him for a double rape/murder, that Matlock had an excellent record. He was a combat tested SEAL in Vietnam. Two tours, a chest full of ribbons, an escaped POW, and more. Now, here's the thing I think you might find interesting. I usually take a pretty close look at the criminal records of the men condemned to the island. I don't think there is a doubt in my mind that they should be there. But since Matlock was ex Navy, I dug deeper. I've got some old Academy classmates who made it up pretty high in the Justice Department and the FBI. I talked with them about Matlock on several occasions. My three friends all concur. Matlock's conviction of a double rape/murder was a put -up job from day one. A judge was bought off, and of course with the country in a boiling frenzy of support for banishment, nothing could be done to save Matlock. Once the DNA sperm evidence was introduced, it was all over. My friends said if they had been free to pursue how that was accomplished, Matlock would have walked. But they were told to stay out of it."

The Captain turned and looked down at the locker again, then said to Chris, "Steady as she goes Quartermaster. I'll be right back." He strolled to the deck area near the top of the gang plank and said something to the O.O.D.

When he returned to Chris, he said, "Okay Quartermaster, I think it's time to get this stuff off my deck. Get it where it belongs. Any questions?"

"No sir. And thank you sir."

"What for?"

"For being the best C.O. any sailor could have."

"Why thank you Chris. That means a lot to me. Carry on."

"Aye Aye sir!"

CHAPTER THIRTY-SIX

Chris reassembled the work party and within fifteen minutes all of the equipment and steel lockers had been wheeled off the *Nolin River* and across the dock into a small warehouse where the Navy bean counters would decide the equipment's fate.

Chris said, "Thanks guys, that's it. Go get cleaned up for liberty. I'll be along behind you. Got to leave some paperwork here for the bean counters."

The work party didn't have to be told twice. They left the warehouse and were heading back to the ship. There was nobody else in the warehouse. Chris went to the steel locker Coon Dog was in and was talking as he worked to loosen the straps and open the locker up, "Matlock, hang on. I'm getting you out. Hang on." Finally the doors sprang open and Coon Dog fell out and would have flopped on the floor unconscious, but Chris caught him in his arms and laid him down gently. The odor nearly gagged Chris, but his first aid training kicked in. He checked Coon Dog's pulse and breathing. They were rapid. Coon Dog's skin was hot and dry. Chris elevated Coon Dog's legs slightly and double checked his airway, then he sprinted to a deep sink he spotted and filled a five gallon bucket with cold water. When he got back he slowly poured half the cold water over Coon Dog and held his head in his lap and began cupping handfuls of water to his mouth.

"Come on Matlock, come on." *Dear God, what have I done?* "Matlock wake up! Come on!" *OH no. I can't believe this is happening.* "Come on Matlock, come on, wake up." He checked his breathing again. It seemed the same – still rapid. *Think!*

Chris took his cell phone out of his pocket, flipped it open and hit the third pre-set in the address book.

"Hello."

"Cindy, it's me, Chris. Are you at work?"

"Yes. What's wrong?"

"I've got a medical emergency. Not me, the guy I'm with. He's .... he's a street person. Heat stroke, dehydration, unconscious. Can't take him to the hospital. It's a long story. Can you help me?"

"I, ... uh, sure. I get off work in half an hour. I'll try to leave now. Where are you?"

"I'm on the base, but I won't be able to get him out of here. I think I'm losing him. Look, if you can come to the West Docks, gate two, bring a filled gas can with you. Tell the gate guard your boy friend's car is out of gas. I'll meet you at the gate. Got it?"

"Yes, I'm on my way. I'll bring ice and an IV drip. Got to go. It'll take me a while to get the stuff."

Cindy had known Chris for six months. She met him at the first 5-k she'd run. She thought he was pretty neat. After winning the race with a time under fifteen minutes, she noticed he'd gone back on the course to encourage the stragglers at the end of the pack. She was one of them. He'd run with her for a couple of minutes and kept her going when she was about ready to quit.

Cindy was a home health nurse. "Mrs. Woodridge, I've got an emergency call. I believe you're all set. Will it be okay for me to leave a little early?"

"Sure Cindy. Thank you so much for the nice bath, and straightening up my meds again. I don't know what I'd do without you. You run along. Is it something serious?"

"It could be."

"You go on now. I'll see you tomorrow at noon again."

"Yes ma'am. Thank you. See you tomorrow."

Cindy stopped at the closest convenience store and threw eight bags of ice in the car, and a fuel can with gasoline. She gunned it the ten miles to the West Docks, gate two.

Chris was waiting for her at the gate. The gate guards let her in and Chris jumped in the car.

"Oh man, he's in bad shape. Turn here."

"Who is he."

"I really can't go into it now. You just have to trust me."

If there was anybody Cindy would have trusted, it would be Chris Remington. He just had a sense of goodness about him, and she'd never seen him betray that image in any way – not even once.

"How long has he been unconscious?"

"Not sure, maybe an hour, maybe longer, rapid pulse, rapid breathing."

They got to the warehouse and Chris had her park close to the door. They hustled inside. Coon Dog was in the same position that Chris had left him in, and he was still unconscious.

Cindy quickly evaluated the situation. "We've got to get his core temp down or he won't make it. We need a tub, something we can pack the ice around him."

"Got it, right here." Chris tipped the steel locker and eased it down to lay flat on the floor.

Cindy said, "Let's get him in it. I'll keep his head and shoulders up, then bring the ice in."

Five minutes later Coon Dog was immersed in ice and water. Cindy had built a mushy head and shoulder support out of the soaked cardboard, enough to prop him up. She maintained support of his head with her hands, but turned that job over to Chris.

"Here, hold his head. I'll get the IV going."

She went to her car and brought in the IV equipment and got the needle in Coon Dog's arm. She opened a plastic bag of electrolyte solution, hooked up the tubes, and had Chris hold the bag high enough to start the drip. She had the flow meter wide open.

Now, it was Cindy saying, "Come on, come on!"

Chris had her hold the bag a few seconds and he slid another steel locker up close where they could hang the electrolyte solution. Chris took Coon Dog's head this time, "Come on Matlock, you're back, come on now. Wake up. You're back in the world." He was softly patting Coon Dog's face with his hands as if to shake him out of light slumber. "Come on, you're back in the world. Come on."

Coon Dog's eyes opened to a narrow slit but they weren't focusing on anything, and he mumbled something unintelligible.

Chris said, "His breathing is slowing down and is getting deeper."

"That's good. Keep talking to him."

"Come on Matlock. You are back. You are off the ship. Talk to me. Talk to me. You hear me? Wake up!"

Coon Dog opened his eyes a little more. A quarter bag of the electrolyte solution was already gone. Cindy was holding his arm with the needle in it, watching more life saving fluid poor into his body.

Coon Dog was moving a little and started talking, "Where's Red Man? He was here with me." He didn't seem to be aware of Chris or Cindy. "Where is he? He was talking to me."

Cindy gave Chris a questioning look, but Chris started talking to Coon Dog, "You're going to be all right Matlock. Just take it easy. You're off the island, you're off the ship. We're going to get you out of here and get you back home to Alabama. Just take it easy. It's going to be all right."

Chris looked at Cindy, "I'll explain everything. You think we can move him now?"

"No, not yet. In a few minutes we'll get him out of the tub, strip him, dry him, and keep ice under his armpits and around the groin. And we'll fan him, but he's got to get more electrolytes. Maybe a half hour we can move him."

While they were waiting on the bag of electrolytes to kick start Coon Dog, Chris had laid out the entire story to Cindy. At first she seemed amazed but then she said she had heard a lot of Vietnam stories from her dad, and that some of them were similar to Coon Dog's background. As far as Coon Dog's record of being a convicted double rape-murderer, she wasn't buying it either. If Chris didn't believe it, and he'd gotten this much involved in freeing Ronnie Matlock from the island, well, she was one hundred percent with Chris, period, end of story.

After a while Coon Dog recognized Chris. "Where are we?"

"In a warehouse, close to the ship. You've had a heat stroke. You were in the steel cabinet up on the deck for over three hours. I'm sorry Matlock. How are you feeling?"

"Kind of like an overdone pancake."

Cindy smiled at Chris, "We can move him now."

Chris hustled back to the ship and got a few things squared away then returned to the warehouse. Cindy had Coon Dog drinking three bottles of gator aide and removed the IV when Chris returned.

"He's ready to go, but nothing strenuous for forty-eight hours. Keep the electrolytes going in. He can have light solids tomorrow. If he has any trouble urinating, let me know."

Smiling at Coon Dog, she said, "Mr. Matlock, it's been my pleasure caring for you. Thanks for all you've done for our country. Welcome home, and God bless you."

Coon Dog said, "Thank you ma'am. It's mighty good to be back."

CHAPTER THIRTY-SEVEN

It was two days after the near fatal heat stroke. Chris and Coon Dog were in the motel room Chris had set up for Coon Dog. They were finishing off a mountain of Chinese food Chris had brought.

"Tomorrow night I'll take you out for good Italian," Chris said.

"I appreciate it, but you've already done more than enough. I'll be leaving in the morning."

"You don't have to hurry."

"I know, but it's time to be moving on. I'll send you the money as soon as I get back on my feet."

"You don't have to, but I'm not going to argue." In the last two days Chris had learned that when Coon Dog made up his mind on something, there was no sense trying to change it.

"The *Nolin River* is going back to the island in, what did you say, three days?"

"Yes, we'll probably stay out about a month."

"Tell me again. What did Captain Weller say?"

"Well, he gave me a song and dance about whether you were worth anybody sticking their neck out for. He didn't say you by name, but he was talking about you. He saw the sweat leaking out of the locker. Then he said he had checked on the details of the double rape/murder two years ago when you were convicted and sentenced to the island. He said three old friends confirmed that the whole thing was a put-up job. Yeah, those were the words he used, a "put- up job," and he said a judge had been bought off. That's about it. No, he also talked a little about your time in Vietnam and escaping from a POW camp. Then he got the OOD to allow the work party to get the steel lockers and equipment ashore. And he asked me if I had any questions. I said 'no sir'."

Chris continued, "Where did you get your nickname?"

"My daddy gave it to me. He taught me everything I know that's any good. We hunted and fished a lot. He knew more about the woods and streams than anybody. We'd gig frogs and grab for fish in the creeks at night. You ever been grabbing?"

"I don't know what you mean."

"Grabbing is wading around a good fish stream at night and grabbing the fish up under the roots and banks where they hide with your hands."

"I've seen that on TV, but they did it in the day time. They'd get hold of these monster catfish."

"Yeah, I've done that too, but in the small streams we did it at night – bass, bluegill, crappie."

Coon Dog finished off his shrimp fried rice and coffee Chris had brought and tucked a big wad of Red Man chewing tobacco up under his lip. He offered it to Chris, but Chris said, "No thanks."

Earlier that afternoon Chris had taken Coon Dog shopping at a Wal Mart some fifty miles away from the naval base. Chris didn't want to take any chances that a crew member might have recognized Coon Dog. It wasn't likely. Coon Dog had shaved his head and was shaving his whiskers clean daily. Not only that, he was wearing shades anytime he was away from the motel room.

The first thing Coon Dog had put in his shopping cart was a Bible, and the second thing was a couple month's supply of Red Man chewing tobacco. Clothes were next and some food he could eat while he was traveling. A large duffle bag would be used to carry everything. He figured that including the cash, the motel, the shopping trip, and the meals, Chris had extended him just shy of a thousand bucks.

"If you ever get back east, you'll have to pay me a visit. I'll take you grabbing, see how you like it."

"I'm from Louisville. Where will you be, Alabama?"

"Maybe, but I been thinkin' about that. It might not be smart going back there. I reckon somebody would be bound to catch me. I'm thinkin' about the Blue Ridge in Virginia. There's still some mighty lonesome backwoods up in there. Or a bit west of the Blue Ridge, a little southwest of Lexington, on the West Virginia line. Build me a cabin, maybe do some truckin'. I've got a lot of prayin' to do, see what God's gonna'do with me."

"It's still crazy you know …. how you carved out the design on the panther skin."

"Maybe not so crazy. Like I said the other day, you just gotta' trust God. Did I say that? Well, if I didn't, I should have. If He means for us to figure it out, trust me, we'll figure it out."

Coon Dog didn't get rolling on religion very often, at least not to others, but he was now. "Here's the thing, Chris. I've lived long enough to know there's only one way to the truth. It's God the Father through His Son Jesus Christ with The Holy Spirit cementing the deal. With me, there's no mystery. Christ owns me. Whatever happens is because of Him. I understand that thoroughly. Never, not once, has He let me down. I remember I used to laugh at the Christians who seemed so sure God was in total control of their lives. I thought it was all a show, you know, they just acted it out so much, them giving up their will to God's will. Well, I don't laugh anymore. I'm one of them. And here's the thing, once you've truly given up your will to God, and the magic gets started, well …. you sort of just expect it, the miracles, the magic. You really do. Unbelievable events, unbelievable things like me making that design of the panther skin, they are not a big thing. Really, you just get so used to miracles and magical things taking place, that it is not a big thing."

"I know, you want to know how it's possible I carved out that design. Me, I already know how it's possible. I'll prove it to you. Tell you what I'm gonna' do. I'm gonna' pray on it real hard and put my old man's excuse for brains to work on it. But they won't do much good. The prayin' will be all I need. You'll see. I'm going to get you an answer. Red Man already told us it wouldn't remain a mystery for long. So now, all we got to do is pray and trust God. The answer will be coming along soon."

"Man I hope so. I'll go nuts trying to figure it out."

CHAPTER THIRTY-EIGHT

Ronnie, Coon Dog, Matlock, free man. He was looking at all the electronic gadgets for sale at a large truck stop just outside San Diego. He was thinking about buying a cell phone. He'd kept Toby's and Jabez' cell numbers in his head the last two years just for this very day. But no, he decided not to. *It's too soon. Let me just get a taste of rambling around again, on my own. I'll be in touch with the JETS before long.*

He ordered a burger and coffee at the fast food stand, and took a seat where six or eight other drivers were scattered around, grabbing a quick meal. *Yeah,* he thought, *this is the way to do it. Stay around truck drivers.* Don't go to the malls and get sick watching aimless and clueless American consumers playing the game. He remembered back in his SEAL days, it was the same thing every time he'd come home from a deployment. He'd get back around normal people, doing normal things, and realized he didn't fit in. Look at them, walking around, not a care in the world, playing the game – buy junk, use it up, buy more. Work a nine to five to pay for it, go bowling, go to the movies, play sports, and raise your kids to do the same. Walk around the malls, act like you care about the next purchase you're going to make. Enjoy the easy life, the good life, it's the American way. What do they know about the sacrifices that have been made for over two and a quarter centuries that allow them to walk around carefree and clueless? Not much. But Coon Dog realized that even though it's natural for returning warriors who have done without, who have served, who have played chase with death and gore and fear, who have become empty and reckless; even though it's natural for them to be disgusted with soft America, he also realized, that he and the others who've given so very much, did so because it was their destiny, their birthright to be givers, to be soldiers, sailors, airmen, marines, coast guardsmen and in his case, in this latest episode of his turbulent life, an escapee from the banishment island.

Yes, he said to himself, *stay around truck drivers. They are givers, too.* He went back to the counter and refilled his coffee cup and sat back down to enjoy being around men like himself.

After awhile he began striking up conversations with different drivers. It was strange, talking with so many people. For the last two years he could count all the people he'd talked to on both hands. He was trying to get a feel for it again. Just small talk, blend in, talk to people. Hopefully the talking would shed light on some decisions he would soon be making, one of which was the decision to forsake his old Alabama woods for the much more remote Virginia mountains.

A burly driver sat close to him with coffee and a sandwich.

"Got a load going east?" Coon Dog asked.

"No, going up the coast to Portland. How 'bout you?"

"Truth be told, I'm outa' a job right now. I'm lookin' for a ride to go back east. I got a couple of things that might work out back there."

"You shouldn't have no trouble getting' a ride. I can put it out on the CB if you want me to."

"Yes sir, that'd be right nice of you."

"No problem. I'll be done here in a minute, and put it out when I get back to the truck. What do they call you?"

The question caught Coon Dog off guard. He hadn't spent any time choosing a new name, or a temporary alias.

"William. Ever'body calls me Will."

"Okay, I'll tell 'em you're in here drinking coffee."

"That's great. Thanks a lot. What do they call you?"

"Oh, most of 'em call me L.T. Left Turn is my handle."

"Nice to meet ya' L.T." *Go ahead and ask him. You know you want to.* "L.T., I was just wonderin'. Have you ever heard of or come across a bunch of Christian truckers called the JETS?"

"I aint' never met none of em', but I've heard some stories 'bout 'em. Why?"

"Aw, I was just wondering. I've heard a few stories too, but haven't run across none of 'em."

L.T. was about finished eating, but went on, "Yeah, ever'body that I've met who knows anything about them has always said they are a great bunch of guys – the real deal. No B.S. with them. Just good Christians that do a little preachin' on the CB now and then. But there's a couple of pretty wild stories going around about 'em."

"Really? What have you heard? Let me see if it's the same stories I've heard."

"Well, as best I can tell, the main story that's been passed around is that about four years back they got involved with some renegade trucker from Montana. This guy was himself involved with a ring of international sex slave smugglers. Some key members of the JETS took it upon themselves to take down the smugglers and at the same time afforded the renegade trucker an opportunity to turn his life around. The story goes, they were successful. They put a rolling blockade around the bad guys up on 90 in Montana, and they stopped a forty foot container that had five girls in it. Otherwise, the girls would have ended up overseas as sex slaves for dictators and drug cartels."

"Wow, that's quite a story."

"Yeah, but that's only half of it. One of the JETS was a guy named Coon Dog. He did a lot of the heavy lifting on the operation."

"What do you mean?" Ronnie was starting to get a little worried. Should he be doing this?

"He was ex Navy SEAL. He tailed the bad guys, saved the renegade trucker, and released the girls." L.T. sounded mighty proud that a fellow trucker could have accomplished all of that.

"Hmm." Ronnie was trying to sound indifferent.

"And guess what he got for all his trouble?"

"What?"

"After the bad guys bought their way out of prison, they had him set up on a double rape/murder. The JETS of course knew he didn't do it, but there was nothing that could be done. Somehow the cops had DNA evidence, and the country was screaming for sociopaths to be sent away to the new banishment island. There is all kinds of stuff going around. I even heard that Hollywood wants to make a movie about it."

"You're kidding."

"Kidding? No sirree! Aw, you've heard about it. You'd have to. Everybody else has. Where you been? On an island somewhere?"

Coon Dog realized he'd gone too far, "Yeah, now I remember. Yeah, I heard all about it. I just don't pay a lot of attention to everything I hear. You know what I mean?"

"I sure do, and the fact is, it's mostly truck drivers that keep the story going. The general public, I don't think, gives a flip."

"I heard that." He was a bit relieved. *Whew!*

"Well, maybe I'll catch you again." L.T. got up and headed out to his truck.

"See ya' L.T., and thanks."

"Anytime."

It wasn't long before Coon Dog spotted a trucker walk in who was scanning the room quickly. The man saw Coon Dog sitting alone with his coffee and walked over, "You the driver trying to get back east?"

"Yes sir."

"That duffle bag all you got with you?"

"Yep, that's it."

"I can get you to Little Rock, but not direct. Gotta' run up to Provo first."

"Yes sir. That sounds good."

"Let me take care of a couple of things. We'll leave in five minutes."

Coon Dog went to the men's room to make sure he was thoroughly dripped and drained, then he waited outside for the driver. The ordinary hubbub was going on. Trucks were jockeying for a spot in the line up to the fuel islands. Others were scrambling to catch an empty parking space as soon as another driver pulled out. He spotted a man pulling the old "run out of gas scam", going truck to truck to get a hand out. He saw another man plying his legitimate trade, polishing wheels and fuel tanks – all the normal truck stop activity which two years ago would many times irritate Coon Dog. Not today. He was enjoying the show, glad to be back, glad to be a part of it.

It was a half hour later. The driver and Coon Dog were in no hurry to engage in any heavy conversation. They both knew there would be plenty of time for that, and they both knew that eventually, good, deep conversation would ensue. They had only shared names so far, both content to settle into the seven hundred miles to Provo, uncluttered by talking.

The driver's name was Terrell Wingshot. He was a hard working truck driver, forty-eight years old, supporting two daughters and a houseful of grandchildren. His wife was strong mentally, but was down in her back and drawing disability after a fifteen year battle with social security to do so. Terrell pulled a flatbed as an owner operator and had the reputation of taking the most difficult loads, hence the pay was usually a little higher. He averaged close to four thousand miles a week running all the lower forty-eight and occasionally getting a load to Alaska. One trip north he came up on a broke down motorcycle near Beaver Creek in the Yukon. Terrell and the biker wrestled the Harley up on the nose of the flatbed and strapped it down. Five hundred miles later they found the part that was needed. The biker was grateful but not surprised at the help he received. Up north, it's a law. You must render whatever assistance you can to stranded or broken down motorists – trucks, cars, even motorcycles.

Terrell aimed his truck up 15 to Barstow. It was late afternoon, and the moonscape appearance of the high desert between Barstow and Las Vegas had Coon Dog feeling a little strange. What if he had been banished here, not on an island in the Pacific? He was wondering if he could survive here. It sure didn't look like it. Not much to see out there. Funny, at the same time, there was very much to see. Mountains way off in at least three directions. How far? Now that was a good question. Distance is a relative concept in the desert. Depending on the angle of the sun and any cloud cover, which rarely happens, you'd be hard pressed to estimate distances accurately. Coon Dog remembered a few years back, he was pretty good at distance estimates in the mountains back east, but out west, he'd usually be off a good deal. He'd kill a lot of time picking a mountain in the distance then measuring the distance to it with the odometer.

Hard to imagine surviving out there. It left him feeling a little low. "Hey Terrell, if you want to catch a few Z's I can take the wheel for awhile."

"All right, we might just do that." He aimed it to the shoulder and let it gradually slow down. When they stopped, Terrell climbed down and walked around to let the truck protect him while he peed. Coon Dog did the same and then he climbed back up, on the driver's side this time.

"You know the way to Provo don't you? Just stay on 15. The Nevada chicken coop is probably closed, but I guarantee St. George will be open. Don't worry though, our weight is okay and I've got PRE PASS." Terrell pulled the curtain shut and stretched out on the lower bunk.

Oh man, this feels good. Coon Dog adjusted his seat and the steering wheel. He locked his seat belt in and checked his mirrors. He checked all his gauges. He pushed the red and yellow parking brake valves in. He put the shifter in 2nd gear and let the clutch catch just a little. He gently tugged on the hand valve for the trailer brakes and felt them pull back just a little and he let the valve go. He ran 2nd out, and 3rd, and all the rest through 10. He settled out at 59 mph because he was still in California. When he crossed into Nevada he'd jump it up to 73. He re-scanned all the gauges and then made sure the jake brake was on high. He eyeballed all the other switches to make sure he knew what was what – the inter-axle differential, the engine fan, air bags, dome lights, floor lights, the loss of power over-ride, turn signals, four ways, variable wipers, washer, head lights and parking lights, the light interrupter, and the various settings for cruise control.

He reached up to the CB and adjusted the squelch. "Break one-nine, radio check please."

"Check's in the mail driver."

"Appreciate it." *I'm back. Been here three days, but now, finally, I'm back. Thank You Father. You are an awesome God. Thank You Father. Thank You Father.*

The next day Terrell and Coon Dog were southbound on 15. Terrell had dropped his load at 10:00 and was now bound for Flagstaff, before turning east toward Little Rock. Coon Dog found himself thinking about the promise he had made to Chris – the promise to pray for an answer to the mystery of the image of the panther, the mountains, and the cross. So, he was silently praying for an insight, even a hint of some understanding where the image came from. He was plenty aware that a rational detailed origin of the image might never be revealed, but still, he prayed, for something.

At mile marker 95 they turned east on route 20. Terrell was driving. They were climbing a five mile grade. Coon Dog was having a great time. The high California desert was yesterday. Today he was rewarded with high western forest, beautiful streams and rivers down in the valleys, the red rock formations that would sometimes run five miles on the horizon and a half mile vertically. The rock formations and spectacular color in this part of Utah is well known but Coon Dog had not seen it before. They were still climbing and there was yet another lofty vista waiting for his eyes. He could see they were approaching the summit and the road signs were already warning truckers of the seven percent down grade on the other side. Up, up just a little more. Getting close to the top. He knew they were about to top the mountain because there was nothing but sky directly in front of him. Up fifty more yards. The big truck was straining to make it. There it is, just in front of them. ZAPPO, over the summit. A hard left or you free fall two thousand feet. *Wheweee! Look at that!* A panorama lying out in front and to the right that nearly took his breath. Mountains so far away he felt like they'd need a space rocket to ever get there. The valley was two, maybe three thousand feet below. A few cattle were way down there in a lush green meadow with an easy moving river running through it. From his spot the cattle were no more than ant-like specks. A two lane was going down. *Good* Coon Dog thought. *It'll slow us down. I'll be able to see it longer.*

On the bottom it was just as good as it looked from above . The river, clean and pure, slipped easily through emerald green meadows, then fell away through canyons strewn with boulders the size of locomotives. Now and then the river would cut through the burning red rock walls and soon again be back in the green fields. It was a river and a country where Coon Dog could see himself living. The farms and ranches scattered along its banks looked like places where people were happy. Well kept places. Horses and cattle and dogs and children. Firewood stacked, waiting for the season. Split rail fences. Big, substantial corrals.

Coon Dog was taking it all in. They turned on 89 south and rolled through several small towns. In two hours the sun would be gone. But there was one more visual treat for his eyes and visceral treat for his soul before darkness and the black night would settle in.

As they drove through the bump in the road called Big Water, a tiny hamlet catering to boaters, they could see the Colorado River to the east. It was backed up into Lake Powell. The cliffs and canyons surrounding it seemed like ranks of Gods protecting it from the sky and the sun. Heavy shadows from the Gods swept across the canyons, and the river and anything on a human scale could not compete. They crossed the river at the Glen Canyon Dam and entered the town of Page, Arizona. The bridge was only four or five hundred feet across, but there was no mistaking what was way, way down at the bottom – the Grand Canyon itself. Very narrow at this, its eastern origin, waiting patiently before it would widen out to seventeen miles. But the mother lode of the visual surprises gifted to Coon Dog today was still a few minutes away. Route 89 continued south out of Page where it would work its way down through the Navajo villages toward Flagstaff. Coon Dog kept looking off to the west to see where the gorge would start widening, and he could see it doing that very thing. As he continued his scan to the west, he wasn't totally aware how much of a grade they were climbing. When he finally looked up in front of the truck, he could see that the summit they were still three miles from had a narrow slit at the top where the last half hour of daylight bore through as a welding arc might. They continued climbing and like a few hours earlier the road signs began their warnings: five mile 8 % grade ahead – truckers use lower gear. The slit at the top didn't widen out. It had maybe ten feet of shoulder on each side of the two- lane, and at the top it towered over the roadway by maybe seven-hundred feet.

Then as the truck limped through the narrow slit at the top, Coon Dog felt as though he might have entered another realm of existence. The sweep of the distant horizon was so vast it couldn't have been a scene from planet earth. Fifty miles, a hundred miles in all directions and so very far down below. The Grand Canyon itself, now off to the northwest, was reduced to imaginable proportion when compared to the scene spread out in front of Coon Dog. He could see the curvature of mother earth, and more than that, he could feel it. Maybe something akin to a fetus in the womb, stretching, kicking, reaching to find the limits. And here was Coon Dog, on this day seeing with his own eyes the absolute limits that God had woven into the creation of the earth.

He wept openly, and Terrell saw it and said, "Are you all right?"

"No, no, I'm not. I'm so undeserving, and …. and look at all this. Look what He's done."

"Yeah, I see. You're right. We don't deserve it."

Finally, they were ready to talk.

"Have you been through this pass before?" Coon Dog was a little more cleareyed now.

"Yeah, several times. It's one of my favorites."

Coon Dog offered Terrell some of his Red Man chewing tobacco. Terrell put a wad of it back in the corner of his mouth, up under his lip. They both found a plastic cup to dribble the poison juice in.

"Sorry …. I just …. sometimes I can't contain it. You know, what God has done for us." Coon Dog was drying his eyes with his shirt sleeve. "Are you a Christian?"

"If you mean washed in the blood and born again and all of that, I guess not. I do believe in a God. I work hard. I try to treat people the way I'd want to be treated."

"The Bible tells us that unless you confess Jesus before men, you can't be saved." Coon Dog was surprised at himself. He would not normally begin a conversation from a confrontational viewpoint, but there was something tugging on him. Here they were, coming down this mountain along the edge of the Echo Cliffs. Coon Dog was assured of a ride all the way to Little Rock, and now, here he is stirring up a religious argument. He kept thinking about it all the way to the bottom. The sun was gone now, but still twenty-five minutes of diminishing remnants of sunset before total darkness.

Terrell hadn't said anything else, but he was wondering when the hard core Jesus pitch would resume. The one all the highway preachers use to eventually beat you down. The one he'd heard a hundred times and the one which made him reject the Bible thumpers more each time.

Coon Dog surprised himself again, where his private thoughts were taking him. *What's the point of coming back to the world if I don't proclaim Jesus to all the people I meet that may not know Him? On the other hand, I know what will happen if I start preaching at Terrell. I'll push him away. He is a good man, just confused. I could walk him through the entire book of Revelations, but to what avail? I'd probably just push him farther away. I could tell him that he'll have another chance to accept Jesus, at the second judgment, the great white throne judgment, but what good will it do? I'm not much of a preacher. I think it will be best to just put Terrell on my prayer list. Let him go his own way. And what is it God is tugging on me to do here tonight? Not with Terrell. No, it's something else. What is it? Coming through that high pass behind us – something happened. What was it? Yeah, I've got to let Terrell go on. I've got to stay here and find out what I'm supposed to do.*

"Terrell, thanks for the ride. I need to get off up here at the next crossroads. You are a good man. I'll be praying for you."

Terrell pulled over where eight or nine Indian shacks formed a little village. There was a trading post with a gas pump and a raggedy sign that said Indian Jewelry and Blankets, and as an after thought, sandwiches. Coon Dog grabbed his duffle bag and was climbing down. "Thanks again Terrell. God Bless. Keep her between the lines."

The big truck wound through the gears and it was gone. Coon Dog picked up his duffle bag and walked over to the Trading Post. The sky was dark gray now, a ribbon of afterglow in the west was all that was left of the sun. There was a naked light bulb hanging inside. Coon Dog opened the door and walked in.

He saw the boy first, nine, maybe ten years old. Round face, dark eyes, and the blackest hair he'd ever seen, cut in a straight line across his forehead and nearly shoulder length in the back. Then he saw the old man look at him. The old man didn't say anything.

Coon Dog said, "I was wondering if maybe you got a room for the night. I can pay you."

The old Indian didn't say anything; he just shook his head no.

Coon Dog looked around the store quickly. Some dusty looking canned goods took up most of one row. Soft drinks, aspirin, cowboy hats and boots and tobacco took up most of the remaining retail space. The blankets were displayed on the walls and some decent leather work lay on a table where maybe the jewelry had once been.

The old Indian man looked from Coon Dog over to the boy who was sitting on a stool. The old man said, "You want the boy, you take him. His father is in prison and will never get out. His mother is dead."

Coon Dog looked at the old man then back at the boy. The boy hadn't moved or changed his empty face in any way. "Look mister, I'm just wantin' to spend the night around here. You got a place outside I can sleep. How much you get for your blankets?"

"Sixty."

"I'll give you forty for that one right up there."

"Fifty."

"Okay, fifty."

The old Indian man had a long stick to reach the top of the blanket where it hung. He released one end of it, then the other and gathered it as it came down.

Coon Dog was looking up where it had come from. There was another blanket behind it still hanging on the wall. Coon Dog stood, staring at the second blanket, his mouth open, his eyes fixed on it.

The old man was folding the first blanket.

"No," Coon Dog said. "I want that one." He was still looking up at the second blanket. *I'll bet the old man wants more than fifty for it.*

But the old man laid the first blanket down and took his stick back to the wall to retrieve the second blanket. He didn't say anything about a higher price. He brought the blanket over to the table and spread it out in order to fold it. The black panther, mountains, and cross on the blanket's design seemed to have Coon Dog mesmerized, but he got his money, counted it, and handed the old Indian fifty dollars.

The old man showed Coon Dog where he could sleep outside. There was a tarp stretched from the back of the trading post. Coon Dog put his duffle bag and new blanket under it, and lay down. He saw the old man and the boy walk from the Trading Post to a rickety twenty-five foot trailer seventy feet away. They went inside and after a while the light went out.

Coon Dog grabbed some clothes out of his duffle bag to make a pillow. He laid his head back against it, and pulled his new blanket up on himself, and lay there with his eyes open, thinking about tomorrow.

CHAPTER THIRTY-NINE

When the sun had been up for nearly an hour, Coon Dog removed his new blanket and pulled himself up to his feet. The Trading Post faced the east, so his sleeping place around back hadn't allowed the heat of the sun to bother Coon Dog, but now it was time to get a new day of freedom started – his sixth, to be exact. He carefully folded up the blanket and placed it inside the duffle bag along with the clothes he'd used as a pillow. He put his new ball cap on his head and put on the sunglasses. He left the duffle bag lying under the tarp, grabbed his plastic water jug, and walked around the Trading Post and across the road toward the east.

The base of the two thousand foot high Echo Cliffs was a half mile away. Coon Dog walked across a dry riverbed and several deep washouts protected from the sun by the cliffs. It was cool in the shade and of course, being the northern Arizona high desert, it was extremely dry. He sat on a rock near the base and thought about the dream he'd had last night.

The dream had been set around 1946, a "period dream" one might have called it. Coon Dog was sure of the time because he heard and saw the big swing bands of the era doing their thing. Tommy Dorsey, Glenn Miller and the others were performing "Stardust", "In The Mood" , and "Moonlight Serenade". Red Man was in and out of the dream, but he didn't have anything to say; he was just *there*.

There was one particularly coherent section of the dream which had a young sailor returning from the Pacific at the end of the war. He was hitching back east and got stranded somewhere in Indian country in Arizona. The sailor had a large Christian cross tattooed on his right forearm. It took the entire space from his wrist to his elbow. As he walked along a desert road at sunset he caught the flicker of a camp fire off in the desert a mile away. He would not have ventured a hike out into the desert to check it out. After all, he was trying to get home. He'd been at Saipan, and Iwo Jima; he wasn't about to waste any time getting back to his family. But he heard a woman's crying from the direction of the camp fire, actually scream-ing in agony. Against his better judgment he tore off through the desert. He found a young Indian woman, maybe twenty, in the last stages of labor, no one to help her. Then he saw the panther's yellow eyes, fifteen feet away. The Indian girl had also seen them. There was no doubt about that. Her screaming might have been as much from the terror the panther evoked as it had been from the labor pain. The sailor went to the fire, removed a burning stick and heaved it toward the pair of yel-low eyes. The panther got the message and scooted out of the area. Later that night the girl delivered a little boy. The sailor stayed with her and the baby all that night and in the morning convinced the girl she had to get the baby to the nearest town. The girl had explained that her people had disowned her and set her out in the desert to parish. The baby she carried, they felt, had been fathered by an evil shaman, and therefore she was not allowed to give birth in the village. The shaman had been known to mate animals with young girls and perform rituals that brought evil spirits out to terrorize the entire reservation. In the morning, as the sailor was admonishing the girl to get the baby to a doctor to check him out, he asked what she was going to name him. She said she'd name him Lonely Bear-Brave Bear. The sailor asked her why that name, and she answered,

"Because, he will always be lonely; his people don't want him. He will need to be a brave bear to face what lies ahead for him."

Coon Dog sat on the rock below the Echo Cliffs and was thinking it all through, the dream and everything else. It was time for a talk with the old man.

He walked back toward route 89, crossed it and went to the door of the Trading Post. It was locked. He went around back and waited. Around ten o'clock the old man made his way from the trailer to the back door of the Trading Post.

The old man let Coon Dog in the back door, unlocked the front door, and took his position on a stool without saying anything. He was counting a few bills from his pocket.

Coon Dog stepped a little closer and was looking at him, "I need to ask you a couple of questions."

The Indian's response was indifferent. He didn't say anything; he was still counting the bills.

"Was there an Indian girl a long time ago that gave birth to a little boy out in the desert? Her people had pushed her away from them for fear the baby was fathered by an evil shaman?"

The old man quit counting and took a rag with him to dust off the shelves and merchandise. He didn't say anything.

"Did the Indian girl name the baby Lonely Bear- Brave Bear?'

The old man continued to dust and piddle around with the canned goods, moving one or two cans here and there.

"Was there a sailor that spooked away a panther that night that might have attacked the girl and the baby?" Coon Dog waited for the old man to show something or say something, but there was nothing.

"What was the sailor's name?"

The old man moved a little closer to Coon Dog and said evenly, "The baby's mother said the sailor had told her that his name was Douglas Remington."

"Are you the baby's father?" Coon Dog asked.

"No, I was his uncle."

"Was that baby boy the same man you said last night was in prison and won't ever get out?"

"Yes."

"I'm sorry to have to tell you this, but he is dead."

The old man looked away, "That is no surprise. Will you take his son with you? I am old. The people around here still think he is flawed because of his grandfather, my brother."

"Yes, I will take him. Can you tell me what it was Lonely Bear-Brave Bear did to get locked away?"

"He murdered his father."

"Who made the blanket I bought from you last night? Lonely Bear- Brave Bears's mother?"

"Yes."

"Is she still alive?"

"Yes, but she lives far from here," the old man said.

"Would you deliver a message to her?"

"Yes, I could do that."

"Tell her that her son died a very brave man, leading others to the Great White Father where he himself dwells for eternity."

"I will tell her."

CHAPTER FORTY

The old man had the nine year old boy ready to travel. He'd prepared a small bag with a few clothes in it, some strands of Indian beads, and some canned meat he'd taken off the shelves. Before Coon Dog and the boy walked out to the road to hitch on down to Flagstaff, the old man gave Coon Dog the fifty dollars back to him and said, "Please use this." He turned back toward the Trading Post, hesitated, and then looked back at Coon Dog, "His name is Michael. Be patient with him. He will talk to you once he gets to know you a little." And he turned and walked away.

"Wait," Coon Dog said. "Can you mail a letter for me?"

"Yes."

"Give me just a minute. I haven't written it yet." He hurriedly wrote the letter. When he finished, he handed the letter to the old man.

The old man turned back toward the Trading Post with the letter in his hand.

The letter was addressed to QM3 Chris Remington, *USS Nolin River*, FPO San Francisco, Ca.

Dear Chris,

Well, it seems like a few answers have already showed up. What I'm about to tell you did not surprise me at all. Remember what I said about the magic you come to expect once you give up your will to God? Check this out:

I'm betting you had an uncle, grandfather, or some other man in your family who was in the Pacific in WW

II, and I would bet that his name was Douglas Remington. What you probably don't know about him because he probably never told anyone is this: When the war was over, he got stranded in northern Arizona, way out in nowheresville. He saw a campfire and heard a young woman screaming. When he got there he saw two things. One, she was in labor and about to deliver a baby. Two, he saw a black panther and ran it away before it attacked the woman. It just happens that this Douglas Remington had a large cross tattooed on his forearm.

Now, that doesn't explain everything, but it should be enough to help you get something of a grip on all that's happened. I'm thinking there are other parts of the puzzle that you know about and I don't.

Try not to run over any island escapees while you're out there driving the ship. Thanks again for all your help. I'll be getting you the money you put on me as soon as I can.
God Bless,
Coon Dog

The big truck pulled up in front of the Trading Post a little later. Coon Dog opened the door and tossed up his duffle bag and the boy's smaller bag. He lifted the boy up to the second safety step and followed him inside. The truck driver directed the boy to the lower bunk in the sleeper and the boy sat down and looked ahead to the windshield.

"Climb on in here fellers. I'm headed down to Flagstaff, then I'm turning east. That help you out any?"

"Yes sir. You bet it will," Coon Dog said.

"Name's Will, what's yours?"

"Junior Neblett, nice to meet ya'."

"This is Michael. His great uncle is letting him get off the reservation for awhile and spend some time with me. He's quiet, but he's a good boy."

"Nice to meet ya' Michael. If you got any questions about this big old truck, you just let me know. And if you want to steer her, I'll set you up here with me, and she'll be all yours."

The boy's eyes sparkled for a second and the hint of a smile sneaked around the corners of his mouth. Coon Dog noticed both, and couldn't suppress his own smile.

The big truck driver worked through the gears and settled into its pace of 60 mph. The road was mostly two lane, with an occasional passing lane every now and then. The Echo Cliffs continued their vigil from the east breaking only three times in the next 80 miles to allow a road to slice through them and cut a path toward New Mexico. Indian shantytowns hugged route 89 all the way to the outskirts of Flagstaff where middle class subdivisions took over.

Coon Dog would glance back at Michael often and give him a reassuring look of confidence. A look that he hoped would convey the message that Coon Dog was going to take good care of him. He noticed that none of the scenery on the way down to Flagstaff seemed to get the boy's attention. But as Humphreys Peak, at 12,633 feet, came into view, the boys eyes stayed glued to it. Coon Dog figured the boy had probably never been out of the immediate area surrounding the Trading Post, maybe a nearby school being the only exception.

"Snow on top," the boy said.

Coon Dog looked back at him with a big smile, shaking his head affirmatively.

After turning east on Interstate 40, Junior Neblett pulled into a big truck stop to top off his fuel tanks with diesel. "You two take your time inside. I'll be over there on the other side of the fuel island."

Coon Dog showed the boy how to exit the cab safely. They walked inside and Coon Dog led the boy to the men's room. After washing up they walked out to the fast food area. Coon Dog recognized immediately the boy was totally confused. He's never been in a restaurant. He sat Michael down and went back to order at the counter. When he returned, he put the cheeseburgers and fries and chocolate shake in front of the boy. Michael knew exactly what to do with the food.

After they were rolling again and were well east of Flagstaff, the interstate traffic had thinned out. Junior Neblett looked back at Michael and said, "Come on up here with me if you want to drive the truck."

Michael looked to Coon Dog for approval.

"Well, I don't know Junior. Do you think this boy might be a good truck driver?"

Junior picked up the game quickly, "Why yessiree dingle bob. No doubt about it. He looks to me like a fine young truck driver."

"Well, okay, if you're sure."

Coon Dog waved Michael up out of his seat on the edge of the lower bunk. Junior slid his driver's seat all the way back and adjusted the steering wheel all the way in. Junior swung his right leg way out wide and Coon Dog helped Michael step in behind the wheel and get perched securely on the front edge of the driver's seat. Junior had his arms around Michael, and his hands were solidly attached to each side of the wheel.

"Put you hands up here and I'll let go. Don't jerk it. Just nice and easy like this."

Michael put his hands on the wheel. Junior kept his on also. Then after a minute, he said, "Okay, it's all yours," and he removed his hands, but kept them close, just in case.

Michael predictably tugged hard and Junior caught the wheel again and straightened them up. "Real easy. You can do it." He let go again. This time Michael held the truck real good in the middle of the granny lane.

They crossed into New Mexico and two hours later were coming down the long grade into Albuquerque. Junior had been back at the wheel, solo driving, for a long time. Michael's eyes were taking in the sprawl of Albuquerque. Coon Dog had laid down on the bunk, and Michael was riding shotgun.

"What's this place?" Michael asked. It was the only thing he had said since his comment about the snow on Humphrey's Peak back in Flagstaff over four hours ago.

"This is Albuquerque, New Mexico, a big city," Junior said. Michael's eyes looked out in amazement. The highway through Flagstaff had revealed little of the size of the place. But here, this place was way beyond anything Michael could have imagined. It frightened him. He left his passenger seat and lay down next to Coon Dog, the only tie that remained that had anything at all to do with his old world at the Trading Post and the old man whom he'd learned for the first time today was his great uncle.

Coon Dog had been catnapping and thinking about what the future might hold for him and the boy. Would he keep him and raise him as his own? Would he turn him over to the authorities who would certainly place him in a state home, or foster home? He knew he'd never do that.

When he felt the boy lie down beside him, he took his hand and held it in his own. A minute later the boy quit weeping.

CHAPTER FORTY-ONE

Jabez was just leaving Duluth, Minnesota. Earlier in the day he'd been up in Winnipeg, Manitoba. His cell phone went off. "Long distance calling for the great road warrior who ceaselessly battles against evil, whose fate it is to lead lost truckers to the light, to redemption they can only find in submitting their flawed souls to the only throne of salvation that exists in this humongous cosmos sometimes called creation."

"Speaking," Jabez said.

Toby Etheridge continued, "It seems, oh fearless leader, I perceive the occurrence of an exceedingly magnificent vibration through the ethersphere, that exalted plain where those like you and I are privileged to enter on special occasions. This particular vibration seems to be an awesome convergence of a tiny lost spirit with a much older, protective, and nourishing spirit. I am calling to see if your great discerning powers have yet detected this same heavenly vibration."

"Yes indeed. The vibration you refer to, I am sure, is the same that has held me spellbound, contemplating another glimpse at the majesty, the grace, the splendor our Father is setting in motion even as we speak. Let us make haste my brother in Christ. We must do all in our power to see that the convergence of the tiny lost spirit with the older, protecting, and nourishing spirit is celebrated properly and with all the support, love, and energy we might bring to it."

"Exactly the response I expected from you. And, oh wise truck driver whom even far off vibrations in the etherspere can not elude your great insight, tell me, to what location should we aim our chariots?"

"That's easy – Big Bubba Buck's Belly Bustin' Barbecue Bliss in Munfordville, Kentucky."

CHAPTER FORTY-TWO

Junior Neblett pulled his big truck into the rest area near Tucumcari, New Mexico a little before sundown. He was out of legal driving hours. He heated up some soup and downed it with crackers. He crawled in the bottom bunk and was asleep in no time as the steady hum and vibration of the big diesel provided cool air conditioning all night. Coon Dog had convinced him that he and Michael would be fine sleeping outside. He took two spare tarps Junior had in his storage compartment under the bunk, a few feet of rope, and Junior's hammer with them. They left the rest area and hiked a half mile to the base of some imposing cliffs. Coon Dog quickly built a lean-to and a camp fire. He and the boy sat down to eat canned meat and oranges.

"I thought you might like sleeping out here tonight. We might be able to talk a little."

"Okay," Michael said.

"I knew your father. I was his friend. Do you know much about him?"

"I don't know anything about him. They would never tell me anything, only he was a bad man."

"No Michael. He was not a bad man. He was a very good man. Like all men, he made mistakes. There were times in his life, I'm sure he was very confused and lost. All men go through those things. I just wanted to let you know, he was very brave, very strong. And I also want to let you know that he died about two years ago. I was very close to him when he died. He was trying to help other men when he died, but they killed him.

Your father taught me some things. If you want, I will try to teach them to you."

"You won't be with me long."

"Oh no Michael. I will be with you a long time, until I am a very old man. I will not leave you."

"Okay, teach me things from my father."

The next morning Junior's truck was rolling across the Texas panhandle. Everything had turned green and flat. Michael had never seen green prairie before or thousands of square miles of crops. By early afternoon Oklahoma City rose up out of the flat green prairie. It had to be explained to Michael that the tall buildings were places where people worked. By four o'clock in the afternoon they were pulling into a truck stop in Fort Smith, Arkansas. Junior had been telling them about his family and his dogs. Coon Dog saw Michael's interest in the dogs, and he made a mental note.

But Junior had to turn off north toward Kansas City on 540. They all said their good byes. Michael told Junior, "Thanks for letting me drive." And Junior said, "You're the best truck driver I've seen in a long time."

Coon Dog got a motel room for the night and before going to sleep, Michael asked him, "Did Junior mean it?"

"Sure he did."

Coon Dog was in no hurry to get out on the road the next morning. They had the continental breakfast at the motel. Coon Dog noticed there wasn't anything wrong with Michael's appetite. There were two young nurses at the table next to them whose attention had been captured by Michael. When they discovered that Coon Dog and Michael were eastbound and on foot, they offered them a ride to Nashville. They had been in California on a three day seminar, and had decided to drive back to Nashville in order to see some of the west. As they drove through western Arkansas toward Little Rock they asked Michael about his school on the reservation. Michael hadn't said anything all morning but he answered them, "My school is okay. I like reading the best."

This got one of the young nurses started, "Oh, me too. I read a lot." She mentioned some of her favorite books, and then she asked Michael, "What are your favorite books?"

"Books about animals, dogs, cats, horses, and cattle."

A little later after gassing up the car, the nurse went into a gift shop and came back with a very nice book about horses and gave it to Michael.

The trip continued on through Little Rock and across the flatland, swamps, and rivers. Michael had never seen so much water. Then they came to the bridge across the Mississippi leading into Memphis. He was awed by the size of the river and more than a little scared as they drove across it, way up above on the bridge.

Coon Dog and Michael were in the back seat. After passing through Memphis, Coon Dog fell off to a light sleep. Red Man showed up in the dream as did Old Soft Shoe. All of the truckers who had previously helped Old Soft Shoe get the children out of Los Angeles were in the dream also. This time they were saving children all across the country - gathering up lost, hungry children from everywhere. Taking them somewhere, but where? There was no place to take them.

Coon Dog awoke frustrated and confused. Then he realized his own situation demanded some decisions be made. They would be in Nashville soon. Would he and Michael turn south toward Alabama and risk being turned in to the law by people who might recognize him, or would they continue eastbound and eventually turn north on 81 up into Virginia? For some strange reason he was sensing that a third option had presented itself – going north into Kentucky.

The nurses deposited Michael and Coon Dog at a truck stop near downtown Nashville, and they gave Michael their address and said they'd love for him to write them a letter every now and then. They promised him they would write back.

It was almost dark and Coon Dog was hustling to get a ride. He felt something tugging on him to keep moving tonight.

"You don't have room for a couple of truck drivers do you?" Coon Dog and Michael were right outside the door between the building and the fuel islands.

"Well now, I reckon I might. Depends on what direction you're headed." The driver was big. He had short gray fuzz for hair, and a week old growth of stubble on his face was the same color. He weren't no spring chicken, maybe sixty-eight or older. He had a big ol' smile and a look on his face that said, "They ain't got me off the road yet."

"Going east or north. I ain't sure which," Coon Dog said.

"You're in luck. I'm headed north. You say this little feller is your assistant driver?"

"No sir. I'm his assistant. He's the lead driver."

"Ten-four, I heard that I did. Let's get a hat."

They came north out of Nashville leading a pack of hard core truckers. All of them long distance, over-the-road types. No day drivers, or regional, or dedicated to a particular route or company. These were men whose family was here, out on this highway tonight, not tucked away in a cul-de-sac in Omaha, or waiting for them in an apartment in Syracuse, in a trailer court in Boulder, or in a farmhouse in Georgia. Oh, they had wives and children in those places, and they loved them. But their family was here, on the highway.

The big truck driver had his yellow W-9 Kenworth humming smoothly at 70, nowhere near the 118 it was said to be capable of running. He and Coon Dog and Michael were listening in on the disjointed CB conversations of four or five in the convoy, rolling north.

"Dagnabit Cornbread! If you go any slower we ain't gonna' make Chicago by daybreak."

"Why, it don't make no difference to me whether we make it at all. I'd just as soon drop this load in a yard somewhere and sceedaddle back to Utah."

The big old trucker in the yellow KW with Coon Dog and Michael looked back at Michael and said, "Look here trucker, we need to get them fellers on the right track. Would you talk to 'em? I'll tell you what to say. All you gotta' do is push this button down and talk right into the microphone."

Michael wasn't sure. He looked up to Coon Dog, and Coon Dog nodded his approval.

"Okay."

The trucker keyed the mike, "All right gear jammers, I think it's time you all get straightened out. I got a driver here with me that's gonna' lay it on you. Listen up good."

He looked back at Michael and winked, and handed him the mike. "Tell them this: Drivers it's about time to eat."

Michael keyed the mike, hesitated, and was looking up at Coon Dog, who said,"It's okay, go ahead."

In the strongest little boy voice he could gather up, he said, "Drivers, it's about time to eat."

"Good," said the big truck driver. "Now tell them this: Quit that yackin' and hollerin' about Utah and Chicago, and pull into Big Bubba's. It's time to eat."

Michael pushed the key button in again and said, "Quit that yackin' and hollerin' about Utah and Chicago, and pull into Big Bubba's. It's time to eat."

Several drivers came back on the CB with, "Ten-four driver. We'll shut it down at Big Bubba's. See you there."

Michael didn't have to be told what to say. He said, "Ten-four."

The convoy slipped through Bowling Green and just a little farther north, up around Mammoth Cave, they picked up a strong CB signal, "Drivers come on into Big Bubba Buck's Belly Bustin' Barbecue Bliss tonight. We've got barbecued pork and hickory smoked ribs. We've got fried baloney, taco salad, fresh fried green maters, fresh fried squash, barbecue beans, and cole slaw. We've got home-made tater salad, pinto beans, collard greens, fried taters, small fries, sweet tator fries, fried corn on the cob, fresh fried zucchini, macaroni and cheese, deep fried dill pickles, sliced shoulder, barbecue tacos, fried pork chops, hamburger, catfish dinner, catfish taco, slaw dogs and hot dogs, blackberry cobbler, and like always plenty of that good ol' down home nanna, nanna, nanna, nanna, nanna, nanna, nanna, nanna puddin'. Just take exit 65 north or south, right at the end of the ramp, and we are a half mile on the right. We've got plenty of truck parking, so come on in and see us."

Coon Dog could see the sign for exit 65 up ahead. The truck driver took the exit and turned right on 31-W at the stop sign at the end of the ramp. A half mile up the road on the right was a big electric sign for the entrance to Big Bubba's. They turned in and saw eight, maybe ten big trucks backed in at the rear of the big parking lot. The trucker backed his truck in. The other five or six trucks they had been running with were pulling in and parking also.

Coon Dog and Michael climbed down from the cab and closed the door. They started to walk up to Big Bubba's, but Coon Dog noticed something stenciled or painted on the door that he had not seen in Nashville. It had been too dark to see it. But here at Big Bubba Buck's, the parking lot had enough light to see all of the details on the trucks. The driver had his CB handle painted on the door – Old Soft Shoe.

Coon Dog stared at the name for a moment to make sure he was seeing what he thought he was seeing. He might have cornered the truck driver and tried to get an explanation from him, but the driver was already half way to the entrance to the restaurant. Coon Dog didn't really need an explanation anyway. Just like he had told Chris, you come to expect these sorts of things.

He and Michael ran to catch up with Old Soft Shoe, and they did, just as he was entering the restaurant. Old Soft Shoe held the door open for them, and Coon Dog and Michael actually stepped inside first. The three of them were walking in, and Coon Dog couldn't believe his eyes. Sitting at a big table were Jabez, Toby, and Windjammer, all three of them looking straight at Coon Dog.

Jabez said, "What took you so long? We been here waiting for you for fifteen minutes. That young driver wouldn't happen to be Michael would he? And is that Old Soft Shoe coming in the door?"

CHPTER FORTY-THREE

It was three years later. Jabez, Toby, Windjammer, Big Montana, and Will (formerly Coon Dog) were out by the horse corral. They were watching Michael do some nifty trick riding on Big Montana's nine year old stallion, Jabez, named after the truck driver who'd gifted the horse to Big Montana just a month before Big Montana had to go to prison.

The prison ministry Big Montana had put in motion had grown from the original fifty members in Deer Lodge in Montana to over six thousand chapters in all fifty states with a membership of over 91,000 jailbirds and prison cons. The state of Montana had offered Big Montana a year off his eight year sentence, but Big Montana didn't take it, saying, "I need to finish my sentence. It wouldn't be right to get out early."

These days Big Montana split his time between returning to the prisons four or five days a month to speak or to help out the ministry in any way he could and being director of Bible Studies here at the Christian Mountain School for Children. It wasn't a big place, but it wasn't small either. Currently there were a hundred and seventy-five students – boys and girls between the ages of seven and seventeen. Jabez's farm in the mountains of northeast Tennessee had proved to be an ideal place to build the school. There was plenty of room for the school's emphasis on animal studies. Actually it was a way of teaching that got the students involved personally with the animals on the farm. They were each given several animals to care for. Strong bonds developed. The children became responsible for the care of the animals, and hence their desire to learn became strong.

Will and Michael would never forget the night, three years ago, at Big Bubba's. What a celebration! Must have been twenty JETS inside waiting for "Will" to return to the world from the banish..... oops, that is, to return from, uh, from a medical leave of absence. After all the huggin' and back slappin' and eating the best barbecue this side of pig heaven, Jabez, Will, and Michael were outside in the parking lot.

Jabez said, "Let's sit down over yonder." The three walked to a picnic table in the grass not far from the restaurant. It was a beautiful Kentucky night, mild breeze, sixty-eight degrees, that old Blue Moon of Kentucky softly shining down.

"Let me see if I can set it out properly." Jabez was looking up into the sky and occasionally stealing a quick peek over at Will and Michael. "It seems to me that you two might need a place to stay for a spell. And it also seems to me that Michael is going to need some schooling. Look here Coon Dog, uh.... Will, I believe you, me, Toby, and some others have been dreaming about children all across the country needing a place to go. Is that right?"

"That's absolutely right."

"Yes. So, I've got a two hundred acre spread over in East Tennessee. Ain't nothing on it 'cept timber, corn, hay, horses, dogs, cats, and cattle. I gotta' feeling we could build a pretty good school for children up there."

He looked over at Michael with a big smile. "Michael, do you think you'd like to play with animals every day and ride horses?"

And so, that's the way the Christian Mountain School for Children began. It took awhile to build the buildings, hire a quality staff, get all the permits, licenses, and legalities squared away, but once all of that was out of the way, all they needed were children. The JETS were responsible for that part of the operation. In their travels all over America they kept a keen eye out for the children that had no place to go – the lost cases, the most severely abused, the most neglected, the throwaways.

It was a beautiful sight to see. And every one of the JETS would pull their big trucks up near the dorms and the classroom building whenever they were in northeast Tennessee. They'd get out and walk on down toward the barns, the corrals and the stockyards. In a minute or so there would be ten, twenty, or thirty children coming to visit with them. And why not? The truck drivers were the children's heroes. It was their money that built the school.

"Would you look at that!" Jabez seemed transfixed. Michael was putting on a show. He was riding Jabez (the horse) full tilt bareback and shooting arrows dead center into a round target forty yards away. Will had taught him how to make an Indian bow exactly like he'd seen Red Man make.

Will said, "Yessir, he's picking it up pretty good. Y'all keep a good eye on him for me. I'm getting' ready to run a load out toward El Paso. I gotta' feelin' I might run into Old Soft Shoe down thata' way."

"Don't you worry about him. We'll keep him plenty busy," said Big Montana.

"All right fellers, see ya' in a month or so." And Will walked a quarter mile down past all the school buildings, dorms, and past Jabez's log cabin, and climbed up in his Pete 309. He would pick up his load in Lexington, Kentucky and then stop at Big Bubba's on his way southwest. There was almost always a JET either inside eating or out in the parking lot.

His search for the promise that America held for all those willing to look would be never ending. Will was, of course, very fortunate. He'd been able to unlock the box to the promise many times. He knew that the key to the lock on the box wasn't in himself. He knew it was God, and every mile he drove, he sought a closer, purer connection to Jesus. He still faltered now and then. He was still a sinner. He was still flawed as all men are. But oh, oh, oh, how he searched for the next miracle, the next victory over the dark side, the next green valley down below the snake's back he was descending on some rugged mountain road in Wyoming or Idaho.

How he still marveled at the beauty in the land! Could there be a more magnificent place anywhere? Yes! Right around the next bend, over that next bridge, on the other side of the town coming up, somewhere out in that high desert, or on top that smoky ridgeline fifteen miles away. How about that twenty mile stretch by the ocean?

There was always a new promise out there somewhere. You just had to keep driving to find it. And you had to believe in your dreams.

EPILOGUE

It was two months after Coon Dog had escaped from the island. He and Michael were very content living on Jabez's farm in the mountains. They were very busy helping Jabez and the contractors begin clearing and prepping the property for the coming school. But there was something gnawing terribly at Coon Dog's psyche. He couldn't shake the feeling that he'd let God down. When he'd been on the island, he'd prayed over and over about witnessing to Toros and his gang of cannibals. But he never did.

He was about to conclude that it was too late. But then one night Red Man had shown up in a dream. He was on the banishment island, but he wasn't being chased or eaten by cannibals. No, everyone on the island seemed perfectly contented. They were all harvesting crops they had grown. There was no need to seek human flesh.

After awakening from the dream, Coon Dog got to thinking. What would it take to make the dream a reality? Well, prayer of course. It always required prayer, but what else? Seeds.

He began corresponding with Chris Remington via the US mail. Chris only had another four months aboard the *USS Nolin River*, so, Coon Dog would have to make things happen quickly.

Two months later, small watertight packages began drifting ashore on the banishment island. Most of these ended up in Toros' hands because his name was on them and not one of the Toros gang members would have wanted to be caught with the package.

Every single package had the same things inside: a letter to Toros, and seeds – seeds of every kind – fruits, vegetables, even herbs. Also, there were simple to understand instructions on how to grow all the plants from seeds, and how to harvest their seeds so that there would always be new seeds.

The first package to arrive in Toros' hands was opened very quickly. When Toros found the letter, he began to read:

Dear Toros,

You wonder how it is possible, how I made it off the island? All I can say is this: With God all things are possible. I will prove it. You remember the Indian you killed and ate? His name was, and is, Lonely Bear- Brave Bear. It is *he* who is responsible for the package in front of you. His spirit came to me and gave me the idea. Think about it, Toros. Even in death, his love for you and your band goes on. He died trying to save your soul, and he continues doing so, even in death.

There will be many back here in the world praying for you and all of the men on the island. But eventually, it will be up to you. I could try to preach at you, or tell you about hell fire and damnation, but as you know, that would be useless.

Toros, I do want to tell you this: When I was faced with the reality of knowing I had no other place to go, when all other routes to survival had come to a dead end, I said four words – Jesus please take me.

Since that moment, I have been a child of God and I know He will love me and protect me forever. It's your choice. I pray I will be with you in heaven. I have forgiven you for everything. But, I'm not the one who counts. God is, and He will forgive you if you ask Him. Start reading the Bibles the new guys bring ashore. The whole story is there.

Ronnie Matlock – The Christian you hunted for two years.

PS – I have buried a considerable amount of dried deer meat. Here are the directions to find it ……..

While Toros was reading his letter, Captain Frank Weller and ops Officer Jerry Cissell were aboard the *USS Nolin River* having a private conversation.

"Sir, I guess you've seen the latest intel from the satellites." Cissell was in the habit of reading the daily reports as soon as they came in.

"No Lieutenant, it's been a couple of days since I've looked at it."

"Well sir, it would seem to me that there's been a big change in things."

"Bring me up to date Lieutenant."

"The lone wolf hasn't been detected in a while, probably close to four months now. Or at least the individual who you and I concluded was the lone wolf."

"Oh yes. Well, honestly Lieutenant, I haven't seen the need to think too much about the so- called "Lone Wolf" or who you and I thought it might be. I mean, all has been quiet lately. No more burning rafts or swimmers. I suppose I'm at a point that as long as those kinds of events don't start popping up again, well…. I just won't lose any sleep over it. If Matlock *was* the lone wolf, maybe it was just crazy on our part to think that he could evade all of those cannibals forever."

Cissell was thinking about it. *That doesn't sound like the attitude the Captain had four months ago. It doesn't sound like it at all.*

And the captain was thinking to himself, *I think I might have a little chat with Remington, the third class quartermaster. He doesn't know that I've been monitoring the postmarks on those small packages he's been receiving lately. Every one of them from some little town in northeast Tennessee. If Remington plans on visiting someone from up in that neck of the woods, I might just want to tag along. Who knows, I might be offered a little of that East Tennessee wild strawberry mountain wine.*

THE TRUCK DRIVER SERIES

Rookie Truck Driver

West Bound, Hammer Down, Trouble in Montana

Truck Dreams

Information on these books is available at the author's website:
garyhbaker.com

Gary H. Baker grew up in Louisville Kentucky and is proud to claim his status as an "original baby boomer". The class of '46 was just that, and it marched off into the '60s as a force to be reckoned with. While some protested, and some sought peace and love, Gary did a four year enlistment in the Navy and pulled a tour of duty off the coast of Vietnam. He later earned an undergraduate degree from the University of Hawaii and a masters degree in alternative education from Indiana University. Along the way Gary worked as a bouncer, bartender, teacher, coach, coffee salesman, insurance salesman, financial services broker, lawn care business owner, and truck driver. Gary currently calls himself a novelist.

In 1986 Gary ran and walked two thousand seven hundred miles in four months to promote the Just Say No clubs, the forerunner to DARE (drug abuse resistance education). Gary sees his writing as an attempt to follow God. Jesus is his Savior, and Gary will tell you quickly that he falls short most of the time, but that won't keep him from trying again.

Made in the USA
Charleston, SC
10 April 2011